Among the Followers

A NOVEL

Joe McCormack

Print ISBN: 978-1-66783-260-9
eBook ISBN: 978-1-66783-261-6

For Anne,
Dorothy and Joe,
and Sayamagyi Daw Mya Thwin

With our minds we make the world.

—The Buddha

Among the
the
Followers

Saint Petersburg

November morning. The moon hung frozen in a black sky. Dank chill lurked along the rivers and canals. The tragic Hero City was still sleeping. But there was a disturbance, a vibration. Irina groped for her phone buzzing on the coffee table. A message from Marina, notorious insomniac and late-night reveler. It was 5:49.

"Can you believe this?"

Light from the TV spread across the room. Irina had gotten home late after posting a final round of memes before the polls closed in the Western states and had fallen asleep watching the results come in. The TV was still tuned to Russia-1, volume muted, so as not to wake her daughter Anya, asleep in the next room.

Irina's eyes drifted to the map of American states on screen, the ones in the middle mostly red, the coasts blue. But several of the swing states weren't decided yet. Russia-1 was running footage from the night before, images of street protests and long polling lines. They showed Americans holding up posters reading "Lock Her Up" and "Don't Shoot Us," with some of the same images she and Marina had used in memes they'd created a few weeks before. On her phone, she checked the Russia Today app and the results were the same. She texted Marina back.

"They're still counting."

Irina knew she wouldn't be able to fall back asleep. The apartment was cold, so she did her morning stretches beneath the covers of her sofa bed. First, knee to chest to release her quads, glutes and hamstrings. Then figure fours to stretch her piriformis and IT bands and one knee thrown over the other to open her hips. It was impossible to stay fit working 12-hour shifts at the Agency leading up to the election. She wasn't as strong as she used to be, not even close, but at least she still had her flexibility.

From a chair beside the bed, she grabbed the thick fleece robe a friend had showed her how to purchase on Amazon, obviously made for fat Americans because it swallowed her up, even though she had ordered a small. The floor felt like ice, so she slid her feet into her purple UGG slippers, another recent purchase.

She stepped into the bathroom, picked Anya's dirty towel up off the floor and put it in the hamper, then turned on the shower, twisting the knob to hot all the way, filling the room with steam. She hung her robe on a hook on the back of the door and stepped under the trickle of hot water, letting it flow from the top of her skull down the sides of her head. If she stood still, the concentrated warmth helped compensate for the lack of water pressure. This was the price they paid to live in Kolomna, amongst the hipsters and away from the tourists, in an old building that had survived the Germans, Stalin's Five-Year Plans and Brezhnev's grotesque urban modernizations. The floor planks sagged and creaked and the windows were no match for the St. Petersburg winters, but after spending 12 hours in a bleak office filled with computers on gray tables, at least when she came home, she felt like she was in a *real* place, built by humans.

After drying off, she let the towel drop and stared at herself in the mirror. Her body was pale and puffy, a ghost of her former self. By February, she'd have the pallor of a vampire. Her paleness made her tattoo stand out, the words "Nothing Is Forgotten" scrawled in a thorny black-and-blue vine running inside her right forearm. When she was competing, she would stare at it to still her mind, standing at the top of the runway gripping the pole, just before the vault. But she felt the tattoo hadn't aged well. It made her look like a woman with a troubled history. But whatever. No point regretting it. Every Russian had a history. To make herself look less ghoulish, she brushed on some dark eye shadow and rubbed some pink lip stain into her cheeks. Her makeup seemed to be slowly disappearing, which meant she probably had to give in and buy Anya some of her own.

She put her robe back on and stepped into the kitchen, a galley with a stove, a counter just big enough for a cutting board. Since she was up early, she decided to make *syrniki,* which Anya loved. She got the eggs and cottage cheese from the fridge, mixed them in a bowl and sprinkled in sugar and a pinch of salt. Then she formed the batter into flat, round dumplings and dropped them into the oil sizzling in the skillet. It was not the healthiest breakfast, but at least it was homemade. On the TV, Pennsylvania flipped from gray to red. The camera cut to Trump and his Russian-model-looking wife waving to crowds, and Hillary looking fat and old. On Russia-1, she was always scowling or tripping over something. Not that it was hard to make her look bad. The Hillary memes they created always got plenty of likes. Hillary in dreadlocks. Hillary in an orange prison jumpsuit. Hillary with horns. Irina didn't feel too bad about it, because she wasn't impressed by a woman who was the candidate only because her husband had been president. She was so boring, no charisma, like a female version of a Russian politician who wins because there's nobody else on the ballot.

At least Trump was entertaining. Or so she had thought, at first. Making up outrageous lies, sleeping with porn stars, every day another episode of American reality TV. Until the Pussy Tape. If he had admitted such things, it meant he had done much worse. She felt guilty for helping such an insatiable, sexist monster, but she needed the job, and they paid her more than three times as much as she'd ever earned as a personal trainer. It wasn't as though she had a lot of options anyway and working 12-hour shifts didn't leave a lot of time for personal reflection. She had missed hundreds of dinners, which meant Anya had to order takeaway and eat alone. Irina couldn't wait for the election to be over, and today was the day. Everybody said Clinton would win for sure if she didn't trip and land on her head. But as Irina stared at the screen, something strange seemed to be happening.

Her phone buzzed again. Another text from Marina.

"The Americans must be shitting themselves."

Marina could be a bit dramatic, but as Irina glanced up at the American map, Florida flipped to red. Florida was one of the states they had focused on at the end of the election. They had reached out to crazy Americans there and gotten them to set up street protests. They had hired an actor to dress up like Hillary in a prison uniform and sit inside a cage. It was amazing the things they had persuaded Americans to do.

But now something was burning. Irina turned to see a tower of smoke rising from the skillet. She threw it into the sink and blasted it with tap water. The dumplings were ruined, black on the bottom.

Anya appeared in the doorway in her Victoria's Secret PINK flannel pajamas.

"What's burning?"

"*Syrniki.*"

"Is it ruined?"

"Yes."

Anya yawned. "Can we go to Starbucks?"

Irina didn't approve of Starbucks, which she considered over-priced, full of sugar and fat. But she'd burned breakfast, and now she was in a hurry to get to the Agency.

"Okay. But we have to go now."

They walked up to Sadovaya Street, past the Yusupov Gardens, ducking their heads into their new puffy jackets against the wind blowing in from the canal. The Starbucks was in the square just across from the Sadovaya metro station. Inside Irina watched Anya observing the other customers with her intelligent eyes. She wondered what her daughter felt there was to learn standing in line at Starbucks. Anya ordered a caramel Frappuccino and an apple muffin, and Irina ordered a black coffee for herself. As they sat down at the counter, Anya snapped a food pic, which made Irina cringe. Was she gloating to her friends? But Irina let it go. She felt guilty for working so much and for breaking her promise, back in the summer, that they would spend a week on the Black Sea.

She sipped her coffee and watched her daughter break the muffin into bite-size pieces. They had a rule: *Food can never be wasted,* so when Anya left a bite on the napkin, Irina wondered if she was being tested.

"Finish. We have to go."

Anya swallowed the last bite and they got up to leave. Outside, they went their separate ways. Anya headed back down Sadovaya Street toward school. Irina cut across the square to the metro station. She got another text from Marina before ducking underground.

"The party is starting. Vodka or champagne?"

Irina got off the metro at Staroderevenskaya Station and walked quickly to the office, slipped the key card dangling from her purple lanyard through the sensor at the gate in front of the elevators, and headed up to the fourth floor. When the doors opened, she was hit with Russian hip-hop coming from a boombox and the tang of meat and vodka. The whole office reeked like a bar in the drunken hours just before closing. She snaked her way through the crowd gathered around the elevators. Teams from the night shift were still hanging around. IT and accounting had come up from the lower floors, most of them wasted, some so young they looked more like boys with their shaved heads, piercings and G-Star jeans. They passed around bottles of Stolichnaya and Novy Svet and plates of sausages, pickles and herring. People were laughing, drinking and shouting above the music. The big screen TVs were turned to RT, Fox News and CNN. Empty plastic glasses and plates littered with food scraps were strewn across the tops of desks. It seemed unlikely any work was going to be done. When Irina got to her desk, she logged in to email and connected to the internet proxy service, but there were no assignments waiting.

Marina brought her a glass of champagne and shrugged.

"Crazy, crazy."

All three networks cut to reactions from people wearing Clinton buttons looking grim.

"Look at them," Marina said. "Guess they didn't see us coming."

Irina took a sip of champagne and stared at the screen. The results were not yet official, but everyone seemed to know the outcome.

She had joined the Agency the winter before on a tip from another fitness trainer. At first it seemed too good to be true, 700 rubles a month for writing silly internet stuff on Facebook. She created a character, Sonechka, an astrologist who interpreted dreams, offered spiritual advice and shared her thoughts on Russian history. At the time, it seemed odd but harmless, just posting stories and predictions that had nothing to do with anything. But after a couple of months, Sonechka started sharing her thoughts on the Ukrainian provocations.

Pretty soon she had thousands of followers loyal to the Russian cause. It didn't surprise Irina that Russians could be so easily manipulated, especially older ones who missed the Soviet glory years and wanted to believe what they were told.

She was relieved when they switched her focus to the American election in the spring. She thought Americans would be harder to influence, because they could think for themselves. But the ones she met and friended on Facebook were different. They wanted to believe the craziest things she could come up with, the crazier the better. It was almost as if they were asking to be manipulated.

Her bosses were basically racists, so they assumed she understood African Americans because she had competed against them as an elite athlete. Perhaps she did, more than most Russians. They had her work on the Black Matters Facebook Page and #blackstagram. She created a blog using the name Shontelle, a single Black mom who worried about her son and told stories about her nephew who'd been killed by the police. In America, those things happened all the time, so Irina didn't have a problem with that part of her work. Even though Shontelle was her invention, she agreed with a lot of the things she was posting.

She was less comfortable with the people she friended in Being Patriotic, Stop All Invaders and the other right-wing Facebook groups. They were angrier and stranger than everybody else. But the work was easy. She didn't have to be creative to stir them up. She tried to see the humor in the ridiculous things she posted: women in Stars and Stripes bikinis resting rifles on their hips with captions like "Go Big Or Go Home!" She competed with the other writers to see who could be the funniest, without getting flagged.

She realized the strategy was more sinister when they started setting up the protests, recruiting Americans to take to the streets. Once, they convinced Black Lives Matter and Support the Police groups to show up on the same street in Houston, at the same time. When the Black protestors started squaring off against angry, armed whites with the Fox News cameras rolling, her coworkers found the spectacle highly entertaining. That's when Irina realized she had fallen into something she didn't fully understand. Turning people against each other with a few clicks: How was this possible?

As the election approached, they had her and Marina work non-stop on Hillary memes with Igor, a scary-looking Photoshop master with several lip piercings and a python tattoo that circled his neck and ran down both arms. They plastered the memes all over Facebook. "Clinton Corruption Foundation." "Hillary's Big Payday: $26 Million." "Everybody Agrees: Chelsea Is A Stuck-Up Brat." "Hillary Pretends She Loves Us." And finally, "F*** The Vote." They had her write a last-minute flurry of posts from Shontelle, saying she didn't think Hillary respected her, so she wasn't going to vote. Still, what difference could a few votes make? Everybody said Hillary was going to win.

But now as she looked up at the screen, Irina saw that many of the states they had targeted—Florida, Ohio, Iowa, North Carolina, Pennsylvania—were lit up red. For months, it seemed like her posts were just tiny pebbles tossed into the cybervoid. But all those pebbles had created ripples that turned into waves.

Across the row of TV screens, Wisconsin turned red. "TRUMP WINS!" started flashing on Fox News. Then CNN. Then RT. The screens showed Trump supporters in their MAGA hats hugging and cheering.

Marina held out her plastic glass for a toast.

"Cheers. Hang onto your pussy."

Irina put down her glass.

"Do you think anybody knows what we did?"

"Hell, yes. They're saying we'll get bonuses."

"I mean in America."

One by one, the networks cut to red-eyed supporters at Clinton headquarters, tears streaming down their faces.

"I don't think so. They look pretty surprised to me."

Rumors of an appearance by Yevgeny Prigozhin, Putin's "Chef," proved untrue, but the two Mikhails who ran the office worked their way through the crowd pouring fresh champagne. Across the room several skinhead boys were dancing, drunk and euphoric. Someone turned down the hip-hop and banged on a bottle to quiet the room, so they could hear Trump speaking to the crowd on TV.

"I want to start by thanking the American people."

"What about thanking Russian people?" someone shouted across the room. Everyone howled.

Maybe it wouldn't be so bad, Irina thought. Maybe Trump would become a typical American president, talking about peace and the need to make the world safe, while dropping bombs and sending drones wherever he wanted. How much worse could he be? But now, staring at his face onscreen gave her an uncomfortable feeling. This wasn't supposed to happen. They had created a fake reality more powerful than the real one. It was hard to predict what might happen next.

To celebrate, the Mikhails gave everyone the rest of the day off. When the vodka and champagne were consumed, people started heading out for the local bars. Irina resisted their offers to go along and left her champagne half-finished on her desk. She got back on the metro, at mid-morning only half-full, mostly women on their way to market with shopping bags and roller baskets. They looked so unsuspecting, the kind of women eager to believe her lies.

She got off at Sadovaya Station, but instead of heading back to her apartment, she just started walking, along the Griboyedova Canal then north toward the Moyka River. The sun had disappeared, and the low, gray sky seemed to press the damp cold down upon the city. She crossed the Pochtamtsky Bridge, walking quickly to stay warm. She realized she was retracing one of the walks she had taken with her grandmother Vera, who was *blodiniki,* a survivor of the blockade. Growing up, Irina spent a lot of time with Vera, and over time her grandmother taught her the geography of the siege. Irina could never make it across the city without running into Vera's landmarks: the apartment on Vasilyevsky Island that survived the bombing; the bakery where Vera had waited in ration lines for hours; the grenade factory where Vera's mother, the history professor, had worked during the first winter of the siege. But Irina didn't want to think about any of that now. She wanted to sit quietly for a minute without someone talking to her or texting her or commenting on one of her posts.

She stopped in a café called I Am Thankful for Today, popular with tourists because of its cheerful English name. She ordered a bowl of *shchi* with a slice of bread and took it to a table along the window. She stared out at the people walking past, hunched against the cold, and waited for her soup to cool. A few feet away was a table of older Americans talking about their visit to the Hermitage. Hearing their voices gave her a strange jolt. While they were enjoying the Rembrandts and sampling the donuts at Pyshechnaya, Irina and her fellow trolls were playing tricks with their democracy back home. Before the election, their tactics seemed trivial, nothing more than spam. Their work didn't feel connected to anything real. Now it was shocking how their actions had influenced events.

Of course, she had never really felt good about the work she was doing. When her fellow trainer sent her a link to the job post on a message board, she had no idea what sort of work it might be. And when the Agency offered her the job and told her the salary, she was so sick of being stressed out every time she wrote the rent check, of course, she couldn't resist. Like most elite athletes, she had spent her life doing one thing: sports. Her only other skill was her excellent American English, cultivated through years of international competition and watching ancient reruns of *Dynasty* and *Baywatch* on Russian TV. She didn't really have "career options." She was a child of the Soviet sports system, but the safety net it once offered had vanished by the time she came along.

Her mother, Tatyana, had been a famous gymnast. When Irina was conceived, her mother was 26, her career officially over, brought down by the darling pixie Olga Korbut, who, in one two-minute televised routine, made the sport off-limits for all normal-sized girls. The first time her mother had seen Olga's beam routine in competition, she was stunned by the incredible elfin springing. She told herself the bouncing and flying above the floor was childish and undignified, but secretly she sensed she was on the wrong side of gymnastics history. Now it would never be enough to learn a new move or add a rotation. Now to be a gymnast you would have to become an entirely different kind of creature. Overnight Tatyana was suddenly too tall, too graceful, too traditionally feminine and, at 19, too old. She went home from the Olympics that year with two silver medals and competed for three more years, but never earned more than a bronze on the international stage. After she stopped competing, she joined the massive Soviet sports apparatus as a Gymnastics Development Specialist, traveling around the country twice a year for weeks at a time, evaluating 7-year-olds' backwards cartwheels and standing flips.

Irina's father, Nikko, was a sprinter—bronze medal in the 200 meters at the European Championships in Helsinki, fourth in the 4 x 400-meter relay at the Olympics in Athens. He trained constantly and was obsessed with his career and status in the party's sports machine. He had no patience for the domestic aspects of parenting, so when her mother traveled, Irina stayed with Vera in the small, 1950s-era flat with the tired yellow panels on the outside, once considered the epitome of postwar Soviet style.

As the daughter of a famous gymnast, even a forgotten one, Irina received special attention and entered the sports machine at 6. By then she could already do a standing flip and taught herself an aerial cartwheel and back walkover in a couple of days. She and her friend Svetlana were pulled from class three afternoons a week to practice and perform physical tests with a few other children in the school gym. This was a relief because she was bored and miserable sitting in a desk, had a hard time listening and preferred starting fights with the boys. Her teachers said she had too much energy for a small package.

On Saturdays, she and Svetlana met with dozens of other kids in a damp, crumbling gym beside the Neva. They were grouped with other gymnasts, some much older. Although she and Svetlana were friends, they were clearly competing with each other. Irina could feel Svetlana's mother pretending to be nice when they walked back to her apartment after practice. She peppered Irina with questions about her diet, her stretching exercises, whether she was practicing at home on her own. It was as if she was trying to discover any hidden advantages Irina might possess so she could neutralize them. She reminded Irina how lucky she was to be the daughter of a famous gymnast, while

Svetlana had to catch the eye of the coaches on her own. During these walks, Svetlana hardly spoke. When they were together at practice, she was more relaxed and they goofed around like ordinary girls, which they often wanted to be.

A few years later, Svetlana's mother was the first to notice Irina's growth spurt. "You look taller. Did you grow this weekend?" Then, "I wonder if you'll be tall and elegant like your mother." And finally, "Soon you'll be as tall as me," a reference to her diminutive stature at five-two and also to Svetlana, who was still a couple of inches shorter than her mother. And it was true: Irina had always been among the best gymnasts, but now she was one of the tallest. Tatyana recorded the change happening to her daughter with pencil marks inching up the kitchen door jamb, four inches in one year. She was five-six on her 13th birthday.

"You can blame me," her mother said.

One Saturday the coaches separated her from the other gymnasts and sent her out with the track-and-field group. After practice, she and Svetlana hugged each other, crying. Irina could feel herself towering over her friend—and the fake sympathy radiating from Svetlana's mother a few feet away.

That evening, Irina came home, refused to eat and spent the rest of the night in her tiny room, furious, sobbing. She loved the discipline of the practices and the freedom of flying through the air, soaring above the mat or between the bars, her energy unchecked, lighting up her body. Did they think she could just turn that off like a switch? On the second night of her hunger strike, her mother brought some chicken and carrots into her room and refused to leave until she had cleaned her plate.

"I spend my life around women athletes and some of them are weird. You can be weird if you want, but not when it comes to food."

Irina spent the rest of the summer at a track-and-field camp with hundreds of kids from all over Russia. The coaches started grooming her for the 400 meters, a brutal event because you had to go out hard like a sprint, then hang on for the last 100 meters—so you had to be fast and have a high pain threshold as well. There were daily three-hour practices, mostly distance running to build strength and endurance. She hated the repetition, the mindless running in circles, and decided she would get even with the coaches by eating like a pig and getting too fat to compete. But the practices were long, and her body burned through the food so fast she just kept getting stronger. She started channeling her anger by pushing herself to her limit, punishing the other athletes by forcing them to keep up. On days when the coaches were feeling particularly sadistic, they would call for an interval line run . Twenty or 30 girls ran single file around the track, and when the coach blew the whistle, the runner at the back of the line had to sprint to the front. When it was Irina's turn, she set a blistering pace, wearing everyone down and exhausting the next runner, who had to sprint even faster to overtake her. Once in the locker room after practice, some of the older girls confronted her. One of them called her a *suka* and they ended up trading slaps across the face and wrestling on the floor. The other girl was bigger and stronger and ended up on top, pinning her down and threatening to break her legs. But the next time the coaches lined them up and blew the whistle, Irina set the same punishing pace. After practice she headed into the locker room and stared the other girls down.

One night at dinner she announced she hated the practices, hated her event. "It's so boring. Running in circles, one foot in front of the other. What could be more boring than that?"

She knew she shouldn't say this in front of her father, who by then was working as a sprint coach. It was a test really, to see if she could get away with hurting him. It was a way to get back at him for being so preoccupied, so distant, a way to say, "I don't want to be like you."

"Boring? Yes, that's what the medals are for. Gold for the most boring."

The moment still came back to her, how childish she had been, intentionally trying to insult him, mocking the sport for which he had sacrificed everything. This was before the serious drinking started and his body fell apart. She guessed he had taken whatever they put in front of him—testosterone, EPO, amphetamines mixed in every imaginable cocktail to avoid detection. He'd swallowed it all because the pressure was always there. Everyone was doing it and sprinters were the dirtiest of the bunch. He never seemed calm or relaxed, and she wondered if he'd ever really enjoyed any of it.

By the next summer, she was five-nine with ropes of muscle for arms. One day toward the end of practice, one of the female coaches pulled her aside. She remembered that both Irina and her mother had been gymnasts. Would she like to try something more specialized, perhaps the pole vault?

Irina had watched the pole-vaulters from across the track, launching themselves into the air. It looked dangerous and they made mistakes all the time. So many things had to be right to avoid disaster: the speed of the approach, the placement of the pole, the timing and position of the takeoff and the vaulter's body control in the air. Women's pole vault was new to the sports world, so she would be the only female vaulter on the team.

The next day the men's coach introduced himself and had her shadow him as he worked with the other vaulters, explaining how to still their minds before the approach, how to adjust their takeoff and lift. He taped a pole to show Irina the proper hand placement and told her to carry it around to become familiar with its heft and balance. He had her start at the top of the approach without the pole and run down to the box to get a sense of timing and distance.

"There are many moving parts," he said. "You have to get the feel of them separately before you put them together."

Obviously, he was underestimating her. One day when the boys were lounging in the infield, she took a few runs back and forth with the pole. Then in a lapse of judgment that bordered on suicidal, she raced down the track, planted the pole too high in the box and attempted to lift herself in the air. Her timing and placement were so far off she skewered herself with the pole and fell hard sideways outside the pit, onto the track. It felt like she had punched a hole in her chest. She rolled around, gasping for air, bellowing like a gored animal. Two of the men ran to her and held her down to prevent her from moving. One of them put his hands on her chest and groped below her breasts.

She screamed, "Stop it, pervert!" She tried to sit up and shrieked in pain.

"Be still idiot. I'm checking to see if your ribs are broken."

The coach and trainer appeared and lifted her onto a stretcher. It felt like someone plunged a hot knife into her chest, and she started screaming again.

"If you're going to scream, do it without moving or you'll puncture your lung," the trainer said.

In the training room, the team doctor gave her two Vicodins and wrapped her in tape from armpit to navel. She felt like a mummy, and it hurt every time she breathed. "You have two broken ribs and almost burst your spleen. So stupid. Never do that again."

As soon as her ribs healed, she trained as if possessed. She watched the other vaulters practice and studied the technique of the men's leading vaulters on tape. With the body awareness she'd developed as a gymnast and the strength she'd built running the 400 meters, her preparation for the sport couldn't have been more perfect. She progressed quickly, and soon the coach used her development to goad the men, telling them her technique was better than theirs. She forgot about gymnastics and fell in love with her new sport, with the sensation of using her power and muscle to fly—the ultimate rush, even better than sticking a double-twisting Yurchenko.

Other women joined the team, but after her second summer of training camp, Irina was the number one female vaulter. When she came home to share the good news, something was different. Her father was moody and irritable. He would come home from practice in a rage over the crumbling asphalt and disappearing lane lines on the track, the weeds growing so wild in the infield they had to clear them with scythes. The locker rooms were filthy and infested with rats. The country was disintegrating, dragging the brilliant Soviet sports machine down with it, so he was lucky to have a job. At work, he kept his thoughts to himself and reserved his outbursts for the dinner table. The evening meal was always tense. Irina could see her mother carefully choosing her words to avoid setting him off, but sometimes the rage would rise up in him seemingly out of nowhere and he'd hurl a glass or a plate full of dinner against the wall above the stove. Her mother told her about the results of his blood test: elevated levels of all four liver enzymes. When Irina asked her mother what it meant, her mother just shook her head.

He started going out every night with other former athletes. Irina and her mother would have dinner together and leave a plate for him. He usually came home after midnight: Irina could hear him stumbling around the apartment. Sometimes in the morning, she'd find him still asleep at the kitchen table. But as the effects of the drugs closed in on him, he became meaner. One night, her mother came into her room and sat on the bed. "He called babbling, then passed out. Just breathing into the phone. I can't do this anymore."

What was Irina supposed to do? By this time, she was 15 and biding her time until she could move away and train full-time with the Russian team that was filling the hole left by the old Soviet system. As much as she loved her mother, she didn't want to be part of her parents' miserable drama. If her mother had gotten herself into this, she could get herself out of it.

That night, Irina was lying in bed when her father came home. She heard him lurching around the kitchen, rattling pans, breaking a glass. He let out a what sounded like a growl as her mother entered the kitchen. Then there was a scuffle and her mother uttered a strange moan. It was a terrible sound, the sound of a woman accepting her pain and something about it lifted Irina up. In a few steps, she was standing behind her father, reaching for the heavy iron skillet on the stove, not thinking, just moving so swiftly and quietly he didn't see it coming. She swung the skillet upward like a kettlebell and caught him on the side of the head. His legs buckled and he fell forward on his face in the middle of the kitchen floor. Her mother shrieked. Irina looked down at her hand still holding the skillet and put it back on the stove. A huge sob escaped from her chest. Blood was flowing from his nose and from a gash above the ear. Her mother grabbed two dish towels, knelt and pressed them against his wounds. She leaned down to check his breathing.

"He won't die. Not from this. But we don't want to be here when he wakes up."

She called the hospital and told them her husband was drunk and had fallen and hit his head on the floor. They left as the ambulance arrived and never returned.

Her mother found a tiny flat through connections with the sports system. Her father never asked how he'd ended up in the hospital with a small crack in his skull, and they never told him. He lived alone in the apartment for a couple of years, until the disease spread to his lymph nodes.

She and her mother visited him together in those last few months and watched the cancer slowly consume him. The last stage, spent in bed and in a wheelchair in the Krasnoselsky Oncology Center, was brutal and brief. His skin and the whites of his eyes turned yellow, and they pumped him full of morphine. His ramblings circled around his achievements and bitterness that he had been a victim of the drugs and the Soviet system. As Irina sat in the chair next to his bed, he repeated his warning: "To them you are a pawn, not a person. When your career is over, they will toss you away like me."

A few months later she won a silver at the European Juniors' in Austria, clearing 4.2 meters, and she kept getting better and stronger. The next year she cleared 4.4 and won a bronze at the European Championships in Munich.

She was consumed, not just with winning medals but physically—how it felt to apply her mind and muscle to a single point and take off, lift herself up, turning her discipline and training into lightness so she could fly. Sometimes she felt like the air was holding her up, as if for a few seconds she had entered some sort of transcendent state like a cosmonaut floating in space, looking down on the Earth. Time slowed as she fell, and when she landed the pad seemed to caress her for her effort. It was as if an escape from the dreary boredom of the world was being presented to her. All she had to do was reach for it.

She spent a year training for the World Championships in Paris. Hitting the weights, improving her flexibility, watching hours of tape to perfect her technique and timing. At the end it came down to her and Yelena Isinbayeva, another former Russian gymnast, two years younger and wildly talented. When the bar reached 4.55 meters, everything else in the stadium stopped. Irina could feel all the energy and attention focused on her as she stood at the top of the runway, listening to the rhythm of her own breathing. She felt in control as she started down the runway, but when she hit the pit she was coming in hot and a couple of inches too high. She tried to compensate by muscling her takeoff, but as she lifted herself up, she felt something in her shoulder pop and she grazed the bar with her hip. When she landed, the pain was shooting from her shoulder down into her arm. She tried to shake it off but it kept getting worse. She was in a cart, being driven off the track, doubled over in pain, when she looked up and saw Isinbayeva clear the bar.

The next day the doctors told her how bad it was: dislocated shoulder, torn labrum and bicep. She was devastated. After the surgery, she had six months of rehab, then another six months of slowly working herself back into competitive shape. Eighteen months after the injury, she was back at the top of her form and stronger because of all the rehab, clearing 4.2, 4.3, 4.4 meters in practice after practice.

Everything was leading up to the World Indoor Championships in Budapest. Women's pole vault was starting to capture the world's attention, and the energy in the stadium was electric. All the best vaulters were there: Isinbayeva and the American Stacy Dragila. They were like rock stars, showing the world how to be sexy *and* ripped. If she did well, it would be on to the Olympics.

Going into the final round, only the three of them were left. Both Yelena and Dragila had cleared 4.7 meters when Irina asked for the bar to be raised to 4.75. At the top of the runway, she focused on her breathing and took off. She hit her takeoff point perfectly, but she had switched to a lighter pole and it shivered in her hand. As she started to lift off, she felt the pain sear through her shoulder down into her bicep. She held onto the pole so she'd fall into the pit instead of backward onto the track. She hit the bar with her hip and tried to shift her body away from the injured shoulder so she would land on her left side. But when she hit the pad, the pain exploded. Her coach and trainer came out and carried her off on a stretcher.

She went through another surgery and another year of rehab. But Isinbayeva became untouchable, and two young women vaulters moved up behind her, so Irina no longer traveled to the major meets. She hung on for another year until she realized her career was over. Only 23 and the best years of her life were behind her. She was angry, depressed and of course she felt sorry for herself. She started partying hard with the other athletes. She used to look down on the partiers; now she tried to outdo them. She moved to Prague, worked part-time as a personal trainer and got careless. She met a Czech tennis player who had just turned pro, six-five and the most gorgeous man she had ever slept with. After a few weeks of Olympic-level sex, she was pregnant. The obvious decision was to get an abortion. But in her unsettled mind, the choice wasn't so clear. She figured she wanted to have a child eventually, and genetically speaking, it was unlikely she could improve on the one that was already inside her. Even after the tennis player's agent made her sign an agreement giving up any claim of child support, she decided to keep the baby. When she saw the ultrasound, she was thrilled and took to calling the fetus "Supergirl." It was still painful to recall how confused she was during that time.

She was utterly unprepared for the reality of her daughter's arrival, but as with everything else in her life, she pushed through it. They let her rejoin the team as a training coach, but because of Anya, she couldn't travel, so they cut her salary. With all the new expenses of having a child, it was barely enough to live on, and when the financial crisis hit in 2008, the Russian team decided her services were no longer needed. She spent the next eight years constantly scrambling for work as a personal trainer, making barely enough to get by.

The fact that Anya had arrived when Irina was still young was part of their relationship from the beginning. On some level, it must have always been clear to her daughter that there was no master plan: They were figuring things out as they went. Despite her superior genetics, Anya didn't appear destined for athletic greatness. She was slender and willowy like the tennis player and didn't possess Irina's coiled, cat-like coordination. That was disappointing at first, but Irina had gotten used to adjusting her expectations. She did her best to put all the worries about the future out of her mind so she could enjoy being with her daughter, watching her become less of a baby and more of a girl. They filled up on eggs and grilled cheese for dinner, and she came up with fun ways to spend time together, scavenging among the sale racks at GUM and dancing to Tutu, Katy Perry, Pink and Lady Gaga.

But living on the edge through the bone-chilling St. Petersburg winters was hard. The job at the Agency felt like a gift. They finally moved from the grim apartment on the outskirts of the city, which she couldn't leave without seeing drunks or drug dealers lurking. For once she could afford to buy herself and Anya puffy down jackets and warm, trendy boots to take the brutal edge off the cold. After all her disappointments, someone owed her that.

Irina's soup had gotten cold. The Americans in the café had become louder, more animated, talking about the election, how shocking it was and who was to blame. They went down the list of culprits. One blamed Hillary because nobody liked her. Another blamed her husband, who was a womanizer and no better than Trump. Somebody mentioned the emails, the FBI and some guy named Weiner who sent dick pics to women from his wife's computer. There was plenty of blame to go around. Of course, nobody mentioned Irina and her fellow trolls, but listening to the Americans made her anxious. She swallowed the last of her soup and left.

Instead of walking back to her apartment, she headed north toward the Moyka, then south along the Griboyedova Canal. Even with the cold and wind in her face, the thoughts kept coming. They had created a fake world more powerful than the real one. That gave her a bad feeling. By pretending to be all those other people, she had crossed a line. But it wasn't all on her. She was nobody. The world was full of powerful people. Why hadn't anyone stopped her?

Irina couldn't even think about preparing a meal, so she stopped at a street stand and picked up some rice and kebabs. It was already getting dark by the time Anya got home from school. They ate while watching an old episode of *Survivor*. When Anya went to her room, Irina changed into her robe and paced between the walls of the apartment.

She stared out the window. The streets were still, frozen-looking. The cold seeped in along the edges of the weathered frames, which made her think of Vera and the blankets she placed along the edges of the windows. When her mother traveled, Irina spent months at a time with her grandmother in her small, modern flat. Except for the windows, it was a nice apartment by Leningrad standards, given to her for her Child Hero status during the war. But Irina remembered it feeling cheap and worn, the vinyl floor buckling in the gaps between her grandmother's thick braided rugs. The worn-down chairs and sofa, survivors from the 1950's, were covered with so many quilts and blankets it felt to Irina that the entire apartment was lined with wool.

Irina would play with her dolls or Legos, constructing worlds among the blankets and beneath the furniture. Her grandmother would make a lunch of stuffed cabbage or meatballs with mashed potatoes and a small glass of blackberry *kompot*, just sweet enough to make her want more. Sometimes they would make lunch together, Solyanka soup with carrots that Irina would dice with a dull paring knife.

"Careful, no fingers in the pot," her grandmother would say.

After lunch they would go for walks along Nevsky Prospect or Vasilyevsky Island, taking breaks on benches from which her grandmother would see a building or a street or an old lamppost that triggered a memory. Vera was 13 when the war began, living in the apartment overlooking a park on Beringa Street. Her parents had a radio, so neighbors came to listen to the announcement that the Germans had invaded. There was a lot of shouting that Hitler was a liar, the Fins were cowards, the Germans were fools and they would teach them a lesson like they had Napoleon. Because it was June, the beginning of White Nights, daylight continued deep into the night, so the neighbors stayed, and her mother served plates of *zakuski* with pickles, cabbage and ham. Her brother, Misha, fell asleep on her shoulder, so she put him into bed still in his clothes and went back to the living room to listen. That night, the war was far away, merely an idea to be discussed. At midnight, the city was still in daylight and the neighbors became more passionate. They talked about the size of the Russian army, its history of destroying its enemies and the inevitable German defeat. But Vera detected something beneath the boasting: fear.

Her father, a psychology professor and almost 40, went away and returned a few days later in an army uniform, carrying a bag of sweets for her and Misha. She could hear him talking quietly to her mother in bed. In the morning, she heard his boots in the hall and slipped out of bed to see him standing with his big canvas duffle on his shoulder. He lifted her off her feet and kissed her on the cheek. She could smell tobacco when she buried her face in his neck.

He said, "Take care of Little Misha Man for me."

She never saw him again.

Within two weeks, the men disappeared from the city. The only ones left were too old or too weak to serve. Academics like her father were conscripted and sent to the front lines. The university closed, which meant her mother, Mila, a history professor, lost her job. The city was already on rations, and her mother came home that day devastated and wondering how they would survive without her Category 1 ration card. But through her connections she got a job in a factory making grenades, which meant she could keep her ration card, so at first, they had enough food. At school they drew posters of Nazi-uniformed monsters grasping children while being shot by Russian soldiers. The city's official radio broadcasts became the event of the day, with news of the millions of Russian soldiers massing along the border to protect the city. The broadcast emphasized the superior strength and determination of the Soviet people working arm-in-arm as equals toward inevitable victory.

Then the bombing began. On the first night, a bomb landed on the school. The next morning all that was left was a hole in the ground filled with broken bricks and splintered desks. Some of the boys picked their way into the crater, looking for traces of their classrooms and cracking jokes. "Look, no desks. School is canceled." To Vera, their jokes were almost as shocking as the crater, because she could see what fools they were.

A thousand bombs fell in one week, and when the bombing stopped the neighborhood was gone. While her mother worked, Vera and Misha went for walks to see the damage. Everywhere were buildings ripped apart, people's possessions scattered in the street, lives torn apart, hands and feet sticking up out of the rubble. With only a few buildings left standing, the streets were unrecognizable. They went to pick up their rations and walked past the bakery before they realized it was gone.

As winter arrived, the broadcasts declared the city safe, but people knew otherwise. Trucks evacuating children from the city had fallen through the ice of Lake Lagoda. People trying to escape to the south were cut off and had to come back as the Germans surrounded the city. German bombs targeted the warehouses where the city's food reserves were stored. Now the food for the winter was gone.

A huge bomb obliterated the park across the street, rattling the building, shattering windows. By then the siege had encircled the city. Their rations were cut, once, twice, three times—less food every week. The food lines grew longer and longer, and because her mother was working, Vera took over the responsibility for waiting in line. Sometimes she waited seven, eight, nine hours, then carried the food straight home on Misha's sled. There were rumors they would close the grenade factory and her mother would lose her Category 1 ration card, but instead they repurposed the factory for repairing rifles. By then her Category 1 war worker status entitled them to a loaf of bread, a pound of kasha and three onions every week. After five days, their food ran out and all three of them were starving.

With the Germans so close, the shelling and bombing intensified, sometimes for days at a time. Only one other building on the block was left standing. The heat and electricity were cut off. They burned up all the furniture for fuel, except their beds. Vera and her brother began spending their days scavenging for broken pallets, slats from wagons, charred ends of logs, and strips of lathe she hacked from broken walls with an axe. It never amounted to much. It was as if the whole city had been picked clean of fuel. Whatever they found they piled on Misha's sled and pulled through the snow-covered streets straight back to the apartment to avoid thieves. When there was no wood to burn, the temperature inside the apartment plummeted—zero, 10 below, 20 below—no warmer than out in the streets. Ice formed on doorways so the doors wouldn't close, and icicles hung down in giant spikes inside the windows. During the day she and Misha spent most of their time in their beds, wearing their coats. When the pipes froze throughout the city, they had another adventure: walking down to the Neva and returning with slabs of ice in buckets for drinking water. They'd return home exhausted and spend the rest of the day staring out the window into the vast, white open space below, where the park used to be, where they had hidden among the trees playing Cossacks and Bandits with their friends. The paths through the park had vanished, and the trees were reduced to splintered stumps sticking out of the ground. Every so often a gray, solitary figure would cross the frozen, empty space, skirting the massive bomb crater filled with snow. Once they watched a woman squat and shit in the open as others walked past. It remained there for several days, until the next snow.

Every week something new would be taken away. Her mother came home every night exhausted, so Vera took over serving dinner. Rations were cut again, so their only meal of the day consisted of three spoons of kasha and a small slice of bread made mostly of sawdust and glue. They soaked it in water to try to make it more filling. She improvised pancakes out of noodles and coffee grounds. It was obvious the three of them were starving to death along with the rest of the city. Food became the single thought, always in everyone's mind. Waiting for rations consumed the entire day. The sight of food, when it finally appeared, was almost unbearable, awakening in Vera a wildness she could barely control, an urge to burst to the front of the line and sink her teeth like an animal into the loaves.

Corpses appeared in the streets. Dogs and cats went missing. An old woman collapsed in front of her in the ration line and died on the spot. Vera sensed the feeling of the first night of the war coming back, a new fear that she could not name, another shoe about to drop. She watched her mother getting weaker, arriving later and more exhausted every evening from her walk from the gun factory. Sometimes she would skip dinner, saying she had eaten at the factory, and give her portion to Vera and Misha. Her eyes became dark shadows sunken in their sockets, eyes Vera no longer recognized, nothing like the clever, confident eyes of the woman whose portrait was on the wall.

One evening her mother didn't come home from work. Vera gave Misha his bread and kasha and put him in bed, then put her boots on to go look for her. She didn't have to go far, only downstairs to the lobby, where she found her sitting on the cold floor, slumped forward at the waist. Vera touched her, then shook her, but her mother didn't respond. She was shocked at how light her mother's body was when she lifted her under the arms and dragged her across the lobby. But there was no hope of getting her up the stairs, so she tilted her mother's body sideways so that her head was resting on the lowest step. Only a few people still lived in the building, so Vera climbed the steps to Mrs. Ruzatski's apartment. The woman followed her back down to the lobby and leaned low, putting her ear to Mila's chest. Then she took off a glove and placed her fingers along Mila's neck. When the woman lowered her eyes, Vera knew her mother was dead. But what did *dead* mean? The actual meaning was impossible, unthinkable, because then what would become of her and Misha?

Mrs. Ruzatski led her up the stairs to their apartment and came back with a jug of water and two slices of bread. Misha joined them and they sat on blankets in the living room eating the bread. They told him his mother had to work late and decided to spend the night at the factory. After Misha climbed back in his bed, Mrs. Ruzatski told Vera to go to the factory in the morning and ask for her mother's job.

"You must have the ration card."

The next day she went to the factory and told them her mother was sick and asked to take her place on the line. The woman at the factory shook her head. Assembling rifles was not acceptable work for children. Her mother had to return to work or she would lose her ration card. Vera wanted the woman to understand the situation. She wanted to explain that, without the ration card, she and Misha would starve to death. But she couldn't bring herself to say the words, "My mother is dead."

It was possible the woman understood, because she said, "I heard there is a hospital where young girls can work on Stanislavsky Street."

As Vera walked back through the city, she kept getting lost. With so many buildings replaced by piles of rubble, she no longer recognized the streets. She wandered in circles, asking strangers for directions to the hospital. Most of them ignored her, maybe didn't hear or even see her because they had lost their minds from hunger.

Finally, a woman pointed to a large building in the distance. As she climbed the steps, she recognized the terrible smell of the dead. Wounded soldiers groaning in their beds lined the halls. A nurse told her she could get a Category 2 status card by reading to them. Vera knew that would provide barely enough rations for one person, not two, but there seemed to be no point in mentioning that. The woman handed her a book to practice reading and told her to appear the next morning.

Vera left the hospital with her mind spinning. Because it was winter, it was already dark outside. Again, she got lost. She couldn't remember which side of the canal she was on. By the time she found her way home, she could barely make it up the steps, and when she entered the apartment Misha was gone. She went down to Mrs. Ruzatski's but he wasn't there. There were stories of children disappearing from the streets, so she went out to look for him. She walked past the bakery all the way to the gun factory and then started back looking for children along the way. She had not eaten all day and had to walk slowly to keep from losing her balance and falling. She started back home, thinking surely by then he must have returned. When she entered the apartment building, she sat down on the steps to rest. She decided she was having a bad dream, a hallucination, that she had fallen asleep on the ground somewhere and Misha was upstairs waiting for her. But when she climbed the steps and entered the apartment, he wasn't there. He wasn't there when she woke up in the morning, but there was no one to tell.

She spent her days at the hospital reading to the soldiers and spent her nights alone in the frigid apartment. The stories she read were printed on pages stapled together, heroic accounts of the New Soviet People who had acquired superhuman powers of endurance and could not be destroyed. Stories of women lifting lorries to save a child, of young boys becoming expert snipers and killing scores of Germans near the front lines. To her the stories sounded made up, but she couldn't be sure. The soldiers at the hospital were too weak and wounded to listen anyway.

But the reading entitled her to the only food she was going to get. So she kept reading even when her eyesight weakened from starvation and the words blurred on the page. This was the math of the siege: Category 2 rations were not enough to keep you alive for long. The hunger was always there, like a scream caught in her throat. She felt like a wild animal. Sometimes on her way back to the apartment she roamed aimlessly, walking past the bakeries looking hopelessly for a scrap of bread someone may have dropped. Every night new corpses appeared in the street and were gone by morning. Because the city was still deep in winter, the days passed mostly in darkness. One evening on her way home, she became disoriented and sat down in the snow in the middle of the street. A nurse from the hospital recognized her and asked where she was going.

Vera didn't answer.

"Where is your mother?" the nurse asked.

Vera stared at her boots in the snow. The nurse took her by the arm, pulled her along the street and up the steps of a large building. It was warmer inside the building and she heard children's voices. The nurse spoke to a woman behind a large desk.

"I found this girl lost in the street."

The woman frowned and shook her head.

"Her family is dead," the nurse said.

Somehow this was new information to Vera. Or something she knew but now understood in a different way. Of course, she knew that her father, mother and Misha were gone, but her mind had refused to complete the thought.

"She's too old," the woman behind the desk said.

"She can help with the younger children," the nurse said. "She can read to them."

The woman behind the desk led her down a hallway and into the kitchen. She smelled food—cabbage, maybe carrots, kasha boiling in a huge pot. The woman said something to two cooks working at the stove. The counter was covered with small bowls, each of which received two spoons of kasha, a carrot and a few ribbons of cabbage. They put a bowl in front of Vera, and she gulped it down in two quick swallows. She sat in the kitchen as they took the bowls into the dining hall, and she could hear the children screaming, shouting, bowls breaking. Later she would witness firsthand the hunger-driven madness that arose at every meal.

Someone led her upstairs to the room where the children slept. No beds were available, so she slept on a pile of blankets on the floor. The next day a girl died, so a bed became available. The children kept dying, three or four every week, the hunger taking them down so that the slightest illness finished them off.

She read to them in the morning after their meager breakfast—a thin slice of bread and a piece of carrot—and after dinner, two spoons of kasha with a clump of cabbage. They ate like animals on the brink of starvation, wolfing down their portions then trying to steal food from each other. Still hungry and anxious from the chaos of the meal, most of them, especially the boys, couldn't sit still for her reading. The quiet ones were usually the weakest and the next to die. She read them Russian fairy tales of *The Wolf and Seven Goats* and the story of *Little Silver Hoof*, the magical deer who made rubies, emeralds and sapphires appear by stomping its hooves. Her favorite was the story of *The Snow Maiden*, about an old couple who wanted a child so badly they made one of snow. Magically the girl came to life and became the most beautiful in the village. Her voice was so pure that when she sang Russian folk songs the whole village stopped to listen, even birds in the trees. But during the Harvest Day festival, the other girls in the village forced her to join them as they leaped across the bonfire. As she leaped, she melted into a small cloud and vanished.

Between her readings, she cleaned the bathrooms. Anything resembling normal hygiene had vanished. The walls and floor were constantly soiled with pools of sickly shit and piss. The staff constantly bickered about how to divide the food between themselves and the children. Some insisted they should have more food, saying if they starved to death the children would die anyway, because there would be no one to care for them. But the director of the orphanage kept everyone on strict rations, which meant they were all on the edge of starvation. Toward the end of the winter, the children started dying faster, up to 10 per week. Vera sometimes saw the cooks stealing bread, but she never reached for a stray morsel and lived in constant fear of being thrown back out into the frozen streets.

One day just before summer, a military truck arrived and the driver unloaded bags of flour, onions, carrots, potatoes and kasha. The entire staff assembled in the kitchen to stare at the sacks piled on the floor. That night Vera was standing in the kitchen when one of the cooks pulled a loaf out of the oven. She could almost taste the smell of butter that filled the room. It was a Stolichny cake, just like her mother used to make when she invited other teachers from the university for tea. The cook sprinkled powdered sugar over the top, cut a slice from the end of the loaf and put it on a plate in front of Vera. The first bite, still warm, awakened something inside her, like a dark room illuminated with the flip of a switch. She fought the urge to shove the slice into her mouth and paused before each bite, making it last. She could smell the raisins, sweet and musky—before that moment, she didn't know they had a smell. She pressed the last crumbs into her fingers and ran her tongue around the plate.

After the war, the story of a 13-year-old girl who had survived the siege and read to wounded soldiers and orphans was useful to the Party. However, to sustain the myth of the Hero City, she wasn't supposed to talk about some of the terrible things she'd seen. But by the time she was taking her walks with Irina around the city, she no longer cared about the consequences of speaking her mind. "The memorial says, 'Nothing is forgotten.' But they are forgetting a lot."

She kept the plaque they gave her hidden on a shelf behind a picture of her parents. Every year on January 27th, the day the siege was broken, she attended the parade with other survivors. But she complained about standing out in the cold and rolled her eyes at the parade of soldiers, tanks, jets and missiles marching through the snow.

Afterward, she would host a little gathering in her apartment. Usually Mrs. Sokolova, another *blodiniki* who lived in the building, would stop by. But sometimes, if Tatyana was traveling, it was just the two of them, Vera and Irina, sitting at the tiny kitchen table, sipping tea and eating Stolichny cake. They ate the cake with their fingers, still warm, a fat slice for each on a faded china plate. Vera had perfected the recipe so that Irina could taste the butter melting on her tongue, and the brandy oozing from the raisins made her mouth feel drunk. The taste was almost overpowering, so rich there was no thought of a second slice. Irina tried to imagine how the first bite would taste if you were starving to death.

Vera's special history lesson explained why her apartment was always unbearably warm, why she hid food in drawers and closets in every room. But for Irina, her grandmother's memories of the war were too vivid and horrible to process. She was never sure what the stories should say to *her*. That she lived a charmed life and should never complain about anything? That the women of her family possessed an extraordinary capacity for suffering? Irina always thought she had a connection to her grandmother, that at least a share of her courage and toughness had been handed down. But now, as she stood at the window and stared into the street with the cold drifting in around her, she realized she'd been flattering herself. Vera had outlasted Nazis and starvation. Irina's adversaries were her own inventions. She was always operating at the wrong frequency, motor running too fast, brain not thinking far enough ahead. She wasn't good at normal life, wasn't the person she imagined herself to be. It was clear to her now: When she fell into the pit that night in Budapest, it was a deeper kind of fall. After that, she was adrift, thrashing her way through motherhood, grinding out a living, never able to muster any real interest in anything she did. Although she loved her daughter, most of the time she was just going through the motions, and beneath it all was a sadness and confusion over what she'd lost.

She looked down toward the busy end of the street and watched a couple stumble out of the nearest bar. The woman struggled along the sidewalk in gold, spiked heels and what looked like leather pants. Her companion swayed as he walked, holding her up, a couple of harmless Russian drunks, distinguished residents of the Hero City. Start letting things slide, thought Irina, and life soon became an icy slope.

She dreaded the morning, when she would have to go back out into the frozen streets and make her way to the office, feeling the weight of the lies they'd spread. She was a troll, a tool. All her high hopes had come to this. How had she fallen so low?

The next morning, when she swiped her badge in the lobby, she felt like the Dostoevsky character whose name she couldn't remember, the one who kills the old lady and returns to the scene of the crime. She spent the next few days working in a trance, posting meme after meme in the Being Patriotic and Army of Jesus Facebook Groups, which didn't require a lot of thought. Find a photo, add "Congratulations President Trump! We look forward to serving you!" in big, bold type and move on to the next one. But she also had to keep up Shontelle's blog with soulful, post-election observations.

"You reap what you sow, baby."

"What goes around comes around."

"I know a lot of people weren't expecting this, but karma's a bitch, amirite?"

There were rumors of layoffs, but toward the end of the week, Mikhail One gathered the hundred or so on her shift to squelch the rumors and explain that, in fact, the opposite was true. Their efforts, code-named Project Laktha, had been so successful they were being funded indefinitely. The millions of followers they had cultivated were assets that years of traditional spycraft could never have delivered. Now the plan was to shift their effort into maintenance mode, keep their new American friends warm until they needed them again. He ended by congratulating them and offering a constricted smile.

"Well done! You made America great again."

People laughed and applauded themselves. Irina surveyed the faces around her. They were all so young and thoughtless. She felt a buzz in the back pocket of her jeans, a text from Marina, who was staring at her from across the room.

"Cheer up! Let's have lunch!"

In over a year at the Agency, Irina had never gone out to lunch. She always brought leftovers from home in a plastic container, which she heated in the disgusting office microwave. She wasn't in the mood for celebrating, but she'd rather be anywhere than at her desk. She texted back a thumbs-up.

"I need something in my stomach," Marina said as they waited for the elevator. "How about some soup?"

They went across the street to a traditional Russian place with worn wooden tables, limp curtains and faded prints of Russian peasant scenes on the wall. They sat near the window, and both ordered Solyanka, for which the menu said the owner was famous. Some people considered it the ultimate hangover cure because it replaced minerals lost during a night of revelry. It came in a small crock filled with chunks of beef, vegetables and sausage.

"This is perfect," Marina said. "It's going straight to the damaged brain cells and organs."

After a few bites, Irina realized she wasn't hungry.

"Do you ever think about what we're doing?" she asked Marina.

"I try not to."

"I wonder what the Americans are thinking."

"I'm ready for a new challenge," Marina said. "We need a new country to fuck up."

When they got back to the office, Trump was on the big TV, suddenly part of the daily coverage on Russia Today. Something seemed different about him, now that he was about to become commander in chief and get his stubby fingers on the nukes. He reminded her of a slicker species of Russian gangster, the kind who concealed his grotesqueness with cosmetic touches. Trump's fancy suits did a better job of hiding the gut overhanging his belt, but he had the same tanning-bed tan and that ridiculous nest of hair. As she stared at the screen, a recurring fantasy came over her. The two of them are having dinner in a fancy St. Petersburg restaurant. He requests a quiet banquette where they sit thigh to thigh. She laughs at his jokes. When she touches his hair, it collapses like a ruined soufflé, but she continues to smile. She leans toward him seductively and reaches under the table, as if groping for his cock. She lets his fat hand move up her thigh. But just as he's about to make his grab, she catches the long end of his tie from under the table and jerks his head down hard. Wine glasses tumble and shatter. Expensive French Burgundy soaks into the tablecloth. Then with his head pinned to his plate like a pig on a platter, she picks up her fork with her free hand and plunges it into his ear. The scene played in her head several times a day, perhaps some feeble self-protective reflex, to make up for what she had done.

To make matters worse, earlier that morning she'd seen a comment from Mark Zuckerberg about how nobody believed fake news, how suggesting that Facebook had influenced the election was "a crazy idea." She felt angry and strangely insulted that the damage they'd done was so casually dismissed. He seemed like an odd character, Zuckerberg: obviously a genius, but with the haircut and social presence of a 12-year-old boy. Maybe he was too naïve to understand what she and her colleagues had done. Or maybe he thought denying it would make the problem go away.

Back at her desk, Irina felt the afternoon pass in slow, grueling increments. She logged back into the project management system and started working on another round of Instagram memes. She downloaded the images from Igor, the skinhead designer, and started working on her copy. She tried to turn her mind off so it felt like only her fingers were doing the work.

The first was Jesus in a red MAGA hat. She typed, "IT'S TIME TO MAKE AMERICA BELIEVE AGAIN. LIKE IF YOU AGREE."

Next was an image of a man hugging Trump onstage after his victory speech. She wrote, "I WISH I HAD A TIME MACHINE SO I COULD GO BACK TO NOVEMBER 8 AND VOTE FOR TRUMP AGAIN!"

There was a photo of Trump giving a thumbs-up on the streets of New York with copy already written by someone else: "TRUMP GETS 65% OF NY SUPPORTERS. THAT'S BEING PATRIOTIC." All she had to do was go to the Being Patriotic Facebook page and give it a "like." But it made her cringe. He'd lost New York by a lot. Didn't everybody know that? They were lying about the results even after the election.

Next there was a meme for #blackstagram, an image of a young Black woman dressed in a crown and long gown, holding a torch. Beside it was a photo of the Statue of Liberty. Under the Black woman, she typed the caption, "REAL LADY LIBERTY," and under the statue, "FAKE LADY LIBERTY." The next meme was an image of Kim Jong-un beside the CNN logo. She typed, "IN NORTH KOREA, PEOPLE ARE FORCED TO LISTEN TO PROPAGANDA. IN THE U.S. THEY DO IT WILLINGLY EVERY DAY!"

To reach her quota for the day, she had only one more meme left, images of two smiling girls, side by side, one Middle Eastern, the other Black American. The notes in the project file explained that the message was to convince Americans to get out of Syria but didn't explain why. She quickly typed, "ALL GIRLS LOVE PEACE. U.S. OUT OF SYRIA," and stared at the photos again. The girls were a few years younger than Anya. She wondered who they were. Chances are the lighter-skinned girl wasn't even Syrian. And the photo of the Black girl looked familiar. The designers were always grabbing random images from the web, especially Igor. She decided to post a message for him in the project file.

"Where did you get these images?"

Irina wasn't that familiar with the situation in Syria, but she knew there was still a war going on. With so many factions it was hard to know who the good guys were or even if there were good guys. But she knew one thing for sure: The president of Syria was definitely a monster. He had actually dropped chemical bombs on villages filled with his own people—and Putin was on his side. So whatever they were asking her to do with these pictures of the girls couldn't be good.

After a few minutes, Igor responded, "Images from Flickr. Why are you asking?"

Flickr was a mess, so finding the images would take a while. It took her 20 minutes to find the image of the Syrian girl, who was actually Moroccan. But Irina couldn't find the image of the Black girl. It looked like a typical school photo, and the uniform was definitely American. Irina lost half an hour searching on iStock and Getty, without success. But the more she stared at the photo of the Black girl, the more she was sure she recognized her braids and her gap-toothed smile. Maybe someone at the Agency had used the image before. She accessed the server and scrolled through memes they had created for Black Matters and #blacktivist but couldn't find the girl there. Finally, on a hunch she Googled "Chicago shooting victims 2016." At the top of her search, an article from the *Chicago Tribune* popped up with photos of people who'd been murdered in the city—90 in the month of August alone, a new record—and there she was, Shameeka Jamison, 11 years old, victim of a drive-by shooting. Irina stared at the image of the dead girl, same braids and smile. She was somebody's daughter. What if her mother or father or sister happened upon Irina's meme? And what was the purpose of this work she was doing? If the Syrians were dropping poison gas on villages and Putin was helping them, was Irina part of that too? Was she using the photo of one dead girl to justify killing others? Irina felt a panic rising in her chest. Her hands started shaking. She deleted the images of the girls from her project file, posted the rest of her memes, then closed the window to the project management system and stared at her blank screen.

She sat at her desk pretending to organize files until the end of her shift. She had hoped the madness would end after the election, that they would go back to doing more trivial things, astrology blogs and recipes from fictional women with political opinions. But now she could see that wasn't the case. Now they were being redeployed to sow chaos elsewhere, as Marina had predicted, layering lies on top of lies until no one could be certain what was real anymore. This was the real horror of their work: They made reality disappear.

She wondered how long they would keep getting away with it before some sort of reckoning occurred. Maybe she would go crazy working there. That would be just punishment, and it was definitely a possibility. She should quit. But what else could she do? What skills did she have? She could go back to life as a personal trainer at a fraction of the salary. Possibly get a job catering to tourists, where her English would be useful. In any case, the money was going to get a lot tighter.

She and Anya would probably end up moving back into some miserable apartment on the edge of the city. It was a grim future to consider, not just for herself but for Anya. There would be no more puffy jackets or leggings from Topshop anytime soon.

Maybe she just needed a vacation. She hadn't had one in two years. And the stress leading up to the election had been brutal. It would be a mistake to make a big move when she wasn't thinking clearly.

Later that night over takeaway curry, she mentioned the idea to Anya.

"I was thinking maybe we could take a vacation."

"Now?"

"We didn't take one this summer. Where would you like to go?"

"A beach would be nice."

"It's November. Too cold for the Black Sea. Maybe Spain."

Anya shrugged. "What about California? They have beaches. And Disneyland."

"Probably too expensive."

Later that night she searched online. Flights were cheaper than she expected, especially at the end of November, just after Americans had their Thanksgiving, and there were cheap hotel rooms to be had that time of year. She found a cheap Lufthansa flight that went through Frankfurt and on to LAX, and a cut-rate travel package: three nights at a no-frills hotel across the street from Disneyland, three nights in LA at a hotel just off Hollywood Boulevard and three nights at the Mirage in Las Vegas, where the heated pool was open year-round.

The thought of such an indulgence was ridiculous, but so was everything else in her life. And after so many days of coming home from school to an empty apartment and eating dinner alone, Anya deserved some kind of reward. If Irina quit her job and money got tight, at least they would have this adventure to look back on.

The next day she met with her boss, Katya, to ask permission for the time off.

"I've been spending too much time away from my daughter. I was thinking of taking her on vacation."

"Where are you going?"

"California. Maybe Las Vegas. Two weeks starting at the end of this month."

Katya smiled. "Market research?"

Irina thought it would be wise to play along. "Exactly. I will record my observations."

Later that day, she applied for their visas, which wouldn't be a problem. After dinner that night, she told Anya the plan.

"So we're going to take that vacation."

"Where?"

"Los Angeles. Las Vegas. Disneyland too."

"Seriously?"

"Yes, I'm going to book the flight."

"What about school?"

"I'll tell your teacher it's a family emergency. You have a long-lost uncle who is dying in Anaheim, California."

After dinner, Irina went online and started making their arrangements. She poured a couple of inches of vodka into a jelly jar and sipped. She opened the tabs she'd saved for each of the reservations and clicked BOOK NOW. When she added it up, the cost was over 100,000 rubles and on top of that would be the cost of their meals. By the time they got home, her credit card would be maxed out. If she quit her job at the Agency, she'd never be able to pay it off, so maybe she would have to stay another six months. Either way, she needed a break.

As she watched the confirmation emails pop up, Irina tried not to think about the possible consequences. Hopefully, being away from Piter (as the locals liked to call her city) would give her some perspective, a chance to think about her next move. She thought about the trip and how much fun she and Anya would have. She had always wanted to go to California, but during her days of competing, the closest she'd gotten was Texas. She wished she had stayed in touch with some of the Americans she had competed against, but that was a long time ago.

There was one person she might look up in America: her old friend Sergei. Sergei was an interesting character, a race walker, the strangest of sports. He was ranked in the top 10 in the world for a while, but he always had a side hustle going. Food supplements, cheap airline tickets, singles cruises. He had somehow gotten access to dozens of treadmills, rowing machines, StairMasters, kettlebells and tons of free weights that had been in storage since the Soviet sports system collapsed. He'd gathered them into an abandoned redbrick power station shaped like an ancient dome and turned it into a fitness center—Red Tower CrossFit. It was a fantastic place, vast, airy and ancient, like a secret underground city. He hired his friends as personal trainers, all former Russian athletes like Irina, and paid them by the hour, taking 10% for himself, or so he said. For Irina it was hardly a lucrative arrangement, but it was great to reconnect with athletes she had trained with over the years. Sometimes her mother would take Anya for the night, and Irina would join Sergei and the other Red Tower trainers at a local bar called Breaking Bad, where they vented about their years of training, the doping, the gangsters, rampant crime, corruption and other post-Soviet mayhem. Sergei was very successful with the women athletes. Irina had slept with him a couple of times after nights of drinking, and she had to admit he knew what he was doing.

Sergei also had connections for recruiting clients: oligarchs and their kids, ex-military, fashion models and others who thought staying fit might somehow lead to fame and riches. But when the financial crisis hit, the whole enterprise instantly fell apart. Clients stopped coming. The heat got turned off. Sergei gave all his staff their final checks, then promptly disappeared. At least he hadn't stiffed them. There were rumors he had sold the building to new owners and moved to California. Someone said he'd landed a job at Facebook, though Irina doubted that was true. There were always rumors of Russians leaving and making it big in America, Germany, Montreal or Rome. Wishful thinking, fantasies mostly.

She logged on to Facebook, typed his name into the search bar, and there he was: Sergei Pavlenko, with his trademark I-am-smarter-than-you smirk. She was surprised to see the rumor was true: He was actually working *at* Facebook, as Director of Fitness & Training, in Menlo Park. It seemed a strange coincidence. At the Agency, she had spent so much time on Facebook. But of course everybody was *on* Facebook.

She sent him a friend request, and within a few minutes, he accepted and they started chatting online.

"Hey Irina, what's up? Enjoying suicide season?"

"Do you miss it?"

"Every winter. We don't have that here."

"Go ahead. Rub it in."

"It's 71 degrees here, 22 centigrade."

"Nice. My daughter and I are coming there for vacation."

There was a pause. Irina guessed Sergei might be wondering if she was fishing for an invitation. Typical Sergei.

"Where are you staying?"

"LA, Las Vegas, Disneyland of course."

"So Russian of you. If you come to Facebook your daughter can take selfies and make her friends jealous."

"She would love that."

Irina remembered how much she had enjoyed the nights with Sergei and the rest of the crew at Breaking Bad. Those were her people.

"So what are you doing?" he asked. "Are you still giving the weaklings our Tough Russian Love?"

"No, I work at an agency now."

"So you're an executive with a big office."

"No, I sit in a room with the other trolls making America great again." She added an American flag emoji.

"Interesting. I'm just the gym guy here." He added a flexing biceps emoji.

"Do you ever see Mark Zuckerberg?"

"Almost every day. Comes in for a 7-minute high-intensity workout. Busy guy."

"Is he really a genius?"

"Everybody says so."

"Does he really think Facebook influencing the election is a crazy idea?"

"Doesn't everybody?"

Irina started to offer a snarky reply but caught herself. It was easy to get carried away on Facebook. She decided to sign off.

"Right. I'll let you know when we get to California."

Sergei signed off, "Safe travels."

Irina scrolled back through her comments. Joking about trolls and the election maybe wasn't her smartest move. But it was just Sergei.

The night before they left, she and Anya had dinner with her mother, who greeted them with hugs and put their winter coats on hooks just inside the door. Irina felt her mother sizing her up in the narrow hallway as she always did and waited for the usual remark, like, "You should wear a blazer to the office" or "What color would you call that?" Irina was relieved when her mother shifted her attention to Anya.

"Nice boots."

Even now her mother never left her apartment without makeup and wore the same outfit almost every day for 30 years—a brightly colored sweater belted at the waist and dark Gloria Vanderbilt jeans. Irina had always thought of it as typical Russian female vanity, multiplied by the pride of being a once famous gymnast—a woman watched by others and expected to perform. But as Irina got older, she realized her mother's choices were a form of discipline, a way of dictating what others saw. Even when she was trapped in a disastrous marriage to an abusive husband, the world would never see Tatyana Zakharova crack.

She led them down the hall into the living space, an aging loft-style room with a sofa, TV and bed at one end and a small kitchen at the other, which smelled strongly of fish, onions and turnips.

"Sorry. At least you don't have to ask what's for dinner."

Her mother almost always served fish and vegetables when she invited them to dinner. For Anya there would be fresh fruit and possibly a small scoop of sorbet. Irina insisted her mother's dinners were too healthy for her to be a real Russian grandmother, but Tatyana assured her otherwise. "I'm the Russian grandmother for the new millennium." And it was true. She doted on Anya and, despite her modest salary from the Russian Sports Federation, sent her indulgent presents every Christmas and birthday, usually clothes from Benetton or Gap.

They sat down near the kitchen at a small table set with silver and cloth napkins for three. Tatyana presented their dinner on small, neat plates.

"So Disneyland?"

Anya nodded. "Very exciting."

"What are you going to do first?"

"Get a photo with Mickey Mouse."

"And after that?"

"We're also going to Los Angeles and Las Vegas," Irina added. She knew her mother had visited these cities as part of her position and was eager to offer her opinion.

"Los Angeles you will like. Las Vegas? Maybe not so much."

"Why not?"

"Americans go crazy there. They don't know how to behave."

Irina could see Anya looked disappointed that their dream vacation might be tarnished. "Fortunately, there is a pool."

"Good, stay by the pool. Avoid all the beer drinkers in tank tops and flip-flops."

After dinner, Tatyana cleared their plates and served them warm pears with walnuts and honey. Anya found her usual spot on the couch in front of the TV to watch her favorite show, *Club of the Cheerful and Sharp-Witted.*

Tatyana brought a pot of tea to the table.

"Your job must be going well."

Irina shook her head. "Not really. I need a vacation."

"An expensive one."

"I might go back to being a trainer again."

"So you're going on a fancy vacation, then quitting your job?"

Irina shrugged.

"Maybe you can find work at some fancy club making oligarchs' kids do crunches."

"We'll see."

"You should be more optimistic. Maybe with Trump the Americans will be nice to us again. No more sanctions."

Irina cringed. "Yeah. He owes us."

"What do you mean?"

"Nothing."

Her mother liked to think of Irina as the fierce, incorruptible one in the family. Telling her how wrong she was would be painful for both of them. So now she was throwing one more deception onto the pile.

By the time the airport shuttle dropped them off at the Anaheim Desert Inn, it was early evening and they had been traveling for 22 hours. Irina was exhausted, ravenous, and knew Anya must be too, even though she kept insisting she wasn't tired or hungry and wouldn't stop talking about Disneyland. So Irina agreed they could drop their bags in the room, freshen up and swing by the Disneyland gates, even though their tickets didn't start until the next day.

They passed rows of touristy gift shops and fast-food restaurants. Families streamed past, kids buzzing. To Irina, the parents looked like children: spent, hollowed out, disappointed that their dream day hadn't come true.

The park was closing as they arrived, so she and Anya stopped outside the main gate. Just on the other side were the Disneyland Railroad and Disneyland City Hall. Sleeping Beauty's Castle loomed in the distance. Seen through her jet lag, hunger and fatigue, the scene seemed both strangely familiar and disturbing, a hallucination, an impenetrable realm separate from the world. Irina worried Anya might be too old to embrace the fantasy of it, but she already had her phone out and was snapping photos through the gates.

"You should decide which rides you want to do."

"I might want to take some photos first when we get inside."

On the way back to the hotel, they stopped at a Mexican restaurant. Even though it was basically fast food, everything on the menu was expensive by St. Petersburg standards. With their drinks and an order of chips, the bill was over $40. Irina decided this must be how the tourist industry worked. They lured you in with the cheap flight and hotels, then overcharged for everything else.

Back in the room, Irina took a long shower. When she finished, she found Anya sleeping face down on the queen-size bed, still in her clothes. Irina half roused her, helped her out of her blouse and jeans, and pulled back the sheets. She stared at her daughter's body as she covered her with the sheet. She was only 13, but her breasts were already bigger than Irina's, and she was almost as tall. With her tennis-player father's genes, she'd probably end up growing even taller and prettier, and who knew what drama might come with that.

Irina dimmed the lights. She climbed in bed next to Anya. The room was clean but kitschy, with floral wallpaper to complement the bedspread; the carpeting was a little worn in spots, but at least it was clean. She couldn't expect much more at this price so close to Disneyland, and Anya was happy.

She closed her eyes but was awakened an hour later by a couple arguing in the next room. The walls were so thin she could hear every word, and with her body still on St. Petersburg time, she was soon wide awake. She started scrolling through the news on her phone. There was an article on BuzzFeed about teenagers in Macedonia creating fake news before the election. But nothing about the Agency. The world seemed to be moving on. She messaged Marina on WhatsApp.

"Midnight @Disneyland here."

"I bet some crazy shit is going on. Mickey and Minnie bringing in Goofy for a 3some."

"You need help."

"No it's true. I went out with a Serb who played Pluto at Disneyland Paris. Total sex addict. In a good way."

"You're too much."

Sleep seemed far off, so she logged on to her Facebook page. One of her neighbors back in Piter had started a discussion about the water pressure problems in the building and triggered a chorus of complaints, which Irina found depressing. The last thing she wanted to think about was the life that awaited her back home.

She wondered if Sergei might be awake and sent him a private message.

"So here we are in California."

"Cool. Where?"

"The Happiest Place on Earth."

"And the most expensive. Bring your own water bottle."

"Yeah, this is costing me $$$$. My Visa card is on fire."

"Come visit, I will buy lunch."

"So generous."

"Yes. Also it's free."

Irina sent an LOL and the crying-tears emoji. She waited a few minutes, but when Sergei didn't respond she logged off. She finally fell asleep at 2 in the morning, then woke up at 6am. Anya was still sound asleep, so she changed into her shorts and went for a run. She crossed the street and started up a running path lined with palm trees, the perfect Welcome to California workout experience, but the path ended after a couple of blocks, and she wound up on a typical suburban street broken up by traffic lights and lined with chain stores, office buildings and more fast-food restaurants. She could have been anywhere in America.

Everybody said it was important to get an early start at Disneyland, so Irina jogged back to the hotel and woke Anya. She took a quick shower and headed downstairs to take advantage of the free coffee and continental breakfast, which consisted of watery juice, hard-boiled eggs, sugarcoated American cereals in tiny boxes, and spongy pastries swirled with gelatinous icing. Irina drank the weak coffee and ate a couple of the rubbery eggs while she waited for Anya to arrive. The other tables were occupied by tense-looking parents rushing their children through breakfast to beat the other families to the gates.

After 30 minutes, Anya finally appeared wearing lip gloss, eye shadow, mascara, a bright red blouse and her nicest Topshop jeans. She moved through the buffet line and joined Irina at the table, holding a cereal bowl and boxes of Frosted Flakes and Honey Nut Cheerios.

"You call that breakfast?"

"We're on vacation."

By the time they entered the park, there were already long lines for Space Mountain, Indiana Jones Adventure and It's a Small Word, but Anya wasn't discouraged and seemed to have her own plan. She led the way to Sleeping Beauty's Castle, where she posed and had Irina snap several photos just inside the arch, making sure the top of the castle tower was in frame. Lines for the *Star Wars* rides were both 45 minutes, so Anya took selfies with Darth Vader and Chewbacca and suggested they move on. Next they circled through the park, with Anya checking off photo opportunities from a list on her phone. They stopped whenever they encountered a Disney character, and before long Anya had selfies with Mickey, Minnie, Donald Duck, Snow White, Ariel, Pocahontas, a Storm Trooper, Cruella de Vil, Buzz Lightyear and the mom from *The Incredibles*.

They decided to stop for lunch. Over $14 skewers at the Bengal Barbeque, Anya started posting her photos and crafting captions on Instagram. She looked up and darted from the table.

"There's Elsa."

She slipped in behind two other girls waiting to have their photos taken with the *Frozen* princess. When it was her turn, she handed the girl behind her the phone, then returned to the table triumphantly. Irina felt her irritation rising.

"So you think this is fun?"

"It's awesome."

"But we haven't been on any rides."

"I thought we could do the rides tomorrow."

Wading back through the crowd, they noticed only a few people waiting for the Mad Tea Party teacup ride. They went inside and sat in one of the pastel-colored cups. When the music started, the cups began to move in unpredictable loops. In the center of the cup was a wheel that made the cup spin. Irina kept turning it faster and faster, so they were whirling and looping. Anya laughed and shrieked as they nearly collided with other cups, then spun away at the last second. Irina threw her head back and turned the wheel. Hopefully, Anya could see that this was more fun than standing beside unemployed actors and posting photos on Instagram. Finally, the cups slowed down and came to a stop. Irina looked across at Anya, who suddenly looked limp and pale.

"Are you okay?"

Anya stood up shakily, staggered out of the teacup and vomited into the shrubbery along the edge of the ride. Irina put her arm around her daughter and led her to the exit. She had forgotten about Anya's motion sickness. In Piter they seldom rode anything but the metro together, so it wasn't an issue back home. They found a bench and sat down. Irina handed her a water bottle.

"Drink. Rinse out the taste."

Anya picked up her phone and flipped through the day's images.

"Can we be done for the day?"

Back at the hotel, Irina tried to stay awake to synchronize her body clock, but they both fell asleep. They woke up three hours later and found a Chinese restaurant Irina assumed would be cheap. They ordered pot stickers, sweet-and-sour pork and broccoli chicken, but the portions were small and they had to pay extra for rice, so the bill came to almost $50. Other families in the restaurant seemed to be headed back to Disneyland for evening shows and concerts, but those tickets were expensive and weren't included in Irina's travel package. They went back to their room and watched reruns of *Friends* and *The Office* until Anya fell asleep. Irina sat in bed beside her, wide awake thanks to her afternoon nap, and skimmed the news of the day on her phone. Around midnight she got a message from Marina.

"Why are you talking to people at Facebook?"

A chill went through Irina. "Sergei? He's an old friend."

"Are you hooking up with him?"

"No. I'm with Anya, remember?"

"I'm not being nosy. People here are asking. I'm just letting you know."

"What? Asking what?"

"About you and your Facebook friend."

"Why?"

"They wonder what you are up to."

"Are they tracking my private messages?"

"No comment. But you should stop with the troll jokes and making lunch plans."

Irina went back and reread her messages to Sergei. She tried to imagine how her boss Katya or the Mikhails might interpret them. At the time, she felt like she was joking with an old friend, but perhaps that made their comments seem cryptic. It was easy to imagine something more was being said between the lines. Clearly, if the Agency was tracking her private Facebook, they suspected her of something. But how bad was one troll joke? Hopefully, they could see she hadn't really revealed anything.

She turned off the lights, plugged her phone into the charger and spent the next few hours changing positions, staring at the ceiling and thinking about how much she dreaded going back to the Agency, especially now. If they were already convinced she'd told Facebook what they had done, her version of events wouldn't matter. Her name would end up on a list of people who needed to be watched. And they had so many ways to make her life miserable. She drifted into a restless sleep around 3 in the morning, then woke up with the alarm at 7. She roused Anya, and after a quick breakfast they headed to the park and arrived before the gates opened, in the hopes of beating the crowd.

They moved counterclockwise away from the herd surging up Main Street. First, they hit Indiana Jones Adventure, where they boarded a battered military transport that took them through stone caverns and darkened tunnels teeming with spiders, bats, snakes and menacing, occult idols. Irina wasn't a fan of the reptile family and had a particular aversion to snakes. Even though these were obviously sculpted out of rubber, their black eyes and flicking tongues unsettled her.

Next they made their way to Pirates of the Caribbean. While they waited, Anya posed for a photo with Captain Jack Sparrow. With his dyed, braided beard and thick mascara, he looked to Irina more like a sexual predator than Johnny Depp, although Irina seemed to recall Johnny Depp was having tabloid problems of his own. Maybe the look-alike actor wasn't so far off.

Anya posed with two zombies outside the Haunted Mansion, and after a short wait, they went inside. They were led in a herd through a series of rooms by an ominous voice until they finally ended up in skull-shaped cars that carried them through an assault of images from the underworld. Flying apparitions swooping toward them, ravens resting on skulls suspended in trees, clocks with snakes for hands spinning backwards, a disembodied head floating inside a crystal ball, a skeleton in a bridal veil wringing its hands. Anya laughed, shrieked and seemed to find the attractions more amusing than terrifying. But with her Russian fear of the supernatural, Irina had no interest in visiting the dark side. She was relieved to step out into the sunlight and follow Anya's lead to Mickey's Toontown, where iconic characters were supposedly always circulating. While her daughter scoured for photo opportunities, Irina sat on a bench and tried to enjoy the sun. She hadn't heard any more from Marina and wondered what was going on back at the Agency, what they might be thinking and saying about her. It was unbelievable a couple of harmless texts could provoke so much attention.

Anya returned with photos of herself with Maleficent, Winnie the Pooh and two chipmunks neither of them could name. From there they headed to Fantasyland, where they waited in line for 20 minutes at the Matterhorn and then rocketed off in bobsleds through tunnels of plastic snow and ice. A roller coaster was always good for getting the adrenaline going, and Irina started to get a second wind. They started across the park for Tomorrowland, but on the way Anya spotted It's a Small World.

"This is one of the classics. We have to do it."

After a few minutes, they were at the head of the line and took their seats. The boats began to move past vivid scenes of tiny costumed characters from around of the world moving in a blissful, benevolent cartoon. Midwestern farm families and Canadian Mounties. French cancan girls and British Royal Guards. Flamenco dancers and musicians in sombreros. Gondoliers in bouncing boats. Organ grinders with monkeys perched on their shoulders. Friendly Russian Cossacks beside onion-domed buildings. Genies on flying carpets and a menagerie of enchanted animals: kayaking teddy bears, leaping kangaroos, koalas and monkeys dancing in trees, goats nodding their heads in time to the music. Creeping along at a pace that would allow a 4-year-old to take it all in, the ride seemed to go on forever and Irina's claustrophobia began to kick in. She found the fixed smiles and repetitive movements of the figures disturbing. The vivid backgrounds seemed strangely ominous against the darkness looming behind them, as the song played, over and over, worming its way into Irina's brain:

> *It's a small world after all*
> *It's a small world after all*
> *It's a small world after all*
> *It's a small, small world.*

She clenched her fists and looked straight ahead, trying to will the boat to the end of its journey, and felt light-headed when she finally stepped out of the toy vessel.

Anya led the way to Tomorrowland, where they took the *Star Wars* ride and got face time with the robots. Anya took selfies with R2-D2 and C3PO. They still hadn't done Space Mountain and the line was almost an hour, so they decided to grab a quick snack at the Galactic Grill and go back while everyone else was having lunch. Anya ordered greasy chicken tenders. Irina did her best to choke down a dry, tasteless veggie wrap, but she kept thinking about her exchange with Marina the night before. She wondered if she should send another message to Sergei, some kind of casual remark about the weirdness of

Disneyland and missing life back in Piter. Maybe find a way to walk back her remark about trolls. She logged on to Facebook and sent him a message.

"There's a problem at The Happiest Place on Earth."

"The lines? Duh."

"No, bad food. They need blini. Cheap, tasty. Americans would love blini."

"Such a good Russian. Do you think Putin is listening?"

Irina froze. Her attempt to make up for her loose talk was backfiring. People were always saying careless things on Facebook, and Sergei didn't have a filter. She logged off. Maybe he would get the hint.

After lunch the wait for Space Mountain was still 30 minutes. As the line inched along, Anya started posting her daily photos on Instagram, and Irina checked her messages. Sergei had posted an image in her feed. At first, Irina didn't understand what she was seeing. It was a photo of a woman on a treadmill in the Facebook gym. She was wearing a T-shirt with the image of a wild-haired troll inside a Russian red star. In bold letters were the words "BLAME THE TROLLS." Beneath the image he had written a message: "You should come visit. Everybody wants to meet a real Russian troll."

As she stared at the image, Irina's confusion gave way to horror. At Facebook, they were putting troll jokes on T-shirts. It seemed impossible her posts could have set that in motion, but back at the Agency, that wouldn't matter. Because this was no joke. They would think she had told Sergei about the whole operation.

It was 2 a.m. back in Piter, but she sent a message to Marina anyway.

"Sergei is posting weird stuff but I didn't tell him anything."

Irina stared at her phone, waiting for a response. Marina usually responded quickly, no matter the hour. But as the minutes ticked past, there was nothing from her friend. Eventually, she and Anya reached the head of the line, where an attendant in a reflective suit summoned them forward. They took their seats in one of the tiny rockets, and he lowered a bar to lock them in. As the ride began, their ship was hurled down a tunnel lined with flashing lights, interrupted by rushing waves of darkness. Then they were hurled into a dark abyss, with nothing holding them up, surrounded by stars and asteroids that crackled as they flew past. Their ship soared, floated as if they were weightless, then turned and jerked, crazily changing directions as if it had lost control of its navigation. A spinning galaxy appeared in front of them and vanished.

As they spun and hurtled through the darkness, Irina tried to calm her thoughts but it was useless. She told herself this was just an illusion created by some diabolical amusement park wizard, but she wanted it to be over—she needed something to hold onto. She needed to get an answer from Marina so she could figure out what to do. She needed to explain that Sergei was just an old friend who was trying to be funny. As they began their descent, she felt herself falling faster and faster, as if she were trapped in one of those fever dreams that arise when infection takes over the body and creates its own disturbing, alien productions. Down and down they went until suddenly lights flashed, they hit the tunnel and were whisked along to the waiting attendant in the reflective jacket on the other side of the loading area. As they came to a stop, Irina glanced at her phone. Nothing from Marina. She struggled to stand up and stumbled out of the tiny rocket.

As they emerged into the light, Anya immediately got back in line to ride again. Irina shook her head. No more rides. She was desperate to reach Marina.

"I'm waiting for a message from work. There is something I need to do."

She suggested Anya get her fill of rides and selfies, and they would meet two hours later near the entrance to Tomorrowland. Irina sat down on a bench and sent Marina a series of texts.

"I know you don't sleep. What's up?"

"I need to hear from you."

"Sorry I know it's late but I'm worried."

She watched people streaming past in various states of Disney euphoria. Senior citizens looking lost but happy. Skipping, galloping children. Anya seemed too old for this. But perhaps that was why she'd wanted to come. One last fling at being a kid before surrendering to the urges and demands of adolescence. And maybe that was why Irina agreed to the plan. She was giving her daughter a happy exclamation point on her childhood before they started the next chapter of their messy lives. Now look where they were.

An hour passed and she heard nothing from Marina. If her only friend was distancing herself, then Irina must be radioactive. Her bosses back at the Agency were not to be underestimated. They had connections running straight to the GRU. In her most paranoid calculations, she imagined she might be only three conversations removed from Putin himself. Katya would talk to one of the Mikhails, Mikhail would talk to the Chef, the Chef would have word with Putin—and she would disappear with a splat like a bug on a windshield.

But what could she do? Go to the Russian press? To the U.S. embassy? Tell CNN? Another troll had come out and spoken to the press a couple of years before, and nothing had happened to her. Not yet at least. But in Russia, everything was a long game. You never knew when payback might arrive. Life was good until the polonium-210 turned up in your tea. She'd spend the rest of her life looking over her shoulder, living like a frightened mouse afraid to leave its hole. She couldn't live that way. She'd rather be like Pussy Riot, saying, "Fuck you, Putin. Come and get us." But that hadn't work so well for them. They ended up in prison, their manager poisoned. The KGB hadn't used enough to kill him, just enough for a trip to the ER and a week in the hospital. Enough to send a message.

She sat on the bench, sent another round of texts and waited for Marina to respond. Nothing. Something was definitely wrong. There was no way to know what might be waiting for her back in St. Petersburg. But slowly a new idea began to form. It seemed ridiculous at first, but her mind kept circling around it. What if they didn't go back? Of course she had to think of her mother. Tatyana would miss them terribly. But her mother was accustomed to playing the hand she'd been dealt. And she still had some immunity for being a once famous gymnast, with two Olympic medals to her name.

Her mind began to seize the idea. They *couldn't* go back. If they went back, her life would be out of her control the minute she stepped off the plane. With every sip of restaurant water, every cup of tea, she would be asking, "Is this the day?" In America, all she had was Sergei, but he had actually invited her to come. She could go to Facebook and tell her story. Tell Sergei and his friends that Russian trolls were not a joke. Hopefully, when they learned the trouble she was in, they would help her. How exactly this would happen, she didn't know, but with so many big brains, surely they would think of something.

She sat on the bench waiting for Anya to return, her heart pounding, her mind swirling around things she needed to do. Book a flight to San Jose. Dispose of her phone so she couldn't be tracked, Anya's too. If she could find a local phone store, she could pick up a couple of burners, like drug dealers did. Eventually, she would have to explain to Anya that they weren't going back, but she couldn't think about that now. If she thought about all the obstacles, she would lose her nerve. She knew it was a risky plan. But even a risky plan was better than getting back on a plane to St. Petersburg. This was her only way out.

Menlo Park

From the San Jose airport, they caught an Uber with a driver who wore headphones the entire ride and dropped them off at the wrong end of the Facebook Campus. They spent 20 minutes wandering through parking lots, and Irina began to doubt her plan, until they spotted a VISITORS sign outside Building 20.

Inside the lobby were two men and a woman in headsets at a massive plywood desk. Behind them the wall was painted various shades of blue, green, black, orange and pink, with drips running downward in long, messy streaks. Overhead were exposed ductwork and girders, as if the building was under construction. Could this really be the famous Facebook headquarters? Irina's stomach clenched as she approached the desk. What if Sergei wasn't there?

"I have an appointment with Sergei Pavlenko."

"Your name?"

Irina hesitated. Giving her name, that was making it real, crossing a line. She glanced over her shoulder at Anya, who had taken a seat across the lobby in an enormous pink chair.

"Irina Zakharova."

The woman smiled, tapped her keyboard and spoke into her headset. "Good morning, Sergei, I have Irina Zakharova for you."

Then she asked, "Was your meeting at 9:30?"

"Yes, I think so."

The woman pointed to a touch screen in front of her and smiled again.

"Can you sign in please? For both of you."

Irina typed in her name, then Anya's. A printer spat out name tags, and the woman handed them back across the desk in clear plastic sleeves. Now they were identified. They were officially at Facebook. If they sent her back to Russia, she would never be able to explain this.

She walked across the lobby and handed Anya her badge. There was something strange about the pink chair she was sitting in. Irina looked closer and saw it was made of dyed cardboard, thin strips stacked and glued together to form the arms, legs and seat.

"Is that comfortable?"

Anya shrugged. Her daughter hadn't spoken to her since the brief, hysterical outburst when she discovered her phone submerged, supposedly by accident, in the sink at the Anaheim Desert Inn.

Irina took the chair next to her. The cardboard was surprisingly soft and wrapped itself around her body. It was more like an artist's idea of a chair than a real one. The messy ductwork and drips on the wall were possibly some sort of cleverness too. She closed her eyes and tried to calm her mind, but the same thought kept coming up, the thought that everything was flying apart, that she had put too many things in motion and couldn't hold them together. And now she was sitting in a cardboard chair in a place pretending to be a lobby.

"Sergei will be surprised to see us," she said.

Anya ignored her.

Irina checked the clock above the reception desk every five minutes. Thoughts came up and she pushed them down. What if Sergei was there but refused to come out? What if he was actually KGB, living under deep cover for all these years? After half an hour, the woman from the desk approached her.

"I left Sergei a message but haven't heard back from him. Are you sure your appointment was today?"

"Yes, it was today. But he might have been sort of loose about the time."

"Okay, I'll try him again in a few minutes."

"Thanks," Irina said, forcing a confident smile.

Did they know she was lying, that she had no appointment? She wondered how she might look to them. A Russian woman showing up unannounced, with luggage and a young girl, possibly a complicated family situation. Such scenes would not be permitted in the famous Facebook lobby. Irina kept an eye on the receptionist, watching for a shift in her demeanor. So far she was still cordial, still smiling, but for how much longer? Irina had no choice but to sit there with Anya until the receptionist told her that Sergei hadn't responded, that she obviously had no appointment, and that they had to leave the building. Then what? Then they would take an Uber back to the airport, fly back to LA, continue with their trip as planned. From there fly to Vegas, hang out by the pool at the Mirage, then back to St. Petersburg, where she would explain to her bosses at the Agency that all her exchanges with Sergei were a huge misunderstanding. She'd simply tried to pay a visit to a friend so they could relive their Team Russia glory days. Nothing wrong with that. Then she would stay at the Agency long enough to ease their suspicions. The story made sense, but who was she kidding? She was a terrible liar. They would never believe her.

Anya stared at the carpet, looking miserable. The clock above the receptionist's desk read 10:31, so Sergei probably wasn't coming. She knew how undignified, how desperate she must look to be sitting there, waiting for over an hour. This was pointless. She stared at the clock and decided they would stay until 11:00, then leave the number of her burner phone in case Sergei decided to call.

Irina watched the friendly receptionist disappear. A few moments later, she returned from across the lobby, followed by a tall man in a blue Facebook polo, a security guard, Irina guessed, but casually dressed because this was California, where even security guards were laid-back. Like almost every other man in America under 50, he had a thin, hipster beard. They were both staring at her. Her heart was pounding. Her plan had obviously failed. She stood up from the chair to show she and Anya would leave quietly, that they weren't going to be a problem. But as the guard approached, she recognized the smirk beneath the beard: Sergei. He stopped a few feet away from her and shrugged, then opened his arms.

"So, you decided to surprise me."

He came forward and gave her a stiff, suspicious hug.

"We thought it would be fun to see an old friend. What a cool place to work."

Sergei stared at her. Irina could see he was processing the situation. He was obviously caught off guard but trying to be polite. He cocked his head and reached for Anya's hand.

"And this is?"

"My daughter, Anya."

"Nice to meet you, Anya."

The receptionist disappeared and they were left to stare at each other. Irina realized she had only thought about getting this far. She didn't know what to say or do next, but somehow she had to get her story out. She had to stick with her plan.

Sergei began to steer them toward the other side of the lobby. "I'm booked for training sessions most of the day, but I have a few minutes now. Would you like to have coffee?"

If they were just having coffee, she was going to have to talk fast. She was afraid to let him disappear, afraid he wouldn't come back.

"Sure. That would be great. I can tell you about some news from back home."

He gave her a fake, flat smile. "News from back home? Okay, but first let's get Anya a smoothie. Traveling is hard on the immune system."

He swiped the badge on his belt and led them into a vast, glass-walled cafeteria. They sat down and waited as Sergei went over to a busy café, where baristas were pulling espressos.

"This is so cool," Anya said.

He came back holding what looked like two coffees and a tall green beverage in a recyclable plastic cup, which he handed to Anya. He put one of the coffees in front of Irina. "Hope you like cortados."

Irina reached for her purse.

"No," he said. "It's free. Everything is free, every day. How's the smoothie?"

Anya nodded and gave him a thumbs-up.

Irina could feel her heart pounding all the way to her wrists. She could tell Sergei's radar was already up. Although he had no idea why she had come, he seemed to sense that whatever she was going to tell him was something he might not want to hear. But she wasn't going to let that stop her.

"I'm going to talk to Sergei for a few minutes, okay?"

He stared at her across the table. "Should we chat outside? It's warm."

They left Anya in the café and sat down in the bright morning sun. He looked at her, then at his fat, black Rolex, then back at her.

"So you survived Disneyland. What else is going on?"

She took a gulp of her cortado, burning her tongue and started speaking Russian, in case anyone overheard them. "The troll thing isn't a joke."

She paused. He smiled, waited. She continued, "There are 200 of us. Making up crazy things on the internet before the election. Mostly for Trump. And it's still happening."

He shook his head. "Please stop speaking Russian. The web is full of craziness. And porn. I think that's why they invented it."

"This is different, more organized. We used Facebook to make things go viral. Facebook ads, Facebook groups. We made up fake stories and created profiles of fake people so they would think we were Americans."

"Yeah, I saw some of it. But do you know how much content goes through Facebook every day?"

She stared at him. He wasn't listening. Was she the only one who cared about this?

"This is bigger than you think. It's like a factory with people working 12-hour shifts, 24/7 every day, going down our list of assignments. We created dozens of groups, hundreds of pages, thousands of memes, ads with fake hashtags and websites. We had millions of followers on Facebook and Instagram. We created fake protest groups, and people actually made signs and showed up in the streets when we told them to. I did hundreds of posts every day, just me. Facebook. Twitter. Instagram. All fake, all for Trump. Super targeted. Things for Blacks telling them not to vote. Stuff for gun freaks to show Hillary is a bitch who wants to take their weapons. Everybody expected her to win, and now she lost because of us. And we're still doing it. Americans have no idea."

Sergei smirked. "So you think you and your friends got Trump elected?"

"Don't laugh. My bosses back home are serious people. They get results."

"People here must have seen it."

"If they've seen it, why does Mark Zuckerberg say it's a "crazy idea"?"

Sergei leaned back away from her in his chair.

"So, you came here to tell me this?"

She nodded. "Also, they hacked my phone and my computer. They're reading my messages. They think I'm telling everyone about the troll factory."

"You sound pretty crazy."

"I can't go back."

He stared at her. "So you came here instead?"

She nodded again.

His eyes widened. "Why? You should go to the government. The *American* government."

"This goes all the way to the top. He who cannot be named. I figured it was safer to come here first. I threw our phones away at Disneyland. Nobody knows I'm here."

He stared at her. "Irina, what the fuck? So now you're some kind of secret informant? What do you expect me to do?"

"Tell someone. Tell Zuckerberg. Maybe he won't think it's so crazy anymore."

"I work in the gym, Irina. I can't just walk up and say, 'Hey, Zuck, you're wrong about the election.'"

"Sergei, think about it. We fucked up a superpower. Don't you think that's a pretty big crime?"

"I can't believe you're dragging me into this."

Five years and 5,000 miles away, he was still the same Sergei, always looking out for number one. She reached into her bag and handed him a sheet of paper, a handwritten list of Facebook groups, Instagram hashtags, blogs and web addresses they had created, and her login information for the proxy server they used. The last sleepless night at Disneyland, her hand had been shaking as she'd written it all down.

He stared stone-faced at the paper.

"So this is what? Evidence?"

"Yes, I wrote it down so there is nothing online."

"Unbelievable. They'll probably poison us both."

He stood up and stared at the list on the table as if it were radioactive. "You should hang onto that." He shook his head. "I don't even know where to start. I guess you can stay here and have lunch. Until I figure out what to do."

He handed Irina lunch passes with his ID number on them so their lunches would be free. She sipped her cortado and watched him walk away. Her heart was still pounding. She thought she would feel better by unloading her guilt, sharing it with someone else. Even if nothing came of her revelations, at least she had tried. But as she watched Sergei disappear into the cafeteria, she realized it wasn't going to be that simple. The real drama was just beginning.

She went back inside and sat down with Anya, who had finished her smoothie and was unfurling a cinnamon roll.

"Don't spoil your lunch," Irina said.

"We're staying for lunch? Cool."

Light poured into the cafeteria from all sides, which made Irina feel even more exposed. An early crowd began to gather. People came in alone and in small groups, and they just kept coming. So many were dressed in jeans and Facebook hoodies, they looked like members of a cult. She could tell Anya was starstruck, being at Facebook, surrounded by people who worked there, and Irina had to admit she felt a twinge of awe herself. She wondered what they did all day, if they had important, interesting jobs. Were they higher-ups or worker bees? It was hard to tell. She wondered how it could possibly require so many people to run a website where people mostly posted pictures of themselves, their food and their pets. But as she watched them streaming into the cafeteria, thousands of them, so young and confident, suddenly it all clicked. During her months at the Agency, she had seen how, among the world's billions of souls, Facebook found exactly the ones they were looking for, the ones who wanted to believe all the outrageous things they were posting. That was its magic, the ingenious code churning beneath the surface of the likes and comments—and these were the wizards behind the curtain. Irina wondered if the reports about what she and her coworkers had done had spread any uneasiness among their ranks, but that didn't appear to be the case. Maybe Zuckerberg's dismissal of the story was good enough for them, the only absolution they needed. Now it was back to business, back to keeping the world open and everyone connected. They were still the good angels.

The cafeteria was organized into different stations like restaurants in a food court. With so many choices, she and Anya didn't know where to start. They circled a massive salad bar with every imaginable leaf, vegetable, fruit, nut and protein, many Irina didn't recognize. They stopped in front of Yumi Sushi and watched two sushi chefs wielding knives through cool bricks of tuna, hamachi, and salmon, but they decided the line was too long. So they moved in an arc along the edge of the cafeteria, past the Righteous Ramen Bar, Planet Pita, Delhi Deli, and finally The Melting Pot for burgers, pizzas and artisanal grilled-cheese sandwiches. As they turned back toward the center of the cafeteria, they discovered several additional stations, each serving a more formal menu.

The Pan-Asian Station
-Black cod in miso with brown rice
-Chinese honey walnut prawns
-Spicy grilled pork with kimchi slaw

Sister Europe
-Braised lamb shank
-Mixed seafood tagliatelle
-Poached halibut with lemon & thyme

Today's Foodie Fantasy: Willy Wonka's Golden Ticket
-Lamb shank with chocolate rub
-Ricotta/chocolate ravioli
-Mixed vegetables with chocolate mole sauce

Irina found the choices overwhelming. "Let's just get a salad and find a table."

"No way," Anya said.

She drifted toward an island filled with an orgy of desserts. S'mores Pie topped with chocolate-dipped pecan shortbread cookies, Molten Chocolate Cake with a swirl of caramel mousse, Apricot-Blackberry Galette with Madagascar vanilla bean ice cream, and the

Call Home Cronut, a mutant mix of donut and croissant, topped with whipped cream, chocolate sauce and orange and yellow Reese's Pieces.

Amidst the decadent sprawl of sugar, Irina almost lost her appetite. She went back to the salad bar, then found a table at the far edge of the cafeteria, away from the crowd. Anya eventually appeared, her tray filled with a falafel pita, a slice of vegetarian pizza, sweet potato fries, a California roll and a lemon bar decorated in the image of SpongeBob SquarePants, with white chocolate chips for eyes.

Irina was annoyed.

"Are you going to eat all that?"

"I'm really hungry."

"We'll see."

Despite the freshness of the ingredients, Irina ate her salad without tasting any of it. As expected, Anya couldn't finish her pita or her fries. Irina tried to finish them off but could only force down a few bites, so the rest remained on the tray, a violation of their meal code. When she took their trays back to the automated conveyor belt that led back into the kitchen, she was disgusted by the amount of food still left on the plates.

By 2 o'clock, the lunch crowd had thinned out. They moved to the outdoor café, where Anya rolled up her sleeves and tried to get some sun. Irina tried to relax, but every time she closed her eyes, her mind started racing. She still felt jet-lagged and had a kink in her neck, so she got up and walked in circles around the perimeter of the café area, rolling her shoulders and neck to loosen the gripping muscles. They went back inside for something to drink. From a rack of 40 different beverage options, Irina chose a Smart Water and Anya selected ginger-apple kombucha, both free, of course.

Back outside, Irina sipped her water and watched the clock. At 3:35 she started worrying again, wondering if her whole plan had backfired, if the police or some other authority had been notified, whether she would be charged with her crimes. She knew nothing about the American criminal justice system, except what she had gleaned from *Law & Order: Special Victims Unit* and *CSI: Miami*. But obviously, she had committed several offenses.

Finally, around 4:30, Sergei returned to the cafeteria, accompanied by a woman in a tight green dress and two men. The taller one looked like a typical geek, hair down to his shoulders, wearing a T-shirt covered with lines of code. The short one—wearing a blue button-down shirt and rectangular glasses—looked more serious.

Sergei introduced her. "This is Irina." She noticed he didn't say, "my friend Irina." An awkward silence followed. No one smiled or nodded.

Sergei pulled Anya aside. "My Russian is getting really bad. I'll buy you a gelato if you help me practice."

The woman led the way back across the cafeteria, past reception to the other side of the building. Nobody spoke. They were obviously making no effort to put her at ease. As they walked, Irina noticed the woman's sneakers, with Gucci stripes and a bumblebee embroidered on the side. Back at the Agency, Marina had been obsessed with designer sneakers, so she knew these cost approximately $600.

They headed down a hall to a small meeting room with "Jar Jar Drinks" on a nameplate. When they closed the door, Irina felt sweat forming on her scalp and temples, as it did sometimes before a vault that didn't go well.

The three of them looked at her, no smiles, as if they wanted to put whatever this was behind them as quickly as possible. The woman appeared to be taking the lead.

"We understand you have information about Facebook content or activity related to the U.S. election."

"Yes. Also Instagram."

The woman stared at her skeptically.

"Could you describe what kind of activity?"

Irina reached into her Longchamp bag and pulled out the list she had tried to give Sergei. She placed it on the table.

"This is the information I spoke to Sergei about. I was part of a group that worked on the American election. We created groups, ads, hashtags and the rest. This is some of them."

The woman picked up the list, stared at it while holding it at arm's length, then placed it back on the table. She didn't seem eager for the information it contained. The Long-Haired Guy leaned forward, lifted the list and examined it more closely. He appeared unsurprised or unimpressed. "Was this operation run by the Russian government?"

Irina swallowed and felt her heart pounding again.

"Sort of. It's called the Internet Research Agency, in St. Petersburg. Two hundred people approximately. Two shifts, people working 24/7, posting on Facebook, Twitter, Instagram."

The Long-Haired Guy looked down the list. "Two hundred people for this?"

"No, this is just a small part. There was much, much more. So many groups. I don't know how many posts. Thousands. Every day I had a list of a hundred things to do. Blogs, memes, ads, posts, likes, comments on other posts."

Suddenly the man with the rectangular glasses looked concerned. "And what was the focus of this content?"

"At first, Ukraine. Then we switched to America before the election, pretending to be Americans."

The woman shook her head. "And why did you decide to bring us this information?"

"I wanted people to know what we did. Some people say Russians influencing the election is a crazy idea. But it's not crazy. We did it."

The woman fixed her with a cold stare. "Do the people you work for know you've come here?"

"No, they think I am on vacation."

The woman continued to stare. "This is quite a journey. Why did you decide to come here in person, with your daughter, instead of reaching out to us online?"

"Some of my...coworkers...I think they hacked my phone and computer. If I just send you an email or a text or a post, that's not a good idea. I thought it would be safer to come here. Safer for me. Safer for my daughter."

Actually saying the words aloud, acknowledging what she was doing there in the room, sent a pulse of anxiety rippling through Irina. What if these people didn't care?

The woman picked up the list. "All these efforts you're describing are violations of Facebook terms and conditions."

Irina was confused at first, then angry, as she let the words sink in. After all she had risked coming there, was this woman really lecturing her about terms and conditions? Was this bitch serious?

"Of course, that's why I'm telling you. I thought you would want to do something about it."

There was a long silence as the three of them stared at her. They were angry at her, that was obvious, but they also looked worried. The one with glasses looked impatiently around the room. "I have a board meeting to prepare for. Chelsea, can you take the lead on this?"

The woman studied the list again as he got up to leave the room. Finally, she spoke. "We need to look into this more deeply and may have questions. How can we reach you?"

Irina gave her the number of her burner phone.

Chelsea raised her eyes. "Is that your personal mobile?"

"It's a burner phone so it can't be traced."

The woman wrote down the number, Irina noticed, instead of entering it into her phone. It was almost as if they were all still unwilling to admit the meeting had just happened.

"Okay, we'll be in touch. Try to enjoy the rest of your vacation."

As Chelsea and Long-Haired Guy stood up to leave, Irina felt panic flooding in. Was that all they had to say? What was she supposed to do now? Where was she supposed to go? She never should have mentioned being on vacation; they seemed to be using that to take her less seriously. She stared at the table and tried to gather herself. Only now did she understand fully what she had done, how complicated and dangerous she had made things for her and Anya.

Sergei came into the room and sat down at the table across from her.

"Your daughter is having some frozen yogurt. With sprinkles. Where are you staying tonight?"

Irina shrugged. On top of everything else, she was running low on cash. "We don't know yet."

He shook his head. "You can stay at my place if you want. But only tonight. And whatever is going on, I can't be part of it. No more discussion."

"Thanks. I understand. That is very nice of you."

She followed him back to the cafeteria to gather Anya. People were coming into the cafeteria, picking up boxed dinners and taking them back to their desks. On their way out, Sergei slipped into the line and picked up something for the three of them. They followed him through a parking lot filled with Mercedes-Benzes, Teslas, BMWs and Priuses. He tapped his key, and the lights flashed on a silver Porsche Carrera a few feet away. Typical Sergei, she thought.

He opened the door for Anya, and she squeezed into the tiny back seat. "It's a bit cozy back there."

"So cool," Anya said. "Is everyone in America rich?"

Sergei smiled. "If they work at Facebook, yes."

Irina sunk into the passenger seat, which was strangely low to the ground, and was enveloped in the engine's deep, caressing purr. Sergei drove fast, down side streets and along a frontage road for a few miles. Then he merged onto the freeway and wove through several lanes of traffic to the outside lane. He kept changing lanes and tailgating, which normally made Irina anxious, but at this moment she didn't care. At least a catastrophic car crash would be a quick death. He exited the freeway and turned onto a winding street lined with sprawling homes surrounded by dark red madrone trees and massive California oaks.

"How do you like my neighborhood?"

"It's nice." Irina was tired. Everything was drier than she expected, almost like the desert.

"Do you know who lives in these houses?"

"No." She had no idea why he was asking.

"Very successful people."

The Carrera rumbled into the driveway of a modern, L-shaped house, nestled among manzanita bushes and clusters of exotic-looking plants with leaves that jutted out of the ground like spears.

"Can you tell a Russian lives in this house? Of course not. Subtle and understated. That's me."

He hit a button on a device attached to the car's windshield visor, and the massive garage door groaned open like the entrance to a castle.

They entered the house through the garage and stepped into a short hallway lined with jackets and caps hanging on hooks. The hall opened into the kitchen, which appeared to be under construction. An enormous chef's island covered with plywood occupied the center of the room.

"Sorry about the remodel. My contractor cuts me a deal, but he only shows up when his other jobs are slow."

Cabinets, many with missing doors, surrounded them on three sides. A band of blue masking tape ran along the perimeter of the ceiling, and a thin film of sawdust covered the floor.

"I'm what you call 'house poor.' I cashed out my stock options and bought this for one million seven. I'm putting it on the market for three-point-two."

He put the dinner boxes down on the plywood counter and opened the giant stainless-steel refrigerator. "Lots of drink choices thanks to Facebook and Costco."

He passed through the kitchen into a high-ceilinged room, where there was a large U-shaped sofa and a massive flat-screen TV.

"We can have our dinner and watch Netflix."

He clicked the remote, and the screen filled with their viewing options, then he handed the remote to Anya.

"You pick."

They grabbed drinks and sat on the sofa with their meals in front of them. Anya chose *Harry Potter and the Prisoner of Azkaban.*

"Good choice, that's the best one," Sergei said.

He went back into the kitchen and returned holding a bottle of white wine and two glasses. He poured Irina a glass and put it in front of her.

"This is what we drink here. No more cheap Romanian stuff."

Irina dutifully finished her grilled salmon. Her mind kept circling back to the meeting at Facebook, the woman Chelsea, her expensive sneakers and sour expression. Why did she end the discussion so quickly? Irina had expected them to react with shock and horror to what the Agency had done. Perhaps even show her some appreciation for revealing the problem. But maybe it was a problem they didn't want to see.

Irina woke up alone on the sofa. The room was dark, and at first she didn't know where she was. Slowly her eyes took in the details of the room, the big-screen TV, her wine glass still full on the table. Someone had covered her with a blanket. She was coated in a light sweat, sticking to her clothes.

She got up, stretched and went looking for Anya, who was sleeping in a huge bed in an otherwise empty room. She was still wearing her shirt, but her jeans, shoes and socks were strewn across the floor. Irina sat on the edge of the bed. The house was silent, so either Sergei had gone out or he was sleeping quietly deep in his bachelor lair.

Irina was wide awake and desperately wanted a shower, something to relax her and wash away the clammy, nervous sweat of the day. She found a bathroom across the hall, and the towels appeared to be fresh. She let the water run until it was warm and then stepped under it. She lathered her body everywhere with Sergei's mango-scented soap, rinsed and lathered her body again. She shampooed her hair twice, then stood under the shower and turned up the water hotter and hotter, as hot as she could stand it, letting the heat melt the muscles up and down her neck and across her shoulders. She imagined her body dissolving into liquid and vanishing down the drain.

She dried off with one of Sergei's big towels and realized she and Anya had left their bags in the car. She cringed at the idea of putting on her sticky clothes. Maybe Sergei would have something she could throw on.

She wrapped herself in the towel and headed to the far end of the hall. The door to what looked like the master bedroom was closed. She listened and heard only silence inside. Instead of knocking and possibly waking him, she cracked the door and heard a whispery snore. When she stepped inside, she saw him sprawled across the bed, deep in his dog dreams. She surveyed the room and stepped inside a walk-in closet filled with rows of drawers and clothes on hangers. It looked like a rapper's closet on *MTV Cribs*. G-Star, Diesel, True Religion, Nike, Adidas, Under Armor, Lululemon and Lucky Brand—nothing she could throw on after a shower. But on the opposite side of the closet was a rack with dozens of T-shirts pressed and arranged neatly on hangers.

She selected the smallest T-shirt she could find—a tie-dye design with "Facebook Over the Rainbow 10K" printed on the front—and slipped it over her head. Then she moved down a row of drawers, starting at the top. Light sweaters. Socks. Boxers (cotton). Boxers (silk). Finally she found a drawer filled with running shorts of assorted vintage. She slipped on a pair of purple Nikes that looked small enough not to fall down and ducked out of the room undetected.

She knew she wouldn't be getting back to sleep anytime soon, so she headed back to the kitchen to search for coffee. There was a machine on the counter that used prepackaged pods, and she found a stash of them in the freezer. She pulled a blue Facebook coffee cup from the cabinet, slid it under the spout, opened the hatch, inserted the pod and pushed the blinking button. What a ridiculous invention. She pulled a tall stool up to the counter. Immediately she felt the worry rise up and tried to push it back down. According to the clock on the coffee machine, it was 3:15 a.m.

There was an open laptop charging on the counter and she decided it would be good to catch up on the news. But she didn't know Sergei's login password so she sat at the counter sipping her coffee, her mind still circling back to the meeting at Facebook. It was almost like it never happened.

She went back to the room where Anya was and slid into bed next to her. She liked to stare at her daughter when she was sleeping. She felt she could see her more clearly when the constant fizz of teenage selfishness and hormones had quieted down, see what she was going to become. In the last year, the transformation had accelerated—her body, of course, but also her eyes and her hair, which kept getting darker and thicker. She moved with the same looseness as her tennis pro father, although she definitely hadn't inherited his hand-eye coordination. Irina wondered if Anya was going to become one of those women who stop conversation when they enter the room. She didn't feel equipped to handle a daughter like that. They'd never had the same soul connection she had with her own mother, the bond fused over the elation and suffering of sports. Anya was from a different tribe. She had a slower motor and kept her feelings hidden from Irina's maternal radar.

Irina thought about the danger she'd put them both in. Maybe Sergei was right: Nobody cared. Not Mark Zuckerberg, not Sheryl Sandberg, not this Chelsea. And if they didn't care, maybe Prigozhin and his gang back at the Agency didn't care either. Maybe truth or lies really didn't matter anymore to anyone. If so, the Facebook people probably thought she was deranged. And maybe she was.

The coffee had been a bad idea. She got up and opened the curtain. There was a crisp chill coming through the opening at the bottom of the window. Maybe she needed a little fresh air.

She got up and grabbed a jacket from one of the hooks in the kitchen hallway, wandered back toward the other end of the house. She'd never been in a house with so many rooms. Another hallway led to the front of the house, where there was what seemed to be a formal living room, unfurnished except for a massive leather sofa. As she started toward the front door, she spotted a black box with a blinking green pin light mounted on the wall. It looked like some sort of alarm system. She stared at it dumbly, afraid leaving would set it off and wake Anya and Sergei. So now she was trapped inside, three hours until daylight. Back at the Agency, her fellow trolls would be sitting in staff meetings gossiping, chatting in the gritty break room or eating smelly pizza at their desks. Knowing she had exposed everything they'd done, now she could never go back.

She lay down on the massive sofa and let it swallow her up. The white leather was cool on her legs. But lying there, falling into the deep uncertainty that surrounded her, imagining the terrifying events that might befall her, was not a good way to pass the rest of the night. She needed something to help her relax.

She crossed the house, listened outside Sergei's bedroom and slipped inside. He was still sprawled across the bed, lightly snoring. She noticed he was wearing boxers now, instead of those ridiculous bikini briefs. She locked the door behind her, just in case Anya woke up and came looking for her, pulled the T-shirt over her head and let the running shorts fall to the floor. She slid under the covers and rubbed her body against him. He turned toward her and groaned as if, even in sleep, he sensed opportunity on an animal level. She slid her hand into his boxers and pulled out his cock. She thought about going down on him to get things started but decided that would send the wrong signal, so she pulled down his boxers and climbed on top of him. Still half asleep, he reached around and cupped his hand on her ass.

"Irina…"

She thought she detected a hint of ambivalence, but she needed to finish what she'd started. She gave him a few brisk strokes and put him inside her. There was no doubt who was fucking who, but he was awake enough to grab her hard with both hands and do his part. It didn't take long for both of them to finish.

Afterward, she rolled off him onto the sheets. She felt better, less anxious—at least for the moment.

"Thanks. Much appreciated."

He half turned toward her, one eye closed.

"No protection?"

Irina snorted. "Catching something from you would be the least of my problems."

He was asleep again in less than a minute. Whatever. It wasn't like she was expecting emotional support. She picked up the borrowed T-shirt and shorts from the floor, slipped them on and went back into the kitchen. She put another pod in the coffee machine and scrambled herself a couple of eggs.

She was still sitting at the counter three hours later when Sergei came into the kitchen. She hoped Anya wouldn't walk in with him standing shirtless in his boxers, but it was his house so she couldn't say anything. He filled his cup without a word, then disappeared, which she took to be a bad sign. She would have to find someplace else to stay until Chelsea called back. She only had a couple of hundred dollars in cash left. She didn't want to use her credit cards because those could be traced, and they were probably going to be denied anyway. And what if Chelsea didn't call back? Then what would she do?

Sergei returned to the kitchen looking sharp but casual in his sweats and a Facebook polo. "So what's your plan for the day?"

"Look for a place to stay. Can I use your computer to search?"

"So, I'm kind of an asshole if I don't let you stay here, right? But this is some crazy shit, Irina."

"I know."

"Two days. Three at the most. After that, you have to figure out something else. The people you work for are too scary. And I have girlfriends, so we can't be fucking every night." He said this with a straight face and ducked into the garage. She heard the Porsche rumble to life and speed off.

Of course, she was grateful. The house was comfortable, and for the next two days she tried hard to relax, lounging with Anya, binge-watching *Friday Night Lights*. But she couldn't stop worrying and waiting for Chelsea or someone at Facebook to call. When she hadn't heard anything by the third day—not a call, message or text— she called Sergei at work and asked him to investigate, but he refused.

"No, please. I'm not part of this. I'm just the guy who runs the gym."

The longer the silence continued, the more anxious and vulnerable she felt. By Day Four she was a wreck, bouncing off the walls. She had given them volatile information, and they seemed unconcerned. Her tourist visa expired in a week. After that she didn't know what she would do.

She threw on the purple Nikes and one of Sergei's T-shirts, laced up her running shoes and took off for a run. It was mid-morning and, even in the last days of November, still warm. It felt good to be running, to be stretching her legs, to feel her heart beating from something other than the stress.

She ran to the top of the hill above the house and along a path that followed the ridgeline. Looking down from the ridge, all she could see were office parks, lined with quiet streets and neat rows of trees. She wondered if this was the famous Silicon Valley. If so, it didn't look like much.

She missed the path coming down from the ridge and by the time she found her way home, she was dehydrated, had run almost seven miles and walked the last two. She pulled two Smart Waters from the fridge and drank them at the counter, watching Anya binge on *SpongeBob SquarePants*. Since they had arrived in Palo Alto, her daughter had devoted nearly every waking hour to television. Irina decided the next day they would have to do something to get out of the house.

That evening she asked Sergei for suggestions. In such a famous place, there had to be interesting places to visit. But he wasn't helpful.

"There isn't much to see."

She didn't believe him, figured he didn't want to play tour guide and didn't want them to get too comfortable in his house. She did some searching online and came up with her own plan. They began the morning by taking an Uber to the Computer History Museum, which turned out to be extremely boring, unless you were a total computer geek. Next they went to the famous Apple Store on the Cupertino campus, which looked pretty much like all other Apple stores but sold more stuff. At first Anya was thrilled with her "I Visited the Mothership"

T-shirt, but she turned surly when she realized she didn't have a phone she could use to take photos and gloat to her friends.

There was still no word from Facebook, and Irina decided she couldn't spend another day sitting around the house watching Anya glued to the big screen. So the next morning, she took Sergei's advice and they went to the Stanford Mall. Irina hated the malls back in Piter. They were all garish shrines to tacky Russian taste, but this was different. Instead of stores crushed into a noisy, oxygen-deficient space, this was all outdoors, more like a park with actual sky overhead. They were free to stroll and browse at a more natural pace, and Irina let Anya take the lead. All the stores a teenage girl dreamed of were there: Anthropologie, Free People, Urban Outfitters, Lululemon and their first stop, Abercrombie & Fitch, where they were greeted by throbbing hip-hop and massive, sexy portraits of shirtless boys with shorts hanging off their hips. Although Irina had to acknowledge the quality of their six-packs, with the pounding music and epic-scale soft porn, it felt more like a strip club than a retail experience. But she kept her observations to herself.

As Anya floated among the displays of merchandise, Irina realized the cruelty of bringing her such a place and not allowing her to purchase anything. So despite the fact she was hemorrhaging cash, she let Anya select a hoodie with a big AF from the sale rack. Next they browsed Urban Outfitters and Lululemon. Irina cringed when she spotted PINK. God knows Irina was no prude, but that store disturbed her. It was always pushing the line, trying to sexualize girls at younger and younger ages. What bothered her most was that it worked. As they entered, Irina tried to steer her daughter to the sweatpants, but Anya veered off toward lingerie and emerged holding a three-pack of pastel-colored thongs. If they were back in Piter, Irina might have put up a fight. But here, with everything else going on, she didn't have the heart.

As they walked down the central promenade, Irina started to notice the other shoppers. They were mostly white or Asian, and even though they were casually dressed, Irina could tell from the way they carried themselves they were obviously wealthy. That was also clear from the selection of stores—Tiffany, Hermès, Louis Vuitton, Kate Spade, Tory Burch—selling not just merchandise, but perfection. You could even buy the perfect car, a Tesla, right there.

As they passed store after store, Irina tried to imagine what was required to maintain such a perfect life. She knew there must be subtle codes of behavior to show you belonged, and she guessed it must be obvious she and Anya weren't members of the club. Although people weren't exactly staring at them. In fact, it was the opposite: Nobody was looking at them. It was as if she and Anya weren't there.

She started to feel light-headed. Maybe she was just hungry or dehydrated since she'd only had coffee and juice before leaving the house. Or maybe she was losing it, buckling under the stress because time was running out and Facebook hadn't called, and their return flight was less than a week away. Up ahead Irina spotted a sign for the Go Fish Poke Bar.

"I think we should have lunch."

They walked up and joined the line leading out the door. Back in Piter, sushi was an indulgence. Here it seemed to be everywhere. They ordered hamachi bowls and found a table outside in the sun. Many of the other customers were young—students, Irina guessed, possibly from Stanford, which was famous for all the tech geniuses who went there, including the guys who started Google, Instagram, Snapchat and WhatsApp. She knew the campus was somewhere nearby. Irina remembered herself at that age. Everything seemed so promising then. She was one of the top five women pole-vaulters in the world, training four hours a day, working her body to exhaustion. These kids seemed like a different species, like the people she'd seen at Facebook, only younger. No doubt in a few months, or maybe a year, many of them would be there. Perhaps the raw fish was part of their training, fueling up on the ultimate brain food, so nothing could stop them.

After lunch, Anya wanted to press on, but Irina decided she'd had enough. As they headed back down the promenade, her phone started buzzing in her pocket. It was a local 408 number.

"Hello, this is Irina."

"Irina, this is Chelsea Howard from Facebook. We reviewed the information you shared and would like to schedule a follow-up discussion. Are you free tomorrow at 11?"

Irina's heart was pounding. "Of course. Eleven o'clock."

"Just come to the lobby at Building 20, same as before. We will send someone down for you."

"Okay, see you tomorrow."

Irina wanted to feel relieved, but her mind was racing. She had been waiting for days for the call, but Chelsea's voice was so casual, as if meeting with Irina was just another event on her busy calendar.

As they waited for their Uber, they saw a strange white object approaching, like a giant egg moving under its own power. A group of girls standing near them giggled. "Here comes the mall cop."

It was a robot, with blinking blue eyes on four sides of its head and a slit in the center of its body designed to look like a smile. Silver letters on its side stated its name, "K5," and its purpose, "For your safety and security." Anya and Irina stared in disbelief. It looked harmless enough, almost friendly. Gentle electronic beeps alerted shoppers as it approached. As she stepped out of its path, Irina wondered what else the robot might be doing. Taking photos? Shooting video? Recording their voices? But she told herself to relax. There was no reason to think a friendly looking robot was anything more than that. Chelsea had called. She was going to Facebook the next day, which meant they might be able to help her, somehow.

Irina woke after only two hours' sleep. She found a curling iron left behind by one of Sergei's girlfriends and spent the morning curling her hair, then trying to straighten it. She put on the least Russian-looking of the outfits she'd brought from Piter—her Hudson knockoffs and a white silk blouse—which she thought seemed too casual but which Sergei said was "fine."

Because she was afraid of arriving late, she called her Uber so far in advance, the driver dropped her off at the campus an hour early. She sat in one of the funky cardboard chairs and focused on her breathing to clear her mind, like she did before a vault. Don't think. Let go. But her composure dissolved the minute the slender male assistant approached her in the lobby.

"Irina?"

"Yes."

"Come with me."

His voice seemed too calm, too neutral, almost like another robot, as if who she was and the information she carried was just another set of data points. They crossed the lobby and walked through two security doors, which he opened with the swipe of his badge. She felt her body trembling on the inside, an odd sensation that had never happened during competition. When she competed, she knew how to transfer the flood of adrenaline into energy and send it to her muscles. If she had a flaw as a competitor, it was that she was too aggressive. Her mistakes were errors of power not nerves.

She followed Robot Boy into a conference room with a name-plate that read, "Death Star," another *Star Wars* reference. Seated on one side of the table were Chelsea, Long-Haired Guy and three others in Facebook hoodies. Irina avoided their eyes, trying to stay composed.

"Thank you for joining us," Chelsea said. She guided Irina to a seat on the opposite side of the table and began the meeting without introductions. Her sneakers, Irina noticed, were Burberry plaid.

"Irina, based on the information you shared, we've begun a content discovery on our platform. I've already shared that content with the team, and they've submitted questions for you, which we will go through today."

Irina nodded. She wanted to make it clear she intended to be helpful.

"We also have some general questions about the strategic focus of your organization."

Irina felt a sharp pain in her gut. "Yes, okay, but it wasn't 'my organization.' I was just a worker bee."

"Of course. The organization you were part of."

A younger woman sitting next to Chelsea interrupted. With the same narrow, penetrating stare and stylishly cropped hair, she looked like a younger clone. "We've booked this meeting to run two hours. But don't worry, lunch is coming."

From across the table, Long-Haired Guy tapped his keyboard, and an image of 55 Ulstina Savushkina appeared on the screen.

Chelsea Junior began the questioning. "So, do you recognize this building?"

Seeing the building gave Irina a strange pang of homesickness. Part of her wanted to be back there, where none of this was happening. "Yes, that's where I worked. Where we worked."

"And how many people worked there?"

"At first, about 150. But they kept hiring. By the election, 200 or more."

"And what was the name of the organization?"

"Internet Research Agency. We just called it 'the Agency.'"

"Was this a government agency or a private company?"

Irina paused. "I would say both. Private but serving the government."

"And was there a structure? Different departments? Different capabilities?"

"Website development was on the first floor. Graphics were on two. Blogs, ads, posts were on three and four."

These seemed like such basic questions. Perhaps, Irina thought, this wouldn't be so bad.

"And what was your position?"

"Specialist."

"Specializing in what?"

"Social media. Mostly writing ads, memes, blogs, posts. Because my English is pretty good."

Long-Haired Guy interrupted. "You posted directly to our platforms through a VPN?"

Irina thought for a second. "Yes, always. Our IT guy set up servers here in the U.S. so it looked like we were posting from here."

Chelsea Junior narrowed her eyes. "And what was the strategy behind your work?"

Irina hesitated. She could feel all eyes on her.

"Do you mean what was the purpose?"

"Yes, the purpose? The mission?"

Irina reached for one of the bottled waters in the center of the table, removed the cap and took a sip. She realized she should have thought about the questions they would ask, so she could have her answers ready. Just blurting out the first words that came to mind was going to be a problem.

"The purpose was to create conflict."

"What sort of conflict?"

"Conflict in American society."

Chelsea Junior looked stunned. The room went silent, as if everyone had stopped breathing.

Original Chelsea cleared her throat. "And how did you attempt to do that?"

"We created Facebook groups that focused on controversial issues, and we did ads that linked to the groups. When people joined, we tried to stir them up."

"Which issues? Which groups? Could you be more specific?"

Irina could feel Original Chelsea's stare. Negative energy surged through the room. By the time this was over, they were going to hate her for sure.

"Immigration. Guns. Black Lives Matter. Pro-cops. Military. Muslims. Super Christians. Gay rights."

"And how did you, in your words, 'stir them up'?"

"We pretended to be Americans and posted memes or likes or comments saying, 'Hey, we're just like you. We're on your side.'"

Across the room people were shifting, fidgeting in their chairs. Irina took another sip of water. She thought the list of groups and names she had given them earlier would reveal what they had done.

But these people were either slow to connect the dots or didn't want to connect them.

Original Chelsea gathered herself. "Let's go through some of the content we've discovered. Hopefully, you can confirm its source and answer questions we have."

Long-Haired Guy tapped his keyboard again, and one of her memes appeared onscreen. A parade of illegal immigrants appeared with the caption "Let's Build That Wall!"

"Was this work done by your Agency?"

"Yes, one team would create the meme. Everybody else would post likes or comments like 'Great idea. America First. Fist-pump emoji.'"

Long-Haired Guy clicked through a procession of memes and posts, one at a time, over a hundred of them. A woman holding a baby and a sign that read, "Give me more free shit." A mosaic of faces with the caption "They're tired, hungry and coming for your food." A series of different wall images: walls made of brick, concrete, steel, barbed wire, images from the wall in *Game of Thrones*, all with captions like, "Let's Do It!" Irina acknowledged each one with a nod or a "yes." There was no point in holding back now.

He clicked through several dozen ads and memes from pro-military and right-wing groups they had created: Being Patriotic, Save Our Heritage, Stand For Freedom. She had worked on all of them. They were all basically the same.

"We discovered hundreds of these," Original Chelsea said.

"Yes, we did so many because they were so easy. Just grab any photo of a guy in military uniform and add a caption, "Like If You Believe in Heroes.' Or, if you were feeling lazy, just 'Thanks Hero.'"

Nobody spoke. The room had become very still. Irina glanced around the table at the blank, numbed faces.

Long-Haired Guy clicked through a series of side-by-side PATRIOT VS. LIBTARD memes. The formula was always the same. On the PATRIOT side, they always chose gun-toting women with large breasts and perfect butts, adorned with the American Flag. On the LIBTARD side, the women were obese or odd-looking, dressed in peculiar, rainbow-colored clothing, holding up drawings of vaginas or deformed penises. She and Marina had done a number of those, each one more ridiculous than the last. Even now with the scorn directed at her from all sides, she found them absurdly comical. True, what they had done was devious and crass. But if Americans were actually stupid enough to be influenced by such things, they shared some of the blame.

Next Long-Haired Guy clicked through memes and posts from #blackstagram, starting with "Black Is Beautiful" images, showing sexy women with long legs and gorgeously coiffed Afros.

Original Chelsea seemed confused by them. "What was the purpose of these posts?"

"At first, we were just trying to get followers. Then we started doing more political stuff."

"Like these?" They showed her a series of posts with photos of black victims: Eric Garner, Trayvon Martin, Michael Brown. She nodded as he clicked through them. She had done them all and could recite their names from memory.

"How did you measure the success of this activity?"

"The usual way. Likes, reposts, more followers for the groups."

Irina took another sip of water. She wondered if they knew about the rallies. If she didn't mention them, they might think she was concealing something.

"Sometimes we would use the Facebook events feature to set up rallies."

Original Chelsea looked at her from across the table. "You mean online meetups?"

"No, street rallies."

"You used Facebook groups to organize street protests?"

Irina nodded. "We used the Black Matters group to set up a protest near the police headquarters in Houston. Then we reached out to a Support the Police group and got them to show up at the same time. They were all screaming at each other. It was all over Fox and local TV."

Irina glanced around the table. She could see them struggling to absorb what she'd just described, trying not to be pulled under by it. She didn't tell them how amused they had been back at the Agency when they watched the two groups squaring off in the streets.

Original Chelsea glared at her. "So this was one of your goals? Stirring up…a race riot?"

Irina avoided her eyes. She had already given them the Hillary ads and memes, but they weren't connecting the dots.

"Not exactly. The purpose changed just before the election. After we stirred things up, we started saying 'Hillary doesn't respect Blacks.' 'Hillary is corrupt.' 'Hillary hates Colin Kaepernick.' 'Hillary doesn't deserve your vote. Hillary is an old white lady who doesn't get us.'"

Another silence filled the room, so she decided to complete the thought for them.

"The purpose was to convince Black people not to vote for Clinton. Or to vote on Instagram instead of going to the polls."

Irina felt the mood in the room turn into a kind of despair. For a moment, even Original Chelsea was speechless. Finally, Long-Haired Guy broke the silence.

"It appears there was a surge in your activity just before the election."

Irina realized it was pointless to hold anything back. "Yes, we targeted Michigan and Pennsylvania. We went after the purple states like Virginia and Florida. In Florida, we used Facebook groups to set up flash mobs in, I think, 17 cities."

Original Chelsea shook her head in disgust.

Irina stared down at the table. Her heart was pounding. Her water bottle was empty. Coming to Facebook now seemed like a terrible idea. She had underestimated how naïve they were, how angry and wounded they would be. She thought she would feel better by coming clean, but describing her actions made her relive them, made her feel how shameful they were, all over again. Maybe they would put her back on a plane to Russia after all. She envisioned all the bad things that might happen to her. Cops coming into the room, arresting her, putting her in jail, then sending her back on the plane. The KGB greeting her at the airport. Hours of grim interrogation. And what would happen to Anya?

Again, Long-Haired Guy broke the silence.

"Can you tell us about this?"

Irina winced. Onscreen was the photo of a man standing in front of the White House, holding a hand-lettered sign that read, "Happy 55th Birthday, Dear Boss." She wished they hadn't found it.

"Is this one of your associates?"

"No. Just a random American."

"So what does it mean?"

"It was a message to our boss, Yevgeny Prigozhin. Sort of like a birthday card from America."

"You had people from the Agency working in America?"

She could feel the hostile energy rising again in the room.

"They went there for research. Before the election."

"What kind of research?"

"Which groups to reach out to. Which states to go for. Which were the purple ones."

"So, was this some sort of coded message?"

"Not really. It was just a joke."

"What kind of joke?"

Irina recalled how hilarious the photo had seemed as it traveled through the Agency. Now she was ashamed of it.

"The joke was getting Americans to wish Prigozhin Happy Birthday. Like we could get them to do anything."

Someone whispered, "Oh my god" and she could feel the loathing swirling around her. Original Chelsea turned toward Long-Haired Guy and put her hand across his keyboard.

"Okay. Enough. No more questions. We will circle back with everyone."

People stood up, shell-shocked, and started silently filing out of the room, stopping to select a boxed lunch or bowl of salad from the cart just inside the door.

Original Chelsea sat texting with her back to the room. Long-Haired Guy stared at Irina across the table. He seemed calm, undisturbed, maybe because he was the one digging up all the terrible things they'd done. He closed his computer and got up to leave the room. Irina wondered if he knew he had barely scratched the surface. There was more, much more, things she hadn't seen, because there had been a second VPN she never used. But this didn't seem like the time to mention it. If he was so smart, maybe he would find it on his own.

Irina leaned back in her chair, closed her eyes and tried to quiet the inner roar. After a minute or so, Original Chelsea swiveled in her chair. Only the two of them were left, but there was no eye contact. Clearly, they were adversaries now.

"I've scheduled a debrief on this with members of senior management an hour from now. I'd like you to join us. Until then, Daniel will keep you company. Let him know if you need anything."

As if on cue, Robot Boy reentered the room. He and Original Chelsea stepped outside, then he returned and took a seat near the door. It was obvious he had been told to keep an eye on her.

"Let me know if you want lunch."

He was trying to be nice. Perhaps that was their strategy for keeping her calm until the authorities arrived. She wondered if she should have requested a lawyer as TV criminals often did. A wave of regret broke over her—for leaving Russia, coming here, bringing Anya. In the last few weeks, there had been moments like this of suppressed terror, when she realized she had destroyed her old life and had no idea what might come next. Would they put her in jail? She hoped it would be one of those prisons they put famous Americans in, that were really just rooms with furniture instead of cells with bars. In any case, wherever they put her would be better than a Russian prison.

Robot Daniel stopped texting and looked up from his phone. "Chelsea says the senior team has to join remotely. She needs another half hour to set it up."

Irina wondered who the senior team might be and if Sheryl Sandberg might be joining. In any case, the meeting had worn her down, and she decided it would be wise to freshen up.

"Could I use the restroom?"

He led her through one of the security doors to a row of unisex restrooms. She stepped inside, locked the door behind her and indulged in a brief escape fantasy. There was one way out: a vent for the HVAC system above the toilet. If she stood on top of the seat, she could leap up, dislodge the vent cover with her fist, pull herself into the vent and crawl her way through the system to freedom. She'd head to Sergei's, scoop up Anya and disappear into the forests of California. But given her lack of wilderness experience, they'd probably get lost. Helicopters would spot them in a few hours. And these thoughts were all nonsense anyway, just her mind coming up with wild schemes. She wasn't Angelina Jolie or the star of *Alias*. She looked at the reality facing her in the mirror, hair hanging in clumps down both sides of her head, pink blotches on her cheeks, deep, anxious furrows across her forehead. She splashed water on her face, took the small bristle brush out of her bag and ran it through her hair. After a few strokes, she decided that was as good as it was going to get.

Robot Daniel was waiting for her. She followed him back through the security door to a break room, where she selected a Red Bull from one of the vending machines. When they got back to Death Star, she popped open the can and finished it in a couple of gulps.

"You must be exhausted," Robot Daniel said.

They went back to waiting at opposite ends of the table. Finally, Original Chelsea and Long-Haired Guy returned. Chelsea clicked the remote, and two faces appeared side by side on the big screen, both men in their early 40s. One was wearing a white shirt and tie and sitting behind a big desk. The other one, with the rectangular glasses, she recognized from her meeting the week before. This time he was calling from a rustic cabin with mountains visible through a window in the background. Every few seconds his face turned to pixels.

"Hello, Drew. Oliver, sorry to interrupt your adventure. How's the connection on your end?"

"Not great. You'd think for $1,200 a day you'd get the fast cable."

"Are those the Torres del Paine in the background?" Big Desk asked.

"Correct."

Original Chelsea cut in. "Must be getting late there. Since you both have questions, I thought it best to do this in real time."

"Is Sheryl joining?" Big Desk asked.

"Too soon. She wants a clearer picture of what we're dealing with before we loop her in."

"Okay, I have a few questions for Irina. Is she there in the room?"

Chelsea pushed a button on the remote, and the camera swiveled on its axis to widen its view of the room. "Yes, she is here."

"Okay, Irina, have you spoken to anyone else about the work you were doing at the Internet Research Agency or discussed any of the content we reviewed with you today?"

Irina looked up at the giant faces. "Only with Sergei."

Glasses raised his voice, "Who the fuck is Sergei?"

"Sergei Pavlenko. He works here in Menlo Park," Chelsea said.

"What group is he in?"

"He runs our fitness center."

"Well that's fucked up. Why is he involved?"

"The two of them were friends previously in Russia." Original Chelsea glared at her for confirmation. "Isn't that right?"

Irina nodded, "Yes."

"Somebody needs to reach out to Sergei and make sure he understands the sensitivities. That's critical," Glasses said.

"We've already done that," Chelsea said. "Sergei understands this is an internal audit and therefore confidential."

"Let's be sure we're not overreacting to this," Big Desk said. "If their ad spend was $100K. That's a rounding error."

"They weren't just doing ads," Long-Haired Guy said. "They created hundreds of Facebook groups. They were all over Instagram too."

"But it's our job to manage this information. Let's be careful how we talk about this," Original Chelsea said.

Glasses reached offscreen and held up a bottle of red wine. "It's late here. Just one more question. Irina, why did you decide to come forward with this?"

She decided not to mention her ill-advised messages to Sergei. Better to appear she was coming from the high ground. "Because I thought someone needed to know what we did. Nobody was taking it seriously."

Her words hung there for a moment. They didn't seem to know how to respond.

"Okay then. Let's review where we are," Glasses said.

"Chelsea's discovery process will demonstrate we're pivoting hard on the issue of the election," Big Desk said. "I'll work on the visa issues."

Glasses interrupted. "Let's not get ahead of ourselves. We're not going public with anything until we complete a full content audit. Are we clear on that?"

Everyone nodded.

"Chelsea, circle back with the team and tell everyone: Voice communication only. No email, no texts, no Slack, nothing electronic. Everybody got that? I'm coming back a few days early, so we can reconnect on this first thing Monday."

"I'll set that up," Original Chelsea said. "Anything else?"

Onscreen, the giants shook their heads.

"Okay, thank you, Drew. Oliver, enjoy the rest of your adventure."

"Thanks. We're going to do some glaciers tomorrow before they melt."

Original Chelsea clicked the remote again, and both men disappeared from the screen. She picked up her phone and tapped out a text. Then she looked directly at Irina—trying, it seemed, to suppress her contempt.

"We would like more detail from you for our discovery. How content leading up to the election was developed, targeted, etcetera."

Irina stared at her. She didn't understand.

"You mean more meetings?"

"Yes. We realize this will complicate your return to Russia."

"My visa expires in a week."

"We know. Drew in our D.C. office is already looking into what can be done."

"So I can stay here?"

"Temporarily. At least until our discovery process is completed."

Irina was having a hard time keeping up.

"So where will we live?"

"Someone from the People@Facebook team is going to join us and take you through the specifics."

Original Chelsea went back to texting and ignoring her. A few minutes later, there was a soft knock on the door. A woman with enormous brown eyes entered holding a file folder. She had the dark, perfect skin of a telenovela movie star and perfect dimples that weaponized her smile. She radiated an almost religious warmth.

"You must be Irina. I'm Ariana from the People@Facebook team. We are moving quickly today."

Irina had no idea what was happening. She nodded anyway.

Glamorous Ariana smiled and opened the folder. "We would like to set up a living arrangement near our campus, so that you can work closely with us. Since you are living with your daughter, we thought a two-bedroom apartment would be acceptable."

"You're giving me an apartment?"

"Yes. You will be working with us as a consultant with living expenses covered. That includes rent, and we will provide an additional $6,000 a month as compensation while you are working with the team."

Irina couldn't believe this was happening.

"What kind of work will I be doing?"

"Assisting with the rest of our discovery," Chelsea said. "Apparently, there is more to discover."

"And we want to make sure you are comfortable while you are assisting with this effort," Ariana said. "We will also provide a laptop, phone, an email address and a personal PayPal account, which you can use for any transactions."

She handed Irina the folder. Inside were photos of the apartment and a list with her phone number, email address, various account numbers.

"So how long will I be staying here?"

"We need to prepare detailed reports," Original Chelsea said. "It could take weeks, months."

"Do you have any questions?" Glamorous Ariana asked.

Yes, of course she had questions. So many they converged into a mental gridlock she couldn't untangle. Irina stared at the folder. "So… what if the visa is a problem?"

Original Chelsea stared at her. "We'll do our best to resolve it."

Irina could see if it were up to Chelsea, she'd be on the next Aeroflot flight back to Piter. But something had changed. No doubt they still despised her, but now they seemed to need her cooperation. For the moment, at least, she wouldn't be going to jail.

"So what happens next?"

"The apartment is fully furnished. You can move in as early as tomorrow."

Irina stared dumbly at the two women but the meeting seemed to be over. Ariana walked her back to the lobby and called her an Uber. By the time she got back to Sergei's, she was numb. She walked past Anya, sprawled on the sofa in a video stupor, watching old episodes of *Buffy the Vampire Slayer*. It looked like a bomb had gone off in the kitchen, with empty Doritos and Chips Ahoy! bags on the counter and a trail of Lucky Charms leading from the sink to the coffee table.

She waved to her daughter as she went past. "I have a bad headache. You need to clean this up before Sergei comes home."

She kept walking straight to their bedroom, peeled off her clothes and threw them onto the floor. She went through her overnight bag and found her earplugs and then rummaged through the medicine cabinet in Sergei's room, where she found all kinds of interesting things: Adderall, Viagra, Cialis, Prozac, Zoloft, Oxycontin. She swallowed an Ambien with tap water, even though it was only 4:00 in the afternoon, and climbed into bed. As the drug took effect, she dreamed of being pursued by some unnamed menace through the streets of St. Petersburg. Vera and Tatyana berated her for neglecting some critical instruction and putting everyone at risk, as they led her down into the sewers of the city to hide until the danger had passed.

The apartment was twice as large and more comfortably furnished than any they had ever lived in. Although the furniture was boxy and impersonal, Irina could tell it was expensive, a step up from IKEA, and the kitchen looked like a page torn from a magazine, with clean white cabinets and counters, and bright steel appliances that looked like they'd just come out of their crates. The oak floors were covered with thick area rugs that caressed their feet as they walked across the room.

The morning they'd moved in, Glamorous Ariana called with the key code and told Irina to text a list of groceries. They would do her shopping and keep the refrigerator stocked. They also gave Irina a new notebook computer and both her and Anya new phones. Until their visa issues were resolved, Ariana asked them to keep a low profile and avoid speaking to the neighbors, which wasn't a problem, because the building was new and none of the adjacent units were occupied. The Russian in her made Irina wonder if their generosity was in part a way to control her. Since she and Anya didn't have a car, they had to Uber everywhere. And because Facebook supplied her phone, the Uber receipts would provide a record of her comings and goings. She wondered if the apartment might be bugged or under video surveillance, but even if they were watching her every move and possibly catching the occasional flash of boobs or ass onscreen in some hidden lair, she figured, *So what?* After the drama of their travels, the golden California light that filled the rooms felt like a drug, quieting the fear gnawing inside her, making her feel like everything might be okay. She felt it most in the afternoon, when the gray chill of St. Petersburg would be creeping into the city's bones. Back home, suicide season was just beginning. While here, even in December, she could sit outside and gaze down at the thick, green patch of lawn below her terrace and let the warmth of the day spread over her like a blanket. It seemed impossible that ordinary people were allowed to live this way.

For two weeks she heard nothing from the Chelseas. Surely they weren't going to put her up in a luxurious apartment without demanding something in return. She called Sergei a couple of times, but he no longer picked up or returned her messages. Her only contact was Glamorous Ariana, who asked probing questions to assess her emotional state, reassured her she would be making a big contribution when the time was right and promised her "things were moving forward."

She also set up a homeschool tutor for Anya and arranged for her to take conversational English with a Chinese girl, Mei, and two East Indian twins, Sari and Neeta, whose parents were Facebook engineers. Ariana even arranged for the families to attend a private screening of *Star Wars: The Last Jedi*. Although the engineers were pleasant and obviously brilliant, Irina could see there was no connection between Anya and the other girls, who made a show of speaking English as they orbited around their parents. Sitting beside them in the theater waiting for the movie to begin, Anya looked several years older and seemed determined to make her boredom known. In the Uber on the way home from the theater, Irina tried to draw her out.

"So how do you like the other girls?"

"They talk too much."

"They're just practicing their English."

"Maybe they should practice saying more interesting things."

While awaiting further instructions, Irina went back to her morning runs, finishing with an hour of crunches, push-ups, pull-ups and stretching to exhaust herself and get through the day. Finally, just before the Christmas holidays, she got a call from Glamorous Ariana and an email invitation to a meeting the following morning, with the subject line "Project P Kickoff." She wore her best jeans and a V-neck sweater, which she thought would help her blend in. The only thing missing was the Facebook hoodie.

Glamorous Ariana escorted her across campus to a small conference room called Force B w/ U. When she arrived, she noticed the interior windows were covered with sheets of brown butcher paper. Original Chelsea and Long-Haired Guy were seated at the table along with the three others from the last meeting. As she took a seat near the door, they kept talking, without looking up, sharing their thoughts on the company's holiday party, held at some San Francisco museum the night before. They compared notes on the fake falling snow ("very realistic"), the Aspen ski gondola suspended from the ceiling ("nice touch"), the actors dressed as elves ("a little creepy"), the booze ("never mix champagne and small-batch bourbon"), the music by LCD Soundsystem ("amazing") and the tab ("had to be close to $2 million"). As she listened silently, Irina felt…what? Small? Envious? Invisible? But then she realized this was the famous Facebook FOMO everybody talked about, radiating from the source. This was FOMO world headquarters.

Original Chelsea glanced at her watch and took control of the room.

"Great party, right? I heard rumor there's a Cristal shortage in the global supply chain. But we're all awake now, so welcome to Project P. As you can see from the windows, what happens in this room stays in this room. Everything we review and discuss here is absolutely confidential."

Original Chelsea paused and glanced around the room, confirming the gravity of the meeting but somehow avoiding Irina's eyes.

"Project P stands for Project Propaganda. As everyone now knows, there were major attacks on our platforms from various organizations to influence the recent election. We don't know the full extent of those efforts yet. That's what we will be digging up."

Long-Haired Guy spoke. "Until now, Facebook never focused on this kind of malicious content. It was easier to assume the world was good. Obviously, we have to rethink that. We're already into the discovery process. What we shared at the last meeting was just scratching the surface."

Original Chelsea frowned. "Let's keep the energy positive. This team is proof of how seriously senior management is taking this."

"Right, the security team will be working through the holidays," Long-Haired Guy said. "We'll have more to share after the holiday break."

Original Chelsea looked at him. Irina sensed there might be some sort of power struggle going on. "We're still deciding on the proper cadence for these meetings. But as we go through this, it's important to remind ourselves of all the good Facebook does around the world. We connect people. Connecting 2 billion people is complicated. But like Zuck says, 'We need to do better.' Any questions?"

Nobody spoke. People seemed to want to end the meeting and get back to talking about the party.

"Okay, I'll give you all 30 minutes of your life back."

Irina stood up and slipped out of the room. Nobody had spoken to her or even acknowledged her, as if they were trying to pretend she wasn't there. She wasn't sure why she had been invited to the meeting or what they expected her to contribute. At the first meeting, she had forgotten to mention the Agency's second VPN. She could tell them about that. Sending an email seemed like a bad idea, so she waited outside the room for Original Chelsea. As people filed out of the room, they glanced at her and looked away. But as Long-Haired Guy drifted past, she caught his eye.

"I wanted to mention something."

He stared at her, curious.

"The Agency had another VPN."

Now he looked more curious.

"I don't know the address because I never used it. But other people did."

He nodded. "Thanks, Irina. That's helpful."

"You're welcome."

She realized it was one of the few times anyone at Facebook had actually spoken her name.

The office was closed for a week over Christmas. Glamorous Ariana sent over an artificial tree and ornaments. Irina sensed the isolation around the holidays was wearing on Anya, so they paid another visit to the Stanford Mall, and she let Anya pick out her own presents: Hudson Jeans, tops and sweaters from Topshop, some Coach boots and another five-pack of thongs from PINK. On Christmas Day, she made *pampushky* filled with cherry jam for breakfast and a pork tenderloin with apples and sour cream for dinner. It was an absurd amount of food for the two of them. For dessert they had Stolichny cake, which only reminded Irina how far from home they truly were.

By now her mother would be worried, but it was too risky to reach out to her. Her old colleagues at the Agency obviously knew something was seriously amiss. Eventually, she would have to tell Anya they were not going back to St. Petersburg, ever. But she wanted to postpone that conversation until she knew what was happening with their visas, and it felt like the clock was ticking. She could feel Anya's boredom and surliness coming to the surface.

Weeks passed without word from Project P but the story about Russians interfering in the election was back in the news. Obama kicked out a bunch of Russians and took away the Virginia mansion where they held their cushy weekend retreats. But the story focused on Fancy Bear, Guccifer and the stolen emails. Irina found it unsettling there was no mention of Facebook. Perhaps people still didn't know. What worried her was the possibility that they knew and didn't care.

Every morning she woke up hoping for something to happen or someone to tell her what to do. When Anya's tutor arrived, Irina headed to the Facebook gym, swiping herself in with the contractor's badge Glamorous Ariana had given her. The gym had every form of fitness machine. Sergei was still keeping his distance so sometimes she'd chat with the other trainers. But otherwise she kept to herself. Between the treadmill and rowing machine, she'd do 90 minutes of cardio, then weights for half an hour and half an hour of stretching. By the time she finished, she could barely lift her arms. She'd shower and then spend a couple of hours in the cafeteria, surfing the web over her smoothie and salad. Every day she checked Russia Today and other sites to follow the exchange of accusations and rising diplomatic tensions. Putin and his cronies dismissed charges of election interference as "an absurdity." If her work at the Agency had taught her anything, it was that repeated, emphatic lying worked.

One morning she got a call from Glamorous Ariana. "Good news. We have gotten your visas extended for six months."

"Okay, good." That was a relief. Irina wasn't sure what else to say.

"Do you have any questions? How is your daughter?"

"She's getting very bored. She needs to meet some other kids her age."

"I understand. Let me see what I can come up with."

"Also, I don't know what I'm supposed to be doing."

"You're working on Project P. That's very important."

Irina knew it wasn't in her interest to debate the significance of her contribution and she was afraid to ask the obvious question: What happens after six months?

The California winter bore no resemblance to any of the St. Petersburg seasons. One night the temperature dropped and frost formed on the grass but the next day it turned warm again. To Irina, it began to feel disorienting, like they were refugees living in a suspiciously comfortable, alien land. But Anya seemed to be adapting. Ariana had arranged for her to take a filmmaking class at the local high school and her English kept improving. Irina arranged a quiet celebration for her 14th birthday and Anya invited an older girl she met in class, Kirsten, who brought expensive yoga pants as a gift.

For lack of anything else to do, Irina intensified her workouts, adding ropes and kettlebells. One day she walked past a row of cardio machines and spotted Long-Haired Guy on one of the ellipticals. He was wearing a light blue Banca di Roma jersey and matching silk shorts, as if dressed for a 1990's Champions League soccer match. It was a strange choice for working out in the Facebook gym, but she had a thing for long-haired soccer players. He had recently shaved, and without the beard he bore a slight resemblance to a popular French midfielder she had vivid fantasies about as a teenager. However, his movements on the elliptical were not those of a finely tuned physical specimen. There was something comical about him. A few days later she spotted him on one of the spin bikes in lycra shorts and a tight orange jersey with the word "Molteni" on the front, as if he were training for the Tour de France. He waved when he noticed her staring, and they exchanged gym nods when she passed on her way to the locker room.

She took a long shower and found her usual spot in a far corner of the cafeteria. She was just finishing her lunch when he appeared, looming over her holding his tray. "Can I join you?"

He sat down before she could answer. "We found the second VPN."

"Good," she nodded. An awkward silence followed. "I haven't heard anything about Project P. I thought maybe I got kicked off the team."

"No, you've done so much already."

Irina stared at him. She couldn't tell if he was serious or joking, if he was referring to the terrible things she'd done or the fact she had the guts to reveal them. She grabbed her tray and stood up to leave.

"Wait. Sorry. Don't take that the wrong way. Just say, 'Fuck you, Dez'. I'm Dez, by the way. I don't think we were ever formally introduced."

"Okay, Dez. Nice to meet you. Bye."

"Wait. One question: Do you know how the Agency paid for the ads?"

She did, because it was the same way they paid for SIM cards, office supplies, light bulbs, vodka, everything. "I think we used PayPal."

He nodded. "Unbelievable." Then he seemed to get lost in thought, and she slipped away. Given Original Chelsea's edict of confidentiality, it made her uncomfortable to be discussing such things in the cafeteria. But this Dez seemed to be his own man.

When she saw him a week later, he was back on the elliptical in bright green basketball shorts and a matching jersey with the name "Havlicek" and a large number 17 on the back. Instead of running shoes, he wore black Converse low-cuts with white socks that came up to his calves. With his long legs thrashing, he looked like a giant praying mantis attempting flight. Irina decided he was a very strange person, but he was the only person at Facebook who ever really talked to her.

He found her in the cafeteria after his workout.

"Can I join you?"

"Plenty of space. As you can see, I'm not the most popular person."

"Popularity is everything."

"Is that the Facebook motto?"

"*The Simpsons*. Season 10, episode one."

Irina watched him organize the items on his tray. Plate, fork, knife, compostable cup, bottle of sparkling beverage. Every item needed to be touched.

"*The Simpsons* is very popular in Russia, except for the episodes about Yeltsin's drinking and the herpes on Gorbachev's head."

"Do you miss Russia?"

Irina's guard went up. "Complicated question. When I do, I just check my weather app."

"How did you know Sergei?"

Irina wasn't sure where this was going. "We trained together."

"He's an interesting character."

"He was a race walker. Not your typical Russian athlete."

"And you were a pole-vaulter?"

Another personal question. "Yes. Back in the day, as you say."

"So, did you have an archrival you competed against? Raising the bar inch by inch, pushing each other higher?"

She wondered if he had been watching footage of her battles with Yelena Isinbayeva and Stacy Dragila, some of which was still online. She decided to change the subject.

"There were lots of rivals. I have a question for you. Why the elliptical?"

"It's efficient."

"Yes, sure. Elliptical is used by people who want their workout over as quickly as possible."

"Sometimes I do the StairMaster."

"Also weird. Do you ever notice how strange it is having all those stairways lined up in the middle of the gym?"

"You mean from a feng shui perspective?"

"If you want to do stairs, go outside and find some real ones. Or try the rowing machine. More dignified. Especially for tall guys."

"I'm actually sort of anti-gym. I only go when I feel my body turning to butter."

Irina had spent most of her life surrounded by alpha jocks. She didn't know many guys who would admit to being lazy and soft.

"Is this why you have these strange outfits?"

"Vintage Boston Celtics, 1960s."

"Why not wear Nike like everyone else?"

"Too serious. Like I'm there to show off my deltoids."

"So the outfit is like a costume? A joke?"

"Something like that."

"You're saying 'fuck you' to the gym."

"Exactly." He readjusted the position of his compostable cup, plate and utensils on the tray, then took a bite of his quesadilla. "I have another question. How did you decide which Facebook groups to create?"

"It was like a test. They gave everybody the polling data and told us to create different pages. Some friendly, some funny, some more extreme. The angriest ones got the most followers, so we focused on those."

"Where did you get the polling data?"

"I don't know. Someone in America."

He stared at her. "Interesting."

And he had more questions. Was the Agency connected to the GRU? Were they involved in posting Hillary's stolen emails? Did they have contact with the Trump campaign? While Project P had gone quiet, he seemed to be conducting his own investigation. It seemed strange he was pumping her for information in the cafeteria. Eventually, she told him about her family history, how her mother's brilliant career was ruined by the pixie Olga Korbut. She told him about her father's death from performance-enhancing drugs but left out the part about knocking him unconscious with a skillet. She told him about her early years in gymnastics before she switched to pole vault, about the injuries that ended her career, about how living in Piter was the opposite of living in California.

In the gym, she noticed he gave up the elliptical for the rowing machine. He still wore the quirky outfits, soccer shorts and matching jerseys with "Fly Emirates" or "Newcastle Brown Ale" on the front. The Frenchman Irina had a crush on had once played for Newcastle United.

Dez seemed embarrassed to talk about his own childhood, growing up in the old section of Palo Alto, in a big house under a canopy of oaks. His father was a venture capitalist and his mother a patent attorney, which meant he spent his childhood moving from screen to screen. His memories were all of TV and video games; he never played sports, which Irina found difficult to grasp.

"Didn't you ever want to go outside and run around?"

"Not as often as you'd think."

"What did you do all day?"

"Zelda, Legend of Zelda, Super Mario 64, Super Mario Brothers 3, Donkey Kong, Tony Hawk Pro Skater, Final Fantasy VII, Metal Gear Solid, Ocarina of Time, Chrono Trigger, Street Fighter 2, Super Metroid, Doom, Myst, World of Warcraft, Guitar Hero, Call of Duty, Grand Theft Auto, Halo and Resident Evil 4."

"A lonely boy with his game controller."

"We thought of ourselves as game developers in training. Playing video games and eating junk food after school every day felt like a pretty full life."

"Boy geniuses from the mean streets of Silicon Valley."

"Like everybody else who works here. This is what happens when you get too many smart people in the same place thinking the same way. Everybody keeps optimizing the algorithm until you end up on the dark side."

Irina knew lots of intelligent Russians, but they were not jokesters like this Dez. He seemed to know something about everything. Vodka production, crime scene forensics, gothic cathedrals, the kinesthetics of thoroughbred horses, the role of mitochondria in muscle training, endangered species of Kamchatka. If she brought up a topic he knew nothing about, like the demise of the Soviet sports system or the physiological basis for cross-fit training, he would show up the next time having immersed himself in it. Irina couldn't predict where the conversation would go, but it was never boring. He asked questions and he could find something absurd or amusing about nearly everything. Occasionally he launched into subjects she found tiresome, like his ongoing experiments with LSD and mushrooms.

"The normal brain screens out so much information, because it's not necessary for survival. What we call 'reality' is like the lowest common denominator. The drugs let things in, so you perceive patterns you normally don't see."

"Like infinity symbols in the sky? I have enough reality. I don't need to see more."

When she was competing, she was always surrounded by men with beautiful bodies. Although she knew it was possible, she never felt the urge to have sex with a guy for his mind. But one night after Anya went to bed, she watched *The 40-Year-Old Virgin* and had a couple glasses of wine. Before she knew what she was doing, she had dialed Dez's number.

"Hello."

"Did I wake you up?"

"No."

"Hi, I just watched *The 40-Year-Old Virgin*. Pretty funny."

"The best of the Judd Apatow movies."

There was a long silence.

"Would you like to discuss other Judd Apatow movies?"

She had called a man after midnight. Anya was asleep in her bedroom. What was she thinking?

"I was wondering if I could see your limited-edition action figures."

An even longer silence followed.

"Okay. 637 Twickingham Court."

She hung up and checked in on Anya sleeping. Irina decided if she were only gone an hour, it would be fine. She put on a black thong, new jeans and a tight camisole top, then applied some foundation and a thin layer of mascara. She took a step back to look at herself in the mirror. She had to admit the savage workouts were paying off.

As she punched in the destination for her Uber, she wondered if Facebook might be tracking her phone data. If so, they would see she had called Dez, which might raise a few questions. But it would be worse if they saw she paid him a visit in the middle of the night. So she entered the address of a bar half a mile from his house. She could walk from there. She left her phone on the kitchen counter so she couldn't be tracked.

The driver dropped her off at the bar and she started walking. It was supposedly only 10 minutes away, but she took a wrong turn and wandered in circles for almost 20 minutes. The homes were all darkened and there was no traffic. A Menlo Park Police cruiser drove by slowly. She realized she must have looked suspicious roaming the neighborhood on foot. She considered asking for directions but decided that might be a bad idea so she smiled at them foolishly and kept walking. Finally, she reached his house, set back from the road, all steel and glass but more modest than Sergei's. The doorbell made a loud electrical noise, which made her jump backward.

Dez opened the door and she stepped inside.

"I got lost."

He was wearing the same T-shirt and jeans he'd worn to the office, no socks. She wished he would have displayed more enthusiasm for her seduction, but it was too late to turn back now.

She kissed him hard on the mouth, then soft. "I only have 30 minutes." She slipped her tongue into his mouth and pulled his T-shirt over his head. He picked her up by the ass. She wrapped her legs around him, and he carried her into the kitchen.

"I don't have any clean sheets," he said.

He sat her on the kitchen island and pulled off her jeans and her thong. When she pulled his boxers off and slid him inside her, it felt like an itch she had been wanting to scratch. Pushing hard against his body, she could feel he wasn't as fit as her usual partners. His muscle tone left something to be desired. But she liked him and it felt good. She needed this.

Afterwards, he picked his pants up off the floor and put them back on. She slid off the counter and found her thong and jeans.

"Do you want a glass of wine or something?"

Irina shook her head. "Anya's at home sleeping."

"How about a ride home?"

"Such a gentleman."

In the car there was awkward silence. She was about to make a joke about action figures, but he spoke first.

"Project P is on hold."

"Why?"

"We completed the discovery of election interference and sent it to senior management. No response."

Irina was afraid to ask what that might mean for her, for Anya, so she came up with a less disturbing question. "What's going to happen next?"

He shrugged and was quiet until he pulled up in front of her apartment.

"Do Russians believe people are basically good or basically bad?" he asked her.

"Basically bad."

"So there you go," he said, looking straight ahead.

When he didn't show up for lunch several days in a row, she wasn't angry but she felt weightless, adrift. Without Project P, she had no idea what would happen to her, to Anya, to their visas. Sex with Dez had been a bad idea, her mistake. It was a nice break from the boredom and he was interesting enough, but he was her only real friend at Facebook. She hated herself for jeopardizing that, considering her situation. But one night he showed up unannounced at her apartment a little after 11.

"I thought you should see this."

He pulled his computer out of a backpack, tapped a few keystrokes, and a PowerPoint presentation appeared onscreen.

Facebook, Russia & The 2016 U.S. Election

He began clicking through his slides.

3,814 Facebook Ads

"Like you said, the Agency placed lots of ads."

7,074,015 rubles = $100,000

"Pretty brazen of you to pay in rubles. Pretty sloppy of us not to notice."

He clicked through a sample of images: Hillary in dreadlocks, Satan wrestling Jesus on Hillary's behalf, Bernie Sanders attacking the Clinton Foundation for corruption, ads telling people to vote for Jill Stein.

"I included some of your greatest hits. We could see how you used our analytics to target specific groups, especially in the last few weeks leading up to the election. Nice to know you found our tools useful. But really advertising wasn't your primary domain expertise, as we say. Where you and your collegues really shined was in your organic activity."

81 Facebook Groups

"You were very prolific," he said.

The slides that followed were filled with names of some of the groups arranged in rows.

Angry Eagle	Angry Patriot	Angry for Jesus
Anonymous News	Army of Jesus	Badass Blacks
Back the Badge	Being Patriotic	Black 4 Justice
Black Matters	Black Edification	Black Excellence
Black Baptist Church	Black Business	Black Rights
Black Power Now	Black Speaks	Blackness Forever
Black and Proud	AfroKingdom	AfrikaNow
'Merican Fury	Carolina Cops	Watch the Police
Stand for Freedom	Pray 4 Police	Progressive Nation
Woke Blacks	Born Liberal	Black4Black
Brown Power	Feminism Tag	Feminist Forever
Muslim Voices	Williams and Kalvin	Snowflakes United
Veterans Come First	South United	Being Patriotic
Stop All Invaders	Clinton FRAUDation	Trumpsters United
Proud Blacks	Stay 4 Police	L for Life
LGBTQ United	Raised in Texas	Cop Block US
Lone Star State Rebels	Patriot's Heart	Ancestral Wisdom
Save Our Heritage	Protect Our Heritage	South Will Rise
Super Sisters	Super Saviors	Righteous Few
Righteous Pathways	Lone Star Lovers	Texas Rises

"All of the groups linked back to VPNs you provided. Much appreciated. We could see how you used our platform's feedback to focus your efforts on the groups that received the most engagement."

Being Patriotic	**387,098**
Black Matters	**257,847**
Woke Blacks	**237,647**
Army of Jesus	**145,976**
LGBTQ United	**124,653**

"You also created lots of content, which you generously shared."

80,000 pieces of Content

29 million likes + shares + comments

Irina stared at the numbers. Back at the Agency, she had worked with her head down, with no real sense of the scope of what was going on around her.

"Twenty-nine million? That can't be true."

"Actually, that's just the engagement number inside the groups. This is how many people saw your content across the platform."

145 million views

"If we factor out duplication, that's roughly 30 percent of the U.S. population. And that doesn't include millions of engagements on Instagram."

Irina closed her eyes. The fact she had been part of something so massive and monstrous was shocking, even now. And she knew the damage wasn't over. They had cultivated an army of millions of spreaders for their lies. It was impossible to guess what they might do next.

"How is this possible?"

"It's the magic of Facebook, the secret sauce. I spent my first eight years on the Growth Team. Smartest people in the world, using every hack to make the Facebook experience as addictive as crack, to keep you locked in and get you to share—the more you share, the more people we reach and the more money we make. You just dropped your twisted content into the system. Our algorithm takes it from there."

"What's going to happen now?"

"Senior management will find a way to bury this or maybe leak it when the world is distracted by some tsunami or nuclear accident. You may be the only other person who ever sees it."

As Dez predicted, Project P was quietly disbanded. His report was scrubbed, reduced to a blog post and a link to a dry-sounding white paper: *Information Operations at Facebook*. Neither Russians nor the Agency was mentioned. Meanwhile, thanks to the efforts of the PR team, *Wired* and *Forbes* ran stories with quotes from Original Chelsea about Facebook's "exhaustive and ongoing" attempts to root out propaganda on the platform. Zuck apologized for his comment dismissing election interference as a "crazy idea," issued another promise "to do better" and embarked on a global listening tour in an attempt to address his empathy deficit. The company unveiled plans for a vast campus renovation that included a rooftop hiking path with a redwood grove and benches for quiet reflection. After taking a brief hit, the stock was surging again.

As weeks passed, Irina floated in anxious limbo. The only things that kept her grounded were her workouts and nocturnal drop ins with Dez. Anya seemed to be making friends at her filmmaking class but their situation seemed so temporary. Their visas, which had been magically extended, were about to expire again.

But a company designed for viral information spreading can't keep secrets for long. By the end of spring, reporters from the *New York Times* and the *Guardian* were circling. Rumors began to drift across campus like a bad smell, and every week seemed to bring revelations of new transgressions for which the company could be blamed. Disrupting the French elections. Ethnic cleansing in Myanmar. And Zuck's empathy tour seemed to be backfiring. The media were merciless, saying he looked like "an alien on his first visit to planet Earth." Just a few months before, people thought he might be president someday. Now he was being mocked for bottle-feeding a calf. But the day the Special Counsel investigation was announced was the day everything changed. The news hit the campus like a chemical bomb, releasing a sinister mood into the air. The Facebook campus was now a crime scene.

Irina was finishing her post-workout stretches when the news appeared on the TVs in the gym. The Facebook employees around her removed their AirPods and fell into grim-faced conversations. Irina's paranoia exploded. After weeks of silence, the other shoe had finally dropped. This was it. Now she was sure they would deport her. She called Dez.

"So the government is doing an investigation?"

"Right. Subpoenas will be coming. But that means our report is evidence, so it can't be buried. Zuck and Sheryl are going to have to own it now."

"What about me? Could I be arrested?"

"No, you're the whistleblower."

"Whistleblower?"

"You blew the whistle. Exposed the operation. Whistleblowers are the new heroes."

"So they'll give me a medal? I don't think so."

On her daily visits to campus, her fears were confirmed. After months of relative anonymity, she began to detect hostile vibrations when she went through her daily workouts at the gym. People strenuously avoided eye contact. In the cafeteria, they gave her a wide berth as she moved through the salad bar and waited in the smoothie line.

With Facebook's image under the microscope, nobody wanted to see evidence of the stain. She became convinced she and Anya would be exiled when their visas expired. Perhaps they wouldn't be so cruel as to send them back to Russia, but there were plenty of other places they could be deported to, Canada or possibly Ecuador. Dez tried to reassure her, but she didn't believe him.

"I was the messenger. You know what happens to messengers, right?"

"Fortunately for you, it's not that simple."

"Something bad is happening. Russians have a sixth sense when plots are forming against them."

"We don't have gulags here."

She stopped going to campus and instead went for long runs in the hills, with her music turned up as loud as she could stand it. She'd run along the ridge for miles, drop down into the nature preserve, then run back up to the ridgeline, anything to escape her thoughts. One afternoon as she circled back to the apartment, her phone started buzzing, interrupting Kendrick Lamar throbbing through her headphones.

"Hello?"

"Are you Anya's mother?"

Irina felt a twinge of panic. Who could this be?

"Yes, this is Irina. Anya's mother."

"Hi, I am Birgit, Kirsten's mother. They are taking filmmaking class together."

"Oh, yes."

She wondered how the woman had gotten her number. Obviously, she was more involved in her daughter's friendships than Irina was.

"I'm calling because Kirsten hasn't come home yet. I was wondering if they stopped at your place after class."

Irina slowed to a stop in the park. "I'm not at home now. But I can text Anya and see if they're together."

"I think they're together. Anya is the only girl Kirsten mentions. She was supposed to be home an hour ago. She's not answering her phone."

Irina didn't like where this was going. The woman seemed like a typical hovering American parent. Now she was implicating Anya in her daughter's deception.

"If you stay on the line I will text Anya."

Irina typed. "Where r you? R you with Kirsten?"

They waited in silence for a reply.

"I normally wouldn't worry about this. But Kirsten just got her license, and she cannot be driving with other girls in the car."

Irina remembered Kirsten as older, but wouldn't have guessed she was old enough to drive. "Your daughter has her own car?"

"She has my Range Rover."

"I'll text her again," Irina said.

"I need to know where u r"

"I'm also texting Kirsten for the 20th time."

Their texts went unanswered, and it became awkward waiting for their daughters to respond. They agreed to call each other if they heard anything and hung up. As she started jogging toward home, Irina's mind circled back to one of her paranoid fantasies. What if Russians had tracked her down, abducted Anya and swept up another girl in the process? She went inside, drank cold water from a thermos and ate a banana as she paced the kitchen. Finally a text popped up.

"We have a flat tire."

Below the text was a photo of a Range Rover with a flat rear tire on what appeared to be a city street. Although Irina was relieved no

Russians seemed to be involved, Anya's story didn't make sense. Irina called her.

"Mom, I can't talk. My phone is almost dead."

"Where are you?"

"The city."

"San Francisco?"

"We're doing a film for class. We're fine, but I have like no power left, and someone is coming to fix the tire."

"Anya, this sounds funny to me. Tell Kirsten to call her mother now."

"Her phone is dead too. I have to go."

Anya hung up and didn't pick up Irina's callbacks. Irina called Birgit as promised.

"I talked to Anya. They are in the city for a project, so she says. They have a flat tire, which someone is coming to fix, and your daughter's phone is dead. This is why she cannot call you. Or at least this is their story."

"The Rover has new tires and two chargers in the center console. They need a better story."

Irina tried to think of what a less distracted mother might say or do in this situation, but she couldn't come up with anything. The awkward silence resumed. They repeated the promise to stay in touch and hung up.

Two hours later, Irina heard a car pull up in front of the apartment. She went to the window and saw Anya coming up the walk and a Range Rover speeding away. Irina was relieved to have her daughter home safely and was prepared to let the incident drop, but the look Anya gave her as she entered the apartment annoyed her. So smug, so casual—as if nothing out of the ordinary had occurred.

"So, sneaking into the city?"

"We weren't sneaking. We were shooting videos for class. We went to the city so ours would look different from everyone else's. We wanted to do something creative."

Irina stared at her daughter. The hint of defiance was new. And using creative passion and dedication to schoolwork as ways to deflect her guilt was an amusing strategy. Irina had to remind herself what the problem was.

"You should have told me you were planning to go into the city."

"We didn't plan it. We just decided."

"Kirsten just got her license and can't drive with other girls in the car."

"How do I know she didn't have permission?"

"You should have called. Let me see your phone. Show me the videos."

Anya hesitated, then tapped her video app and handed over her phone, which had half its charge.

"I thought your phone was dead."

"I charged it on the way home. Obviously."

Irina swiped through a series of short videos of the girls posing and holding paint brushes in front of vivid street murals: a French bulldog wearing an Elizabethan collar, a scaly dragon with the face and claws of a tiger, a snarling wolf with sections of skeleton, nerves and muscles exposed. There was a hallucinatory intensity to the images that Irina found both intriguing and concerning.

"You drove to the city just to shoot videos."

Anya rolled her eyes. "We're going to speed the videos up so it looks like we painted the murals. Don't worry, we didn't buy drugs."

Now Irina understood. They were going to post the videos, which Anya knew she wasn't supposed to do.

"Anya, you can't post these on Instagram."

"I'm not. I'm helping Kirsten."

Irina stared at her. She doubted Anya was telling the truth, but suddenly she didn't have the energy to find out. She'd forced her daughter to leave her friends and join her desperate, vagabond adventure. What difference did it make if Anya lied about posting videos and letting air out of some rich woman's tire? Irina was convinced Facebook had no use for her and they'd be on the move again soon. Anya's little video adventure wasn't worth fighting about.

As summer began, Irina stayed away from campus and relied on Dez for updates on the plummeting morale. The story divided Facebook into the faithful, who still believed Zuck's assurances that the company's role in the election had been minimal, and the doubters, who were certain the opposite was true. They had sacrificed, given up nights, weekends, months and years pursuing his lofty mission of "making the world more open and connected". It was the best job in the world, until now. Now it seemed Facebook's role in the election was deeper and more nefarious than anyone could have imagined. Now they were grieving. Their innocence, their belief in the goodness of what they were doing, had been taken away. Of course, they still had their stock options, which for many of them were worth millions, but now they had to feel guilty about that too.

The People@Facebook team sensed employees were struggling, knew they might be getting questions from friends about all the stories coming out, so they sent out a list of talking points to help them respond. The main thing to remember was that Facebook was a platform, not a media company. They weren't creating all those fake news stories and toxic posts and they weren't responsible for the actions of their 2 billion users. To rally the troops, one of Zuck's lieutenants wrote a memo reminding everyone about the goodness inherent in their mission: They were about connecting people, no matter what. Even if terrorists used Facebook to launch a plot that killed a lot of people that wouldn't change Facebook's sacred mission. Needless to say, the media went into a feeding frenzy. Facebook was basically supporting terrorism. Its reputation was in free fall, and the stock price was plummeting with it.

That was also the week Irina got the call from Glamorous Ariana.

"Irina, we have some good news for you. Your O-1A Extraordinary Abilities Visa has been approved."

Irina was stunned. O-1A? They were giving her the same visa as the rock star coders. "Amazing. I was not expecting this."

"We would like to make it official and offer you a full-time position. Can you come in this afternoon?"

She still couldn't believe what she was hearing. A weight had been lifted. She called Dez and told him about the meeting, her visa, her new job.

"Wow. Interesting. Did they say what you'll be doing?"

"Not yet. I'm going in this afternoon."

Glamorous Ariana was waiting with a young East Indian woman when Irina arrived.

"Hello, Irina, today is a big day. This is Kiara Martin from the Facebook legal team, who has been assisting with your visa."

Kiara reached out and shook Irina's hand. The three of them sat down. Glamorous Ariana reached across the table and presented Irina with an open folder filled with forms to be completed.

"Welcome to Facebook. We would like you to join the new Content Moderation Team as a Senior Specialist. The starting salary is $120,000 per year, with full benefits, of course."

Irina stared at the number in disbelief. "Fantastic. I accept."

"Excellent," Ariana said. "We'll make that effective today."

Irina scanned the responsibilities listed below her salary. There was only one: "Review content to ensure compliance with Facebook Community Standards."

"So I only have one responsibility?"

"Yes, but it's a big one. As you know, there is a lot of content on Facebook."

"Of course. I will have to become familiar with the standards."

"Those are being revised."

Irina looked down at the information in the folder. The space beside "Reporting To" was blank.

"It doesn't say who I will be reporting to."

"Don't worry. That's because we are still building out the team."

Kiara leaned across the table. "In the meantime, we'd like your help with our response to the Special Counsel's investigation."

"The government investigation?"

"Yes. With your knowledge of the Internet Research Agency, we think you can make an important contribution."

Irina stared at them. "But I've already provided everything I know."

"We've spoken to the Special Counsel's office. Because of your knowledge of the Russian operation, they would like you to testify in person."

Irina froze, heart pounding. "So I'm part of the investigation?"

"Only as a witness. They feel your testimony will be invaluable."

"What am I supposed to do?"

"Don't worry. We have a few weeks to prepare. And now that you're a Facebook employee, I can represent you."

"As my lawyer?"

"Yes, we'll help prepare your testimony, then we'll fly out to D.C. together."

The idea of traveling to Washington and suddenly needing a lawyer activated Irina's terror all over again. In Russia when the government called you in to answer questions, it was never good.

"I have to go there?"

Kiara widened her eyes and reached across the table for her hand. "Don't worry. They are grateful you came forward and want to make sure you are safe. But they have additional questions for you."

Irina left the office holding her folder. She tried to remind herself of the good news. That she and Anya were not being deported, that she now had a high-paying job. She told herself, *This is America, not Russia.* But Americans were getting pretty weird, posting stories about pedophilia rings in pizza shops. The whole country seemed to be losing its mind.

She called Dez to get his assessment of her situation.

"You know that Special Counsel thing everybody's talking about? They want me to go there."

"What? Go where?"

"To Washington. To testify."

"They're sending you? Who else is going?"

"Kiara from legal and the guy with the German looking glasses."

"Oliver? What about Zuck and Sheryl?"

"Nobody mentioned them."

"Total chickenshit move."

"Kiara said I didn't have anything to worry about. You're kind of freaking me out."

"They're using you as the trophy witness. Having someone from the inside of the Agency makes it look like Facebook is taking responsibility. Your testimony will deflect attention from everybody else."

"Is that why they gave me the job and the visa?"

"Exactly. Welcome to Facebook."

Over the next four weeks, Kiara helped Irina prepare her answers to questions she would likely be asked. Beneath her polished grooming and manner, Kiara was cool and relaxed, possibly something she had picked up at Stanford Law. She did her best to put Irina at ease, sending her links to outfits that would present an appropriate look: silk blouses and tailored slacks, conservative, expensive, mostly from Nordstrom. They were nothing Irina would ever wear again, but Facebook had given her a $1,000 clothing allowance, so she bought them anyway, hoping the clothes would buy her confidence when she walked into the room.

Three days before their flight to Washington, the team gathered in Sheryl Sandberg's private conference room—the one with the nameplate that read, "Only Good News." The Chelseas spent the morning verifying numbers and making small edits to the slides. Two designers were brought in to visualize the data.

"This is a legal document, not a sales presentation," Original Chelsea said. "Do we really want to use 3D graphs to show 3 million users engaged with a fake post?"

She was wearing ripped jeans and a faded Facebook hoodie, hair pulled back in a ragged ponytail. Her white Balenciaga sneakers looked too big for her body, like something a Russian ER nurse working long shifts would wear.

"Kill the graphs," Kiara said.

Late in the afternoon, Irina caught a glimpse of Sheryl outside the room. She was wearing a tight black skirt and a red silk blouse made all the more striking by her amazing legs and black, shoulder-length hair. Everything about her whispered, "Watch and learn." Irina kept expecting her to step in to review the presentation. But when the revisions were complete and they left the room at the end of the day, Sheryl Sandberg was nowhere to be seen.

They were scheduled to fly out on Monday and spend Tuesday taking the Special Counsel's lawyers through the discovery presentation. Irina was scheduled for three days of testimony, which concerned her because she didn't think she had that much to share. Depending on how her last day of testimony went, they would fly back late Friday or possibly Saturday morning. Glamorous Ariana had arranged for an executive nanny to drive Anya to her classes and spend the evenings at the apartment while Irina was away. She said goodbye to Dez the night before and left Anya $80 spending money.

A limo picked her up and took her to a swanky private terminal at the San Jose airport, where Kiara and Oliver were waiting. Due to the sensitivity of the trip, Facebook gave them use of the private jet usually reserved for Zuck and Sheryl. Irina kept trying to remind herself how amazing it was to be flying across America in Mark Zuckerberg's private plane. Her only points of reference were the private planes in hip-hop videos, which were much bigger inside and filled with strippers and champagne. This was more modest, but the leather seats were luxurious and the lunch was a delicious salad with grilled chicken, served on a real plate. Kiara was obviously enjoying the experience and tried lightening the mood by sharing her headphones and playing "Like a G6."

But somewhere over the Midwest, Irina's composure abandoned her. The flight path of the smaller plane gave her a better look at the country below, and she couldn't help thinking about the insanity unfolding there. Neo-Nazis marching with torches. Men with AR-15s shooting at imaginary helicopters sent by the Deep State. All the assorted chaos the Agency helped stir up.

By the time they checked into their hotel in D.C., she was feeling scattered and anxious, so she was happy Kiara hadn't invited her to dinner at the fancy Georgetown restaurant that Drew from Facebook Government Affairs had booked. She changed into her favorite Lululemon sweats, ordered scallops and a half bottle of sauvignon blanc from room service. She noticed the bill was over $100, but that didn't matter. Facebook was picking up the tab. She drank the wine, finished her scallops and channel-surfed, sitting on the giant king-size bed. She woke up around midnight with the lights and TV on and then couldn't get back to sleep. Her alarm woke her at 6:00 in the morning on, by her estimate, three hours' sleep. She showered, blow-dried her hair and put on one of the outfits Kiara had recommended—navy silk blouse, caramel-colored slacks, dark-brown flats. From room service, she ordered scrambled eggs and toast with coffee. Just lifting the silver dome on the room service tray made her nauseous. But she forced her breakfast down anyway.

Kiara was waiting for her in the lobby. "Perfect. You look very professional. Very earnest."

Oliver and Drew were waiting in the limo.

"I got some intel from my contacts at the Special Counsel," Drew said. "You'll be interviewed by Catherine Hughes. She's part of the D.C. inner circle. Argued three cases before the Supreme Court. And she speaks Russian."

Kiara shifted in her seat. "Hopefully, she won't be asking the questions in Russian."

"No, the interview will be in English, and you'll be with Irina in the room. We cleared that."

Irina stared out the window and watched Washington float past. The streets were wide, and traffic moved briskly. They drove past an obelisk, the name of which she couldn't remember—something she'd seen in films. In the distance were buildings with columns and domes. She wondered where the White House was, what sort of madness might be going on there. By now Trump had exceeded everyone's expectations for how unhinged he would be, how much damage he could do. Putting children in cages. Promoting Ivanka's jewelry. Sucking up to Putin and white supremacists. If she were still back in St. Petersburg, watching all the little fires they had ignited flare up and set America ablaze, she might have lost her mind.

Kiara pointed to a building in the distance, a nondescript square of cement and glass. For an instant it looked to Irina so much like 55 Savushkina Street that she felt a flash of confused panic, thinking, *They're taking me back.* But then she realized it was just her mind spinning, that she was in Washington, D.C., 8,000 miles from Piter. She closed her eyes and tried to slow her breathing.

"The lobby is usually full of press, so we're going in through the side," Drew said.

The limo slipped into the semi darkness of an underground garage. They got out of the car and took an elevator to the fifth floor.

Drew approached the receptionist. "We're from Facebook."

To sign in, Irina had to present her passport, sign forms and stand for a photo, which they retook three times because she kept blinking. The receptionist led them to a windowless conference room with a long table in the center and only three chairs, which Irina found somehow ominous. The gray carpet and neutral, fabric-covered walls were also disorienting. The room could have been anywhere. She took a bottle from a row of Evian waters on a credenza and sat down in one of the leather chairs, reminding herself, *I am in Washington, D.C.*

Kiara took a seat beside her and touched her arm. "Try to relax. This will be fine. They've already reviewed our discovery presentation. That should make this go more smoothly."

The door opened and a woman entered, about the same age as Irina. She was wearing a dark business suit and had thick black hair in a blunt-cut, shoulder-length style. She reached for Irina's hand, then Kiara's.

"Hello, I'm Catherine Hughes, representing the Special Counsel's office."

She looked at Irina and sat down. Seeing how relaxed the lawyer was had the opposite effect on Irina. She had been bracing herself for someone more intense, more adversarial. Now, even before the questions started, she was off her game.

"Irina, we're going to be asking about the work you did at the Internet Research Agency, as well as other questions relevant to our investigation."

"Yes, I understand."

The lawyer placed a tape recorder in the center of the table.

"Our discussions will be recorded."

Irina swallowed. They had warned her about this.

"I understand."

"We've set aside three days for your testimony. It may take a bit more or a bit less than that. If it's helpful, I also speak Russian. I studied at the State University in St. Petersburg. You're from Piter, correct?"

Irina nodded. "Yes." This lawyer was slick; usually only locals called it that.

Suddenly Kiara seemed nervous. She removed her sleek, thin laptop from her bag and placed it on the table. "Would it be helpful if we began by going through the discovery presentation we forwarded?"

"We've already reviewed your discovery and will have questions about that later."

She pushed the record button on the tape recorder.

"This is Catherine Hughes, assistant special counsel for the Mueller investigation. It's July 25, 2017, 9:03 a.m. Eastern Standard Time. This is an interview with Irina Zakharova. Irina, can you please identify yourself, first and surname?"

Irina took a drink of water and cleared her throat. "Irina Zakharova."

"Thank you. Irina, today I'd like to start by asking you a few questions. Please be as direct and factual in your answers as possible."

The lawyer started with questions about her childhood back in Piter. It was obvious from her questions she knew things about her past, which made Irina uncomfortable.

"So you grew up at the end of the old Soviet system. What was that like?"

"It was difficult but it could have been worse. My parents were athletes."

"Your mother was a gymnast?"

"Yes, a famous one."

"And was your father an athlete too?"

"Yes, a sprinter. He ran the 100 and 200 meters."

"So you were destined to be an athlete?"

"You could say that."

The lawyer asked the questions in a polite, unwavering voice. Her eyes stayed locked on Irina's except when she jotted down an occasional note on the legal pad beside her.

"Were you close with your parents?"

"Yes. Especially my mother."

"Was it difficult for your parents when the Soviet system fell apart?"

"Yes."

"How so?"

"They almost lost their jobs. The conditions of the training facilities deteriorated."

"Your parents had a hard time with that?"

"My father did."

"How old was he when he died?"

"Forty-six."

The lawyer let her answer hang there.

"It was probably the drugs," Irina said. "All the sprinters took them back then."

"That must have been difficult."

"Yes."

Irina could feel her neck muscles tensing. She couldn't remember the last time she was in the presence of someone so focused, someone who wasn't constantly fiddling with an app or checking her phone. It was unnerving. She kept drinking from her water bottle even though she wasn't thirsty.

"Were you close with your father?"

"Not so much. He was always training."

"Was he strict?"

"Not really."

"Was he abusive?"

Irina's heart was pounding. She had never spoken about her parents' relationship to anyone. She stared at the lawyer. "Not to me."

"To your mother?"

Irina let her eyes drift around the room, but when she looked across the table again, the lawyer's eyes were waiting for her.

"Sometimes."

She could tell the lawyer sensed she was protecting something.

"I'm sorry if these questions are painful. But in a case like this, we need to know as much as we can about the background of a witness."

Irina began to realize that, beneath the formality, this was an interrogation. The lawyer was learning to read her by applying pressure, and Irina could feel herself giving in to it.

"Was there any other close family when you were growing up?"

"My grandmother."

"Is she still alive?"

"No, she died six years ago. She was 82."

"Was she *blodiniki*?"

It was clear to Irina she already knew the answer.

"Yes."

The lawyer seemed to be doing some math.

"So she was 13 when the war started. Did she ever talk about the siege?"

"Yes."

They looked at each other. Something beyond words—images of unspeakable things—passed between them.

The lawyer paused and looked down at her notes. "Let's move on. I'd like to ask about your athletic career."

Irina wasn't sure why that history mattered but she wasn't the one asking the questions. "Okay."

The lawyer's questions went all the way back to the beginning: the gymnastics camps and competitions, Irina's growth spurt, her switch to the pole vault and years of success.

"So why did you give it up?"

"I was injured. Twice. After the second time, I knew it was over."

"Was that difficult?"

"Of course."

"What did you miss the most?"

"Everything. The feeling of it. The feeling of flying."

The lawyer nodded. "Who wouldn't miss that?"

They broke for lunch. Kiara got up from the table. "You're doing great."

Irina had forgotten the Facebook lawyer was in the room. She could feel the muscles locked at the base of her skull. "Do you have any aspirin?"

Kiara shook out two pills from a small container in her purse. "We didn't anticipate that personal line of questioning. Hopefully, she will move this along."

After lunch, the government lawyer picked up where she'd left off. Irina knew she was probably revealing things the lawyer would find useful, but she decided there was no point in trying to filter her answers, even if she knew how.

"So after your injuries you left the Russian team?"

"Eventually, yes."

"And how did you support yourself?'

"I worked as a personal trainer."

"How did you end up at the Internet Research Agency?"

"A friend told me they were hiring people with English skills."

"So you were recruited by someone who worked there?"

"Just another trainer. Being a trainer doesn't pay much, so we were always looking for other work."

"So working at the Agency was a better opportunity?"

Irina shrugged. It all felt so shameful now. "Much more money. And I have a daughter. So…"

The lawyer finished the day asking about her life back in St. Petersburg. Did she have close friendships? Was she romantically involved with anyone? How often did she see family? She asked about Anya and how she was adapting to America. The lawyer seemed to sense she was fading again.

"One last question for today. Help me understand why someone with your personal history, your family history, with such deep connections to their country, would come to us?"

Irina wondered if she should recount the messy truth of her decision, sending foolish texts to Sergei without anticipating the likely consequences. She suspected they would treat her better if she claimed more noble motives. But how could she escape the lies she'd been a part of if she was still telling them?

"When I started at the Agency, it just seemed like silly internet stuff, sort of harmless. But after the election and some other things that were happening, I felt pretty bad. I mentioned to someone what we did. Made some jokes about working at a troll factory, and then things just got out of control."

"You were afraid for your safety, so you flew to America with your daughter?"

That sounded close enough, Irina decided. No point in mentioning Disneyland.

"Yes."

"And why did you decide to go to Facebook?"

"A friend of mine from Russia worked there. Most of what I did at the Agency was posted there. I figured they would want to know."

Irina felt Kiara nodding and leaning across the table. "We did, of course. That's why we are here today."

The government lawyer reached forward and turned off the recorder. "Thank you, Irina. I think we will conclude our interview for today."

By the time they got back to the hotel, Irina was exhausted. Once again, Kiara didn't invite her to dinner, but that was fine with her. This time she ordered grilled salmon, brussels sprouts and more wine. She thought about ordering a full bottle, but the way the lawyer was getting into her head, a hangover would be a disaster. She wondered who this lawyer was. If this Catherine Hughes was digging into her past, why not do a little digging herself? So she dug her laptop out of her bag and googled her. Just her Wikipedia page explained a lot: Rhodes scholar, degrees from the University of St. Andrews in Scotland and Harvard Law. A profile in a D.C. law magazine suggested she might be Supreme Court material if a liberal ever became president again. No wonder Irina felt overmatched. But nothing she dug up explained what the lawyer was doing to her, why Irina found herself liking her, wanting to please her.

The lawyer began the next day with the questions Irina had been expecting, the ones she had rehearsed with Kiara. What was her title at the agency? Her focus? How did they assign the work she was doing? What were the qualifications of her colleagues? What was the structure of the organization? How was it funded? How did they determine which groups to focus on? Did they target particular states? Were there contacts in the U.S.? Were there contacts with Russian Military Intelligence or the GRU? Were there any contacts with the Trump campaign? Had she ever heard of Cambridge Analytica?

Although Irina anticipated the questions and had practiced her answers, giving them to a government lawyer in Washington was very different from rehearsing them back in Menlo Park. She was nervous and on edge by the time they broke for lunch. The lawyer returned, and the recorder was back on, in precisely 30 minutes.

"Irina, can you take us through your process for creating fake identities on Facebook?"

"How we did it?"

"Yes, take me through the steps."

"Basic equipment was laptop, monitor, Samsung Galaxy 5 phone and three or more SIM cards. I use my laptop to connect to the VPN, so it looks like I'm in the States. Go to Facebook, click 'Create New Account.' Come up with a name, usually a woman's name, because women were considered more trustworthy. So maybe I pick Emily Wilson, a very normal-sounding name. Then I download a picture of a woman I think looks like an Emily. The right age, white, Black, city person, suburbs, farmer, whatever. Then I insert one of the SIM cards into the phone and wait for the ID confirmation code. Type the code into the Facebook ID page, and Emily is good to go. She's sending posts about how she's afraid of immigrant criminals, loves her AR-15, hates Hillary. It usually took about four minutes."

"That's it?"

She felt Kiara beside her shifting in her seat.

"Yes, very easy. With five SIM cards you could manage 50 to 60 accounts. The hard part was keeping track of who was who. What they like, what they do. All day I went back and forth making comments, posting videos or links to something they would enjoy. Chatting with followers who posted comments. Sometimes I made mistakes about who I was, but nobody seemed to notice."

"How many fraudulent identities would you estimate the Agency created?"

"Total? I don't know. Thousands."

Kiara interrupted. "But many of those were on Twitter, not Facebook. Isn't that correct?"

Irina paused. Now she knew why Kiara was in the room. She was there to protect Facebook, and now she was reminding Irina that she was on the Facebook team too.

"Yes, I didn't work on Twitter much, but they created many accounts. Thousands. They were also using bots."

The lawyer studied them both, then redirected her attention to Irina.

"Why don't we shift gears and go through the discovery you provided? I have questions for both of you here."

She opened her laptop and brought up the presentation they had created back at Facebook. They went through it slowly, starting with the ads, then the list of Facebook groups with examples of their pages. The lawyer was obviously well-versed in the ways of social media, so she kept moving back and forth between the summary and the appendix, where they had provided the numbers of followers and views. She seemed to be directing her questions at Kiara.

"When did Facebook become aware of the scope of this operation?"

"Our discovery began immediately after the election. It was completed a month ago."

"And what measures are now in place to identify and block this activity?"

"Yes, we're creating a new content integrity team. When fully staffed, it will include several thousand people. Irina will be part of that team."

Irina chimed in occasionally to provide context on a particular ad, group or post, but she was relieved to have the lawyer's attention focused elsewhere. She could feel the energy leaving her body like air escaping from a balloon.

The next morning Irina detected a hint of warmth in the lawyer's greeting. "We're very grateful for your cooperation, Irina. Just one more day."

Then she turned on the recorder.

"Your testimony has provided some very valuable details about Agency operations and helped us understand how your organization manipulated social media. But we need you to tell us more about the Agency's structure and leadership."

Irina didn't like where this was heading.

"I told you about the structure. Four groups. There was also finance, but I didn't work with them."

The lawyer leaned forward. "We need additional information. We need you to identify the Agency principals by name."

Irina pressed her lips together and looked away. "As I mentioned, it was funded by Yevgeny Prigozhin. He was the boss."

"We have that information already, as does everyone who reads the *New York Times*. We need the names of others in the organization."

Irina shook her head. If she gave them names, they would come for her, hunt her down for sure, which would be child's play for them.

Since she hadn't returned, no doubt they suspected her already. Names she could not do.

"They will kill me."

The lawyer seemed to look into her. This was the connection she had been building. Her expression was sympathetic, but Irina could see she wasn't going to back down. She was determined to get what she needed.

"Your testimony has been very helpful, but cases like this are built on facts. We need you to tell us everything you know about the Agency operations, including the names of the people in charge."

"I can't give you names."

The lawyer looked her in the eyes again, locking her in.

"Irina, we understand your situation. We deeply appreciate you coming forward. We do. But a serious breach of our democratic process has occurred. It's the duty of the Special Counsel to use everything in its power to determine who was responsible, so we can prevent it from happening again."

"You can't prevent it from happening again."

"We have to try."

Irina turned and looked at Kiara. She wondered if she knew, all along, where the government's questions would lead. What better way for Facebook to repair its reputation than turn over an informant who exposed the Russian scheme from top to bottom. She thought about the names of her collegues and what they might do to her. No doubt something creative enough to make a sensational news story—a cautionary tale to deter future informants. An unexplained fall from a building, a mysterious poisoning, perhaps the usual radioactive isotope in her TV remote or lingerie drawer.

"And if I don't give you the names?"

"You are currently on an O-1A Extraordinary Abilities Visa that expires in 11 months."

"So you'd send me back to Russia?"

"If you fully cooperate with our investigation, we can offer you and your daughter full protection. New identities for you and Anya, a new place to live."

"Where would I go? What would I do?"

"We would relocate you through our Witness Security Program."

"What about my mother?"

"We believe your mother is safe. We would arrange for one final contact with her. After that, any contact may be risky for you."

Irina stared at the lawyer across the table, then closed her eyes. She had been naïve not to guess what her testimony would require, that they would ask for names.

Kiara reached for her hand. "Can we take a break and resume this after lunch?"

Irina shook her head. "Give me some paper. I will write the names down."

They left her alone, then the government lawyer returned with a yellow legal pad and a silver pen with a Department of Justice seal. She printed the names in bold capital letters, jotting down their roles and whatever else she could recall about them.

YEVGENY PRIGOZHIN (Putin's Chef)—The Boss. Personal friend of Putin. Paid all the bills but never showed up. Named Agency after some high-rise in St. Petersburg (Project Lakhta), so it looked like one of his real estate deals.

MIKHAIL BYSTROV, General Director—He wasn't around all the time but everything that needed money had to go through him.

MIKHAIL BURCHICK, Office Manager—Always there keeping the Agency running, getting people what they needed. Phones, laptops, SIM cards, whatever.

DZHEYKHUN NASIMI OGLY ASLANOV, Strategist—He was in charge of election strategy. His English was excellent. Went to NYU. He knew a lot about social media and how to talk to Americans.

ROBYERT SERGEYEVICH BOYDA, Manager Facebook group—He tried to go to the U.S. but there was a problem with his visa. Tough guy. Always demanding more memes, more posts, more comments, angrier against Hillary.

KATYA ANATOLYEVNA (My Boss)—In charge of research and strategy. She traveled back and forth to the U.S. She read all our posts to make sure they sounded American.

ALEXSANDRA KRYLOVA, Manager—Worked on Ukraine situation. Switched over to American team before the election.

ANNA BOGACHEVA, Data Analyst—Provided information from America and GRU to tell us which groups and states to target.

VADIM VLADIMIROVICH PODKOPAEV, Specialist— Worked with Fancy Bear, Guccifer and kept track of what GRU was doing. Set up DC Leaks account that posted stolen emails from Democrats.

GLEB IGOREVICH VASILCHENKO—Lead Graphic designer. Very creative at finding weird photos and creating good memes.

VLADIMIR VENKOV—Manager of Twitter group. Coordinated what we were doing on Facebook and Instagram.

SERGEY PAVLOVICH POLOZOV—IT Manager. Set up VPNs. Fixed all our tech problems.

When she finished, she spread the pages out in front of her. At Facebook, she was surrounded by people who asked questions but didn't want the answers. They let them float in the air, batted them around like balloons, so they'd never land or stick to anything. But the government lawyer had demanded the truth and here it was. Irina looked down at the names and what she had written. She felt like she'd jumped off a cliff.

After an hour, the lawyer returned to the room with Kiara. She took the list and came back again with the names printed on large index cards. She had Irina go through the names one by one, asking additional questions, taking notes, having her match some of the names to photos. They asked her to arrange them to show how the Agency was structured, until the wall became a montage of names, faces and scribbled descriptions, the sort of thing TV detectives assembled to solve a crime. But now she was actually part of the story, swept up by forces beyond her control. And slowly she began to understand that it wasn't just a feeling: It was true. Her life, the one she had been living, was over. She wasn't going to be the old Irina anymore. She was going to become someone else.

Irina and Kiara returned to the Special Counsel's office the following morning. It was Saturday but the building was buzzing with activity. Waiting with the lawyer in the conference room were a man and a woman, both stone-faced and wearing suits, possibly armed.

"Irina, given the sensitivity of the information you've shared, we believe you should enter Witness Security immediately."

"What does that mean exactly?"

"As we mentioned, you and your daughter will receive new identities and begin new lives in another city."

"So I can't go back to Facebook?"

"No. Under the circumstances, we can't guarantee your safety there."

"So where will we live?"

"We're working on that. You'll stay here for a few days, and your daughter will join you. She'll be escorted by a Justice Department agent."

"Is that like the FBI? That will totally freak her out. She's been through a lot already."

"If there's an adult in California who could fly out with her, that would be fine. We will also send along an agent as a precaution."

Irina felt her paranoia spiraling all over again. "Precaution for what?"

"It's just standard procedure," the woman agent said. "We've never lost a witness in our program. We want to keep it that way."

The lawyer explained she could have a few final calls with friends and family members. The full impact of the path she had chosen was finally sinking in. They gave her a private office and one of the agents brought in a special phone that scrambled its location, so her calls could not be traced. She called Dez first. She was afraid he wouldn't pick up because he didn't recognize the number.

"Hello?"

"It's Irina."

"Somehow I thought this might be you. How did it go?"

"Yeah," she paused, holding back a sob. She imagined this would be the easiest of her conversations and she didn't want to start crying already. "I ended up giving them lots of information. So, they're putting me in witness protection."

"Wow. Like a new name? New life? The whole thing?"

"That's what they said."

There was a long silence on the line.

"New boyfriend?"

The moment was so surreal, so complicated, she didn't know what to say. "I don't know."

"When is this happening?"

"Now. They want to have an agent fly out with Anya, but I think that will be too traumatic for her. I was wondering if you could do it."

"Sure."

"They will send somebody with tickets."

"So, this is really happening? Unbelievable. I'm trying to come up with an appropriate but lighthearted remark."

"I know. I can't even think straight." Irina wanted to get off the phone before she started crying. "Thanks for doing this."

She took a few minutes to gather herself before she called Anya. Her daughter loved California and was just beginning to make friends. Irina decided it would be better to break the news they were moving in person. She had never told Anya the truth about her work at the Agency. That would have to wait too.

Anya picked up on the first ring.

"Hello?"

"Hi, it's me. How are you doing?"

"I thought you were coming back yesterday."

"I had to stay longer. Washington, D.C., is great. So…Dez is going to bring you out here to meet me."

"That's cool, I guess. But why don't you just come back here?"

Irina tried to hold her story together, as always, making it up as she went along. "Since we're going to be staying in America, this is a good chance for us to visit the Capitol. It will help us feel part of it."

"Mom, this seems really weird."

"I know. But we're going to become American citizens. We have to come here first."

"Okay, so Dez and I fly out. Are we going to, like, tour the city? How long are we going to stay?"

"I'm not sure."

"When are we coming back to California?"

"We have to see."

"Mom, I hate this. If we just keep moving around, I'd rather go back to Piter."

"Anya, this will be fine. You and Dez will have a nice flight. I think it will be business class." Irina wasn't sure about that, but she figured it was the least the government could do.

"This sounds crazy, but whatever," Anya said, and hung up.

Her last call, the one she really dreaded, was to her mother. The agents had suggested she keep it short, since there was a good chance her mother's phone had been tapped.

"Hello?"

"Mom, it's me."

"Ah!" The sound her mother made was almost a shriek. "I was so worried. I thought something happened."

"No, I'm okay. Anya too. But we can't come back home."

"What do you mean? Why not?"

"I can't really talk about it. It's because of the work I did in Piter before I left. If someone comes to talk to you, just tell them you don't know where I am, which is the truth."

"Oh, they already came. I told them you went to Disneyland, but I think they knew that already."

Irina felt a flood of panic. "Have they done anything else? Are you safe?"

"They don't bother old ladies anymore. They are trying to improve their image."

"I hope so."

"Irina, where's Anya?"

"She's with me. She's fine. I have to go soon."

"So when are you calling back?"

"I can't call back. I just wanted to let you know we're safe. I love you. I'll always love you." Irina started crying softly.

"Irina this must be serious."

"Definitely."

"What did you do?"

"Mom, I can't really talk about it. But I'm safe here. We're safe here."

Tatyana started crying. Irina couldn't recall a time when they were crying at the same time.

"And you're not coming back?"

"No, I wish this wasn't happening but there's nothing I can do."

"I will be thinking of you and Anya."

"Okay mom, I have to go now."

Irina hung up and sobbed uncontrollably for a several minutes. Afterward, she felt numb, as if in a trance. A limo drove her to an apartment not far from the Special Counsel's office, where they would bring Anya and work out the details of a new life. They were clear: It had to be a clean break. The only people allowed to join her had to enter the program themselves. If Dez wanted to join them, he would need a new name, a new life, just like her and Anya. No matter how he felt about her, she couldn't imagine him wanting that. It was too much to ask.

Witnesses weren't allowed to select their new cities, but they were allowed to request geographic preferences. When they asked Irina, she simply said, "Someplace warm."

Gilbert

They warned her how strange it would be to look in the mirror and see a different face. But when the scars had healed and she looked at herself for the first time, the real shock, why not just say it, was how good she looked.

The Witness Security team kept reminding her how fortunate she was. Plastic surgery was rarely part of the program, but it was safe to assume the Russians who might come looking for her would have the latest facial recognition technology, so in her case they made an exception. The surgeon had tightened the flesh around her eyes, so they were more almond-shaped, and Botoxed away the furrows that had started to form across her forehead. Ironically, she looked even more Slavic now, but that was consistent with her new identity, Irene Kaits, from Estonia and more recently Bergenfield, New Jersey. She had a daughter, Tanya, and an ex-husband who worked at the Estonian consulate in New York. She dyed her hair blonde and didn't have to feel vain about doing it, because the American government suggested it. She tried to imagine she was looking at a younger version of herself. But more often she saw a woman she didn't quite recognize, an acquaintance she couldn't name.

"Kaits" meant guard in Estonian, a reminder to keep hers up. They warned her about the strangeness of living with a new identity, having to conceal who you are from everyone around you. And they were right: It was disorienting to wake up every day asking, *Who am I?* They actually encouraged people to retain their first names, so they would answer when called. Of course, her tattoo had to go. They told her it would take at least six sessions. It was impossible not to feel the irony of the laser slowly erasing the words "Nothing Is Forgotten". Obviously she wasn't heeding their message. The pain—like a thousand bee stings, one after the other—felt like punishment she deserved for betraying herself and her grandmother or for the things she'd done. But even after the final session with the needle, shadows lingered where the ink had penetrated her skin, so in the bright Arizona sunlight, she could still see the ghost of her tattoo, even if no one else could.

In her WitSec orientation, they explained they would choose a new city that would give her and Anya the best chance of fitting in and starting a new life. In her case that turned out to be Gilbert, Arizona, formerly a small town but now a suburb 30 minutes from downtown Phoenix, thanks to 25 years of urban sprawl. According to her orientation packet, it was rated #33 of America's Best Places to Live by U.S. News & World Report, based on the excellent schools, job opportunities, access to parks and nature, and low cost of living.

The house was in a new development called Superstition Springs, popular among young families moving to the area, despite the lack of character and mature landscaping. When Sarah, her Witness Inspector, told her the address on the way from the airport, she thought it must be some bureaucrat's joke—a Russian living at 1227 North Buckaroo Road. From the outside, the house appeared drab and unwelcoming, a low, ranch-style rectangle of rough stucco, painted a dull beige that matched the desert sand. In place of a lawn were wide beds of tan lava rocks with a few alien-looking plants sticking out. Along with the new name, personal history, a Social Security number and an Arizona driver's license, they also gave her a new Prius, which she practiced maneuvering through the treeless streets out past the edge of the development.

Although Irina was grateful they honored her request for a warm climate, she and Anya were not prepared for August in Phoenix. Temperatures inched up over 110 degrees Fahrenheit. Going outside felt like stepping into an oven. They could feel the moisture being sucked out of their skin, as if humans didn't belong there. They never left the house without bottled water and quickly learned the consequences of parking in the sun. Vinyl seats, steering wheels, door handles and seat-belt buckles became lethal objects that burned welts into their flesh. Locals rushed through their errands in the morning to avoid the withering afternoon heat. In the middle of the day, the neighborhood became a dead zone. Nothing moved.

To establish a routine and give her new life structure, she woke up at dawn each day and went for a run. The morning air was cool, and in the distance the Superstition Mountains looked like a pagan church. It was the best part of the day. She'd run toward the mountains at least five miles, sometimes more. By the time she circled back toward the house, the heat of the day was rising.

To help Anya navigate her new school, new friends and the drama that went with being 14, they showed up at the Mesquite High School Gym for freshman orientation, the day before classes began. They sat through presentations on the school's curriculum, rising academic standing, extensive range of sports and after-school activities, tips for making friends and the standard list of high school perils including drugs, STIs, bullying, cyberbullying, and eating disorders. Obviously, Irina didn't know any of the other parents and didn't feel ready to mingle or strike up the "Hi, we're new here" conversation, so they left as soon as the presentation ended. As they headed across the parking lot, Irina tapped the key to the Prius, savoring the metallic thunk and sensation of effortless power she got from the remote-unlocking feature.

"Excuse me."

Irina turned and saw a short, fit, blonde woman with a deep, tennis-player tan standing a few feet away. Next to her was a girl about Anya's age.

"Hello, hi. I think we're neighbors. Do you live in that tan stucco house out on Buckaroo Road?"

Irina felt a surge of panic. She took a deep breath and remembered to smile.

"Yes, we do."

"I think I see you running out there every day on my way to CrossFit. You look like a serious runner."

Irina's guard went up. Again, she told herself: Breathe. Short answers.

"That could be me. We just moved in about a couple of weeks ago."

The woman nodded. "We're just around the corner on East Melody, near the park."

Irina had never seen the park but decided it was better not to mention that.

"I'm sure that's nice."

"It's fine. Just another ranch-style place with a few skinny cacti scattered out front. Kind of like your place. I'm Tara and this is Celeste."

The woman smiled, kept smiling. Irina smiled back.

"Oh, sorry. I'm Irene and my daughter is Tanya."

The two girls gave each other wary nods.

"Where are you guys from?" the woman said.

"New Jersey."

"We just moved from Scottsdale. We needed more space, and you get a lot more bang for your buck over here. We're ex-military."

Suddenly Irina was flashing back to her time in the Being Patriotic Facebook Group. Military women were a no-bullshit group, but they could also be a little crazy. Now she was meeting one in the flesh. She tried to think of something to say.

The woman smiled. "Is that a New Jersey accent?"

Irina's guard went up again. "Actually, Estonian. With a little bit of *Jersey*."

"Ha! You hear a lot of accents when you're military."

Irina wanted to change the subject. "Have you heard good things about the school?"

"Yeah, that's why we're here. We homeschooled before, but now we've got a 2-year-old, so we decided we'd give this a shot. Right, Celeste?"

The girl stared at her sneakers. Irina noticed Anya was mirroring her.

"Anya did homeschool too. Back in New Jersey."

From the corner of her eye, she could see Anya giving her a look.

"We should get the girls together."

"Definitely," Irina said, opening her driver's-side door. She wanted to end the conversation, jump inside the car, but the heat was pouring out of it like a furnace.

"Great. Are you on Facebook?"

Irina smiled. A surreal moment. She remembered all the different people she had been on Facebook. Now she was becoming another one, using the new profile Witness Security and Facebook had created for her.

"Yes, but I'm not on it much."

"Cool. What's your last name?"

Irina hesitated. She had no idea she would have to become this new person so quickly. "Kaits."

"Don't worry, we're not stalkers. Are we, Celeste? We have a solid group. We'll get you some friends. There's only one Tara Ferguson in Gilbert. Nice meeting you, Irene Kaits. We'll see you around."

"Nice meeting you too." Irina tossed her a wave and slid into the driver's seat. The burning upholstery stuck to her thighs. She forced a smile as Tara drove past.

"That went well," Anya said sarcastically—her default mode these days.

As Irina drove out of the lot, she reminded Anya how important it was to embrace their new life, never talk about their past. After dinner they went over details from the folder Sarah had given them. Anya rehearsed answers she would need to give at school later that week. Then they spent an hour watching *Survivor* and practicing their new signatures.

After Anya went to bed, Irina went online and logged on to her new Irene Kaits Facebook Page. She already had a friend request from Tara. She hesitated, knowing all the unwanted connections and unintended consequences just clicking "Accept" could set in motion. But she decided making friends would help Anya make friends, and given how seriously this Tara seemed to take her CrossFit workouts, maybe they would actually have something in common. So she clicked "Accept" and within minutes started getting friend requests from all over the world: Japan, Afghanistan, Italy, the Philippines, Alabama, Missouri, Kansas and Virginia. As the requests popped up, she wondered if she'd messaged any of them when she was pretending to be Alison Garber or Jean Shamanski on the Being Patriotic Facebook Page. Given that the group had grown to almost 400,000 followers, it wouldn't be such a far-fetched coincidence. She had interacted with hundreds of followers in the group, posted dozens of memes, gotten thousands of likes. So it was possible these were old Facebook friends who had commented on her posts or forwarded links to conspiracy videos about the Deep State, which she then forwarded to others.

She decided to work on her new Facebook profile. She knew how to use mundane personal details as a kind of armor, how to make her new identity appealing but not so unusual as to attract unwanted attention. She decided to muffle her Russian cynicism and present the Irene she wanted people to see—a quiet advocate for the fit, healthy life. She had to admit the government's investment in plastic surgery helped in that regard. She didn't look like a tortured Russian troll. She looked like a woman who was crushing it.

She started by posting a series of motivational quotes:

"The successful warrior is the average woman, with laser-like focus."

—Bruce Lee

"It's the last three reps that make the muscle grow."

—Arnold Schwarzenegger

"The only place where success comes before work is the dictionary."

—Vidal Sassoon

She posted workout playlists, photos from her sunrise runs in the Superstition Mountains and a list of Irene's favorite movies.

1. La Femme Nikita (French Version)

2. Mad Max: Fury Road

3. Alien

4. Atomic Blonde

5. Wonder Woman

After realizing the first few all had bad-ass female action heroes, she threw in some comedy and romance to suggest more mainstream taste.

6. Bridget Jones's Diary
7. Jerry Maguire
8. Casablanca
9. Die Hard
10. Bridesmaids

She decided she would keep her Facebook interactions simple, maintain a low profile. No edgy memes or insensitive jokes. Given a new life and a pleasant house in a warm city, perhaps she could become the thing that eluded most Russians: a positive person.

Once a week, she met with Sarah, who listened to her concerns and offered suggestions to ease the transition. Irina had never thought of herself as needy, but she could have used a little more warmth from Sarah, who was an exception to the caricature of the overly friendly American and always began their sessions the same way.

"So, what's the latest?"

"We enrolled Anya in school."

"Mesquite High, right? Good school."

"Seems like a lot of military."

Sarah nodded. "You'll find that over on the East Side. Have you met any of the other parents?"

"One. She's kind of nosy."

"That's natural. You're a new face. People are curious, especially nonworking moms. They're bored—what else is new? Have you been to the national forest? The sunsets are amazing."

"Yes, beautiful."

Irina had been so busy getting Anya ready for school and learning her way around the sprawl of suburban Phoenix, they hadn't visited any of the parks. But she was tired of everyone telling her about the natural beauty and sunsets; and because she didn't like having every detail of her life monitored by Sarah, she wanted to hold some secrets, however small.

"So how's Anya?"

"Moody."

"She's a high school girl. That's her job."

"I think she needs some space. We've been so connected through all this, through everything. It's too much."

"Hopefully, she can make some friends. Is she on social media?"

"Of course. Mostly Snapchat and Instagram."

"You should follow her so you can see what's happening there."

"Yes. Girls can be terrible."

"You should try to keep an eye on it. For her own protection. And yours."

Irina nodded. She didn't like the idea of cyberstalking her daughter. But she was curious about what Anya was doing all those hours in her room every night.

"Good news. I have information about your new job," Sarah said. "You'll be working for Cogniture Solutions. Really hot tech firm. You start at the end of the month."

She handed Irina a folder with the Cogniture logo on the front. Irina opened it and thumbed through a brochure inside.

"I thought I was going to be working for Facebook."

"Cogniture does outsourcing for Facebook, so in a way you are. Your title is Content Moderation Manager, and you'll be working on the Facebook account."

"But I'm not actually working for Facebook?"

"No. This needs to be a clean break from what you were doing before. And Cogniture is growing incredibly fast. This sounds like a great job. You'll have people reporting to you."

"What will I be doing?"

"Moderating Facebook content, I guess. Whatever that means," Sarah said. "The salary is generous: $110,000 a year."

Irina nodded. "Great."

Sarah smiled, as if congratulating herself for setting up Irina for the good life. "That will go a lot further in Phoenix than it would in Silicon Valley."

On Irina's first day in the office, a young woman named Melanie in a sleeveless blouse and jeans greeted her in the lobby. "Welcome to Cogniture. We're so glad you're joining us." She handed Irina a security badge as they rode the elevator to the fourth floor. "I have six more new hires this morning, so I'm going to do your orientation pretty fast."

The doors opened into a long hallway lined with lockers. "These are for your phone and personal belongings. For data security purposes, there are no phones at desks. No food or drink. Small personal items must be placed in a clear plastic bag on the desktop. This applies to managers too."

Irina was surprised at the locked down conditions. This was not Facebook. "So how does someone reach me if there's an emergency?"

"They can message you through your Cogniture account."

She led Irina through a set of glass doors, into a sea of desks pushed against each other, manned by people, none older than 30, all staring at screens. They finally stopped at a desk set apart slightly from the others. "This is your spot, which is good because it's close to the window. Trevor, who you'll be reporting too, will handle the rest of your orientation."

For the next half hour, Irina watched the people around her, silent and expressionless, fingers tapping keystrokes, hands scrolling. There were desks as far as she could see in all directions. She guessed there were more than three hundred people in the room. Eventually, she was approached by a guy in a maroon Arizona State Sun Devils polo. He introduced himself with a firm handshake.

"Hi, I'm Trevor. Welcome to Cogniture. Do you have any questions?"

Irina looked at him, confused. "Sure. Nobody has actually explained what I'm going to be doing."

"Whoa. Okay. Let's start there." He looked around and led her to a glass-walled conference room in the center of the sprawl.

"Things are moving so fast here. This is the Content Moderation Services Division, totally dedicated to Facebook. It feels like we're working for Facebook. That's the feeling we want to convey. We're their eyes and ears. Any content flagged by Facebook or Instagram users in the U.S. comes here."

"Flagged for what?"

"All kinds of things. Since the election, Facebook is under a lot of pressure to monitor what's on its platform. We get over a half a million pieces of content every day. The people at these desks review every single one. They block it, approve it or ask a manager for a ruling. That's where you come in. As manager, you make the call."

"Based on what?"

"Facebook Community Standards. You'll need to be extremely familiar with those."

Irina flipped through the information in her folder. "Are they listed here?"

"No. They're only posted online. You'll have to review them every week with your team because they keep changing."

"So how many people am I managing?"

"On any given day, 30 people will be coming to you. But things move fast here and we have a lot of turnover."

"Why is that?"

Trevor seemed irritated at the question. "It's a demanding job. It's not for everybody. Moderators have to work fast. And some of the content is pretty disturbing."

"Disturbing? In what way?"

"There's a ton of hate speech. Conspiracy theories. Child pornography. Animal cruelty. All kinds of bizarre sex stuff. Violence. But we have counselors you can talk to if you feel the need."

Irina felt her neck muscles tightening. She had seen such things posted before.

"So that's the kind of content I'm going to be looking at?"

"You probably won't see the really bad stuff. Most of that is pretty obvious, so the moderators just take it down. It doesn't get to you unless the moderator has a question."

"But I'll be seeing some of it?"

"Yes, definitely."

Irina tried to let this sink in.

"Also, very important, we're protecting Facebook user data. Which, with everything going on, has become a sensitive issue. That badge you're wearing. You need to wear it everywhere. If you don't have your badge when you show up in the morning or come back from lunch, you will not get in the door."

Irina nodded. "I understand the importance of security."

Trevor stared at her blankly. "I feel like I'm forgetting something. Oh right, you came to us through Facebook, so corporate is covering your salary. Obviously, you need to keep that confidential. Most people here make minimum wage. Fifteen dollars an hour. But, hey, it beats flipping burgers or stocking shelves at Walmart, right?"

Trevor led Irina back to her desk.

"I'll send you a list of your team members. Tomorrow you'll probably see different faces around you here. Everybody floats to the available stations, so your people will be scattered around this area. They log out when they leave their desks, so you can keep track of them."

As Irina took her seat, one woman looked up and smiled. Others kept their eyes locked on their screens, as if they were working against an invisible clock. Irina read through the Facebook Community Standards, which detailed the different reasons for removing content: Violence and Criminal Behavior, Safety, Objectionable Content, Integrity and Authenticity, Respecting Intellectual Property and Content-Related Requests. A lot of the distinctions seemed narrow and complicated, as if they were written by engineers. There were elaborate diagrams detailing the steps required to reach a decision on whether something violated the ever-changing standards. Reading between the lines, Irina understood that Facebook believed removing content should be a last resort. After everything, their position still seemed to be that users were responsible for the content they posted, not Facebook.

When she finished reading the guidelines, Irina decided to explore the office. She walked to one end of the space, which was just a row of windows looking out on the parking lot, then she turned around and walked to the other end. The only area not occupied by desks was a grim break room filled with Formica tables, microwaves and vending machines. Even the motivational wall posters seemed discouraging.

It is possible.

Forgive yourself.

You'll get through it.

Be the person you want to be.

When she explored the other floors, she found people congregating in stairwells and along the narrow hallway lined with lockers.

Everyone seemed trapped. This was nothing like Facebook. No free lattes or haircuts. No yoga or meditation classes. No free breakfast, lunch and dinner.

She went back to her desk and stared out at the sea of faces locked on their screens. She followed the prompts for setting up her email account and other in-house apps. She got a "welcome" message from Trevor with a link to Facebook community standards and sent him a reply. "Excited to be here."

He replied back, "It's definitely exciting."

While she waited for whatever might be coming, she logged on to Facebook and saw she had a comment from Tara on one of her playlists.

"Great tunes. Why don't you stop running from us and join the CrossFit Crazies?"

Two other women, apparently friends of Tara, chimed in.

"Yeah, we need some fresh blood."

"C'mon Irene, don't be shy."

At first, she was going to reply to Tara with a "Cool, glad you liked it" and ignore their invitation. But the truth was she was getting tired of running alone. Sarah and the other people at WitSec said it was a good idea to start making friends. After a few minutes she replied, "I might be up for that."

Tara responded immediately. "Meet us tomorrow Hellfire CrossFit @ 6:30 ready to sweat."

A 6:30 workout would give her time to shower and get to the office. She'd have to leave the house a little after 6:00, which meant Anya would have to get herself ready for school. But as long as Irina made sure there was something tasty for breakfast, Anya would probably welcome a little independence.

Irina responded with a thumbs-up emoji.

The next morning Tara and two other members of the "Crazies," as they called themselves, were waiting for her outside a converted car dealership with a Hellfire CrossFit sign above the door. Justine and Vita, who she recognized from school orientation, introduced themselves. Irina reminded herself to seem like a newbie. She didn't want to arouse suspicion by seeming like a CrossFit veteran.

"Cool space for a gym."

"First of all, we call it a box, not a gym."

Tara went on to explain the CrossFit-famous acronym WOD, which stood for Workout of the Day. "There's a different WOD every day, all named for women. Cindy, Diane, Elizabeth and Grace."

"Why are they named after women?"

"Because a CrossFit workout is like a hurricane and hurricanes are named for women. Or at least they were until all this PC BS."

Irina, of course, knew all this from her days at Red Tower CrossFit back in Piter. Yelling at rich Russians to do five more reps. Going out for beers with Sergei and the crew afterward. She could hardly believe that had been her life, so she tried not to think about it.

A trainer named Christina introduced herself and led Irina to a quiet corner of the space so she could demonstrate the exercises and routines.

"I could use a little refresher," Tara said as she tagged along. "I feel like I'm getting a little sloppy."

The two of them stood facing Christina and mirrored her movements. She demonstrated a pull-up, muscle-ups on the rings and the proper technique for the rowing machine, movements Irina could have done in her sleep.

"You're making this look too easy," Tara said.

When they were finished, Irina tried to keep her distance in the locker room. Tara was waiting for her outside.

"So what do you think?"

"It's good. Hard."

Tara shook her head. "I can't believe how fast you're picking it up."

"Thanks, now I'll go collapse at my desk." .

Although she sensed a red flag in Tara's curiosity, the cult-like CrossFit culture offered at least one familiar activity in her strange new life. The speed of her progress was a recurring theme for Tara. "You must be the Bionic Woman. Are you sure you haven't done this before?" She asked lots of questions about Irina's past, and Irina stuck to the simple storyline Witness Security had given her. As a child, she was a good athlete but hardly competed because her family moved a lot. She always acted as if her efforts were unworthy of mention, but sometimes she wondered if Tara was stalking her online.

Once Tara spotted the pale ghost of ink on the inside of her right forearm.

"Did you have a tattoo?"

"In my tough-girl days."

"Cool. What did it say?"

"Too embarrassing to mention."

Irina wondered if it might be wise to ease her way out of the friendship, but it seemed as if Anya and Celeste were becoming friends. The last thing she wanted to do was make Anya's life harder. She mentioned the situation to Sarah during one of her check-in sessions.

"So that CrossFit friend keeps asking questions."

"Unfortunately, this happens. There are a lot of homegrown conspiracy hunters out there. They see cover-ups everywhere. If they can't find something, they make it up. What's she into?"

"Sometimes she mentions the Deep State. I think maybe she was a Pizzagate person."

"See if she settles down. If she starts putting you in awkward situations, you might have to get away from her."

But Irina found herself getting hooked on the workouts. Although she wasn't as strong as some of the other women, she excelled on the rings, rowing machine and pull-up bar and she was one of the few people in class who could do handstand push ups. She could feel herself getting stronger by the week, and it was pretty much the only social life she had.

One curious thing was that she wasn't attracted to any of the men. She found their chiseled swaggering a turnoff. Instead she now found herself staring at the tall, gangly, slack-muscled guys and realized it was because of Dez. Not just that she missed him—it was more than that. Somehow their connection had reprogrammed her code of sexual attraction, which made it hard not to think about him, his apartment with the symmetrical arrangements of dishes, pots and kitchen utensils, the rows of vintage T-shirts on hangers. She missed his stream-of-consciousness observations, the way he was funny without trying to be. She had no idea what he was up to, whether he had moved on.

She would never have guessed she would find someone like him attractive. All her prior relationships had been with athletes. The tennis player, a pentathlete, downhill and Nordic skiers, a speed skater, plus a female Canadian ice dancer and a French 200-meter sprinter. They were charismatic, confident moving through the world. Athletes knew their bodies better than anyone, so the sex was usually great, but she often felt like she was dealing with someone too much like herself. At the end of the day, they were all narcissists, trying to win medals and amass enough fame to carry them after their glory days were over.

Dez never seemed to be competing with anyone. He always had a way of disarming the tension, of bringing down the energy so she could think more clearly. When they were together, the usual chaos in her head seemed almost manageable. That was what she missed.

She kept circling back to the last time she'd seen him. After her testimony, he'd flown out to D.C. with Anya, and they'd spent a few days together. It was obvious how much he cared about her, but she was in crisis mode, thinking only of Anya and their safety and all the unknowns that awaited them, of how surreal it would be to become a different person and start a new life. When they said goodbye, she wasn't really there. But when he left and it sunk in that she would never see him again, she wondered if she was making another mistake she couldn't erase. Of all the things she'd given up by entering Witness Security, this was the toughest. But she couldn't ask him to give up his life in California. She doubted he would even consider it if she did. And she had Anya to think of. It was too big a risk to leave Witness Security and go back to Facebook, especially when they didn't seem to want her there. She had to stick with the plan.

So she threw herself into her new life and her new job, even though the work wasn't easy to love. Every month, Cogniture increased the moderators' quota, so they had to work more quickly. But Facebook demanded accuracy. Removing Facebook content could not be taken lightly, and they expected moderators to always make the right call. In the first few months, three of Irina's moderators' accuracy dipped below 95%, and she was required to "manage them out," as if they were faulty machines. What made it worse was that Facebook revised its Community Standards every week, posting random PowerPoint presentations that contradicted each other, so the rules for eliminating content kept changing. It was clear they had no idea of what the world should or shouldn't see and were making up the rules as they went along. To try to improve efficiency, Cogniture reorganized content teams around specific categories, like General Violence, Child Abuse, Animal Cruelty, Terrorism, Human Trafficking, Narcotics, Suicide and Self-Injury, Propaganda and Misinformation. But that meant moderators were subjected to one particular kind of horror, child abuse for instance, day after day.

The strange undercurrents Irina had first detected around the office began to bubble to the surface. Every week, the content Irina's team reviewed grew darker, more disturbing, and she could see them buckling under the pressure. Farhan insisted they were sending him all the ISIS torture and beheading videos because he was Muslim. He started pinging Irina every time one arrived, at least three or four every day. She would wade through the sea of desks to find him, but she had him pause the footage before the grisly ritual started. The other moderators started complaining about Ozzy. Although he was fast and efficient, he kept forwarding memes and videos about the "Holohoax" and telling everyone 9/11 was an inside job. And Irina was particularly concerned about Destiny, who kept reaching out to the on-site mental health counselors and spent an extra 30 minutes away from her desk every day. Following office procedure, Irina was forced to give her a warning for not meeting her quota and failing to review flagged content to its completion.

"Maybe you can just let the content play without actually watching it," Irina suggested.

"Okay, if you think I'm going to watch a guy set fire to a bunch of piglets? No way. And if I get one more video of somebody dropping a baby, I'm out of here. I have a child."

At weekly leadership meetings, managers discussed ways to improve morale and reduce turnover, but nothing changed. Irina was too familiar with all the bad things people posted. She had posted some herself, so she welcomed the responsibility for taking some of them down. But there were things out there she couldn't have imagined, monstrous scenes of torture and cruelty, first posted in the festering hives and warrens of 8chan, then copied onto Facebook, where they multiplied exponentially, so it was impossible to take them all down. It was staggering how much abhorrent, revolting content there was, how it never stopped spreading, how for every suicide video they took down, five more cropped up.

Publicly, Facebook kept insisting its amazing AI and machine learning were purging toxic content from the platform and keeping its users safe. So the moderators weren't supposed to talk about what was really going on. The truth was Facebook's machine was built for speed, and it wasn't human. It couldn't fathom the depth and range of the world's depravity. That job had to be left to the humans themselves.

By early December the insufferable heat had cooled. The desert air was clear and crisp. Everywhere she went, Irina heard people mentioning "the poor suckers in Minneapolis and Chicago." With the holidays approaching, she suddenly felt the pressure to come up with a plan to mark the first Christmas in their new home. People at the office talked about their plans for skiing and snowboarding in places like Utah and Colorado. The more she thought about it, the more it seemed perfect, something they could do together, that Anya could brag about to her friends.

But when she started looking at prices, she was shocked. Most hotels and resorts had doubled their rates for the holidays, and when she factored in the cost of lift tickets and equipment rentals, it was outrageous. But the idea of spending two weeks at home staring at their separate screens seemed grim. So she found a package deal and booked four nights at a resort called Purgatory in Colorado.

They had a quiet Christmas Day at home, opening presents in the morning, and Irina made *syrniki* with cherry jam. For dinner she made beef stew, and they watched *La Femme Nikita* again. The next morning, they got up early and drove east through the Petrified Forest. There was ice on the roads as they drew closer to their destination, and Irina stayed in the right lane while hulking SUVs rocketed past her at 70 mph. The drive took almost 10 hours, and they arrived at their tiny resort condo exhausted and miserable from eating gas station food.

The next morning, they went straight to the mountain and waded into the long rental line. The makeshift hut smelled like a human stable, and the laborious rental process predated the digital age. They ran out of pens, which added to the chaos, and gave Anya the opportunity to remind her that they should have rented their equipment back in Phoenix, as her friends had suggested. They were both wearing their ski jackets and pants and covered in a full body sweat by the time a red-eyed boy, obviously stoned, grabbed the forms from Irina's hand and slapped down two boards and two pair of boots.

Irina had ridden a snowboard once 20 years before, while traveling with the Russian ski team in Slovenia, but it all came back to her quickly. For Anya, however, it wasn't so easy. She struggled trying to push herself along the flat stretch to the bunny hill, so Irina suggested they pick up their boards and walk to the lift. While they were waiting in line, Anya lost her balance and fell twice. When it was their turn to board the lift, she wasn't paying attention, so Irina had to jerk her by the arm to pull her into the chair as it swung around behind them. Getting off, Anya lost her balance and stopped dead in the path of the riders deboarding behind her. Irina pulled her to the side to prevent a collision.

"Stop jerking my arm."

Irina stared at her, sensing already that it was going to be a challenging day. "When you get off the lift, you have to keep moving or people will run into you."

"That's their problem."

Irina guided them to an easy run with just enough of a slope to generate a smooth, effortless glide. Anya would build up speed, panic, try to sit down, spin backwards and fall face-first in the snow every 20 feet.

"Don't think so much," Irina said. "Let your body do it."

Every time Anya fell, Irina had to take off her board and walk back up the hill to help her. She tried having Anya go ahead so she could watch from behind. Seeing her daughter flail and fall was like observing an alien creature. She wondered what sort of genetic accident had caused her to give birth to a child with a total lack of physical coordination. The grace Anya exuded at rest disintegrated when her hips, knees, legs and arms tried to work together. There was little evidence the dance lessons were having much effect. After a couple of hours, she sat down in the middle of a run with her goggles, jacket and pants crusted with snow.

"I hate this. I want to go home."

They picked up their boards and walked the last hundred yards down to the lodge for hot chocolate. Irina forced herself to be upbeat.

"Snowboarding is always hard the first day."

Imagining the two of them might enjoy a sport together was possibly her worst idea ever. But spending $800 and giving up after a couple of hours on the mountain was out of the question. She had to find a way to salvage the situation. Her daughter was a klutz. Doing face-plants while watching your mother glide downhill was no doubt making things worse. What Anya needed was what every klutz needed: confidence. The kind of confidence that only came from being surrounded by other klutzes.

"We can't give up now. Maybe I'm not a good instructor. Tomorrow we will get you a real lesson."

The next morning Irina handed over her credit card, paid an additional $130 and enrolled Anya in a beginner's group lesson. The instructor was a girl named Sam with pink cheeks and the sports-camp energy required to justify the expense.

"Hey, Anya, cool. Glad you could join us."

It was a motley group: two fearless 10-year-old boys, a husky couple in Wisconsin Badger ski hats, and thankfully, two girls who looked about Anya's age. Sam waved goodbye to Irina.

"We got this, mom. We'll see you back here at 4. By then we'll be shreddin'."

Irina slipped her boot into her board and headed back to the main lift, hoping for the best. If this went well, she'd probably have to spring for two more days of lessons. This was costing her a fortune, but if Anya came away thinking she could snowboard, the trip would be a success.

She worked her way into the singles line and studied the trail map as she waited for the lift. She wanted to get up higher on the mountain, among the black runs and away from the crowds. The first run she took was Crescendo. She carved a smooth line, making wide arcs, gaining speed, getting the feel of the board and catching a few bumps. Then she took a different lift up to Little Johnny's. She rode down from the lift and stopped to take in the view, a jagged line of sawtooth peaks cutting into the sky, so vast and outrageously beautiful, it was impossible to take it all in. Maybe it was the thinness of the air, but suddenly she felt light-headed, exhausted and had the urge to lie down in the snow. Her life, so full of effort and struggle, was not a life she had chosen. This was what happened to people who weren't paying attention: Life chose you. And it was wearing her down, especially her nightmare of a job. Such madness. If she was ever going to escape the feeling of being held captive, she would have to start making better decisions. She shivered, felt embarrassed to be feeling sorry for herself, wrapped in expensive rented ski gear so she could admire the spectacular view. She turned around and rode back down the mountain.

At the end of the day, she came back to the base of the mountain a little early so she could watch Anya return from her lesson. She spotted the group slowly cruising down the hill. First the 10-year-old boys, cutting back and forth, then the Wisconsin couple heading down in a straight line and finally Anya and the two other girls, swerving too close to each other, crossing each other's lines, slightly out of control. The three of them came to an awkward stop a few feet away and sat down in the snow, laughing.

"How was it?"

"Okay. Cool, I guess," Anya said.

"Everybody had a great day," Sam said. "I think we should keep this crew together and do some more shreddin' tomorrow."

The other girls waved to Anya when they left, so it appeared some connection had been made and Irina would be coughing up another $130.

The next day they got dressed, took the shuttle bus to the mountain and ate overpriced waffles in the lodge, so they could be there in time for the start of the lesson. Anya's new friends seemed happy to see her and escape their parents for another day.

Irina headed to the other side of the mountain. She had hoped the trip would be a way to connect with Anya. Instead, she would probably spend the next two days riding the mountain alone. She moved through the lift lines quickly, got in seven runs in the first couple of hours and headed into the lodge for an early lunch to beat the crowd. She sat by the window and ate a bowl of soup with a large black coffee.

When she went back outside, it was cold and windy, and there was no line for the lift. As the chair swung around, she slid on next to another single, a tall, fit-looking man on skis. He was wearing a custom black jumpsuit with a Day of the Dead skull embroidered on the back and a scorpion on the sleeve. He turned and stared at Irina.

"Where is everybody? Too windy for wimps?"

His accent was Russian. Irina nodded and looked straight ahead. She knew this kind of asshole well, the kind who thinks, "I am handsome. Stop pretending you don't want to talk to me."

"Are you skiing alone?" he asked.

"I'm here with my daughter. She's taking a lesson."

"And you're Russian."

Irina tried to smile. "No, I am from little Estonia."

"Really? I would have guessed Russian, like me." He stared at her. "Are you from Tallinn?"

Irina's guard went up. As part of her orientation, she had studied the history of the Estonian capital but was less than knowledgeable about current events. She was going to have to wing it. "Yes."

"You've been to Café Moon?"

"No."

"Too bad. It's the best in town."

Suddenly the lift jolted to a stop. Irina felt a wave of panic. This was too strange. Now she was trapped. What if the guy's Russian accomplice had stopped the lift so that he could interrogate her or push her off?

"Why are they stopping?"

He smiled at her. "Probably the wind. And so we could have a nice conversation."

Irina tried to recover. "Yes, this is nice. I always enjoy sitting on the lift in freezing wind."

"But the weather is terrible back home, right? You must be used to this."

"Maybe I'm getting soft. I've lived in the States for a while."

"Really? Where?"

Irina felt another surge of alarm. She looked down. The chair hung 30 feet in the air, too high to jump, even for a former pole-vaulter.

"New Jersey first, now Phoenix."

"With your husband?"

She almost said "yes" but decided it would be a mistake to start piling lies on top of each other. The lift started up again.

"With my daughter."

He smiled again. "The one who's taking lessons. We could ski together."

"You'll be too fast on skis."

"I like taking breaks. We can talk about Russian-Estonian relations."

In other circumstances, Irina might have been amused by his flirting. He seemed too charming to be KGB, but of course, she couldn't be sure. Maybe he was some oligarch's nephew. Either way, Irina wanted to escape from him as quickly as possible.

"It's cold. I'm going to take one more run and call it a day."

When they reached the top of the lift, she could see he was leaning left, so she leaned to the right.

"Stay warm," he said as they slipped off the lift. She watched him jet down the hill.

After a long day of boarding, she was cold and the wind was blowing hard on the exposed side of the mountain. She took her time gliding down the run, found a bar at the base of the mountain, left her board outside and went in and ordered a hot spiced rum. She sipped it sitting by the window, waiting for Anya to finish her lesson.

Irina hoped they could snowboard together the last day, but Anya wanted to join her new friends for another lesson. Irina reminded herself that the real purpose of the trip was for Anya to learn to snowboard and have fun, so she had to say it was a success. She wasn't really in the mood to get back on the mountain, but couldn't get a refund on her lift ticket, so she spent the day on the runs favored by snowboarders, trying to avoid the handsome Russian. She saw him once below the lift, skiing fast with the skull on his back.

After the holidays, Irina sensed a different energy in the office. Perhaps people had seen the massive ad campaign for Facebook Live and discovered the irresistibility of video streaming, how it made them the star of their own show. Or maybe it was the reach of the satellites Zuck launched to extend Facebook's domination deep into the Third World. But whatever the reason, suddenly the flow of disturbing scenes and images turned into a torrent—horrible things that couldn't be unseen, that took their toll on Irina's team. Destiny went back to her old job at Walmart. Justin locked himself in the lactation room for an entire afternoon. Another moderator had to be treated for panic attacks after watching a drone mow down an Afghan wedding party. Someone saw Ozzy put a handgun in his locker. Even the mental health counselors started calling in sick.

One day Irina was reviewing a series of flagged posts that looked like human trafficking, when a news notification popped up on her screen. She clicked on the link to the story. The headline read, "Mueller Indicts 13 Russians for Election Interference". Irina's body broke into a sweat. The Agency was mentioned in the first paragraph. She scrolled down the page, looking for the names and there they were, a few paragraphs later, exactly the list she'd given the Special Counsel lawyer. Months had passed since her testimony and she was beginning to feel like it was behind her. Now her heart felt like it would burst from her chest. She had imagined the secrets she revealed would remain confidential, that they were helpful background to spur the investigation. Now they were being broadcast to the world. She felt betrayed, like someone had painted a target on her back. Although she knew her failure to return to St. Petersburg would be damning back at the Agency, she had allowed herself to imagine they wouldn't take it seriously enough to come after her. But a lead story on the world's major news sites gave her every reason to believe they would.

She got up from her desk, grabbed her phone from her locker, went down to the parking lot and called Sarah.

"Did you see the story about the Special Counsel?"

"Of course, you should feel good about being part of that."

Irina's mind was racing. "Feel good about it? Seriously? I gave them the names. The Agency will know it was me."

"Not necessarily. This is an exhaustive investigation. The Special Counsel has hundreds of sources."

"I wrote down 13 names. Today they announce 13 names, all the same. Do you think that's a coincidence?"

A couple of moderators were leaning against a car, smoking and looking in her direction. She walked across the lot to her Prius and got inside.

"Irina, everyone understands the importance of your contribution. That's why you have the full support of WitSec. We've never lost a witness. We will make sure you're safe."

"Easy for you to say."

"I understand you're feeling vulnerable right now. But we know what we're doing."

"Nobody told me this was going to happen. Do they think they can just go to Russia and arrest them? That's not going to work."

"No obviously not."

Suddenly a terrifying new possibility occurred to Irina. "Are they thinking of some kind of spy swap? Like sending me back to Russia in exchange for some of the other trolls?"

"No, no, no. But you sound upset. Would you like come in and talk about this?"

"I've done too much talking already."

"Irina, I understand how you're feeling. But as long as you stick to our protocols you and Anya will be fine in your new life here."

Irina closed her eyes and took a few long, deep breaths. "I hope so. Since that's the only choice we have."

She hung up, rested her head on the steering wheel and tried to make her mind go blank. When she opened her eyes, the dashboard clock said she had been away from her desk for almost 30 minutes, so she had to get back.

A few weeks went by without further news of Russians. Irina was relieved to see the investigation shift to Trump's money-laundering cronies. She kept up her morning workouts with the CrossFit Crazies which helped her relax. Her schedule didn't allow for many home cooked meals, but in the evening, she tried to leave the office behind, so she and Anya could eat dinner together and talk about the day.

Then the Cambridge Analytica story broke. According to the *New York Times* and the *Guardian*, the data intelligence company—created by Steve Bannon and a secretive right-wing billionaire named Robert Mercer—had gotten its hands on the data of 87 million Facebook users before the election. They hadn't stolen the data; Facebook had given it to them. But the shocking thing was what they did with it. They had gotten all the Facebook users to answer a long, detailed questionnaire that probed the depths of their psyches and unearthed their darkest needs and fears. The data was so rich, so deep, so detailed, they knew these people better than their own spouses. So when the Trump campaign started crafting ads and messages, they knew exactly which levers to pull. Instead of creating dozens of ads, they created thousands, each one using a different image or turn of phrase to trigger the right response. Using the Facebook platform as a perfect feedback loop, they could see what worked best, which buttons to push and hone their efforts as they went along. The campaign became the ultimate hyper-targeted, data-driven juggernaut, especially in the final weeks. Now it was impossible to deny Facebook had played a decisive role in the election, had in fact, blown up American democracy. And they had been denying it, lying about it, for months. What Irina and her collegues at the Agency had done was bad enough, but this made them look like amateurs. The nightmare scenario of what an evil genius could do with your personal data—this was it. They had made human beings hackable.

Irina wondered what Dez must be thinking or doing, if he would resign. All day she resisted the urge to call him. She told herself if he had wanted to talk to her, he would have called her. After six months, of course, he had probably moved on. She pictured the scene on the Menlo Park campus. People gathering in small groups around their desks to rant, possibly cry. They had lived their lives moving from one bubble to the next. A gentle, orderly suburb. An elite college. And finally, the fabulous Facebook campus, designed to their generational specifications. It was very different from growing up in a city where half a million souls had been exterminated, where you learned at an early age what monsters human beings could be, what terrible urges lurked in their hearts. You didn't enter adulthood believing a benevolent world awaited you, like the innocents she'd met in Menlo Park did. Perhaps Mark Zuckerberg would have been more careful about moving fast and breaking things if he'd had a Russian grandmother who told him stories about the siege.

Days after the Cambridge Analytica scandal hit Facebook, it was on its way to Cogniture, moving like a hurricane that gathers full force when it reaches shore. Now Facebook was squarely in the government crosshairs, under pressure to clean itself up. But Facebook had been built for growth, not policing itself, so the cleanup would have to be outsourced. With 2 billion Facebook users posting their darkest thoughts, that was an impossible task—but for Cogniture, a lucrative one. They hired 300 people in one month, rushed them through training and increased the moderators' quota to 500 pieces of content per day.

While keeping daily watch over the darkest corners of the internet, Irina couldn't help but worry about Anya. At least five times a day, they took down videos of young girls cyberbullying each other, cutting themselves or sharing their suicidal urges. The Web was a virtual encyclopedia of the disturbing thoughts of teenage girls. So she thought it was a good sign that Anya seemed to quickly make friends. She seemed to enjoy the modern dance classes she took with Celeste and another girl, Alexis, three days a week. In fact, the three of them spent their free afternoons practicing their routines and shooting videos at Alexis' house. Irina would have loved to catch a glimpse of the three of them working out their choreography, but Anya said they needed more space.

After they'd been so locked into each other for the last year, maybe "space" was exactly what Anya needed. Irina thought of herself at 15—angry, defiant, feeding on confrontation. Anya ran with a slower motor, which seemed healthier. According to the teachers, she was reserved in class but an excellent student. If she had secrets, she kept them to herself, and Irina was okay with that. All teenage girls needed secrets.

But one afternoon a moderator called her over for a ruling on a video of teenage girls dressed like strippers dancing to "Bandz a Make Her Dance" by Juicy J. The video was shot with a cell phone and poorly produced. It was a tricky call because even though the girls were mimicking the usual stripper moves, there were no nipple or nude shots, which meant it didn't violate Facebook Community Standards. But after 10 seconds of watching the girls caress their own breasts and shake their asses, Irina had seen enough.

"Take it down," she said.

The moderator was a woman in her 20s, a new hire concerned with following the rules. "I'm not sure about that."

"Those girls are too young. Take it down."

When she returned to her desk, Irina decided she needed to learn more about Anya's dance class and the videos they were shooting. She would make a home-cooked meal for a change, and they could catch up on everything that was happening.

At the end of her shift, Irina climbed into the Prius and drove to Whole Foods. She never shopped there because of the ridiculously high prices, but Anya mentioned the store often, as if having a mother who shopped at Whole Foods was a form of social currency. Irina decided talking about the importance of going organic would be a good lead-in to a more serious conversation that evening.

She pulled into the lot, and as she started toward the store, a couple pulled up beside her. They looked Slavic and spoke rapidly to each other, but with the car windows up, she couldn't hear what they were saying.

Irina took her time in the store. She bought a plump organic chicken, yellow potatoes that looked like scrubbed pebbles and carrots with leafy tops. As she moved through the aisles, she stopped looking at the prices and loaded her cart with beets, apples, oranges, spinach, quinoa, bread, a couple of salmon fillets, organic raspberry-fig bars, chamomile and echinacea teas, non-GMO Kettle chips, individual blueberry and lemon yogurts—all the treats Anya liked. When she reached the personal care aisle, she decided to replenish Anya's shampoo, conditioner and lotions. She was sure her daughter would appreciate that. She felt foolish as she watched the prices flash on the screen above the register. Thirteen dollars for almond butter? Six dollars for a cantaloupe? The total came to $221.39, far more than she'd ever spent on groceries. But she reminded herself of her purpose: This indulgence was a gift to Anya, an investment in their mother-daughter bonding.

As she pushed the cart across the lot, she noticed the Slavic-looking couple still sitting in their car. The man seemed to be checking his rearview mirror, which seemed odd. The woman's gestures looked so familiar, Irina was sure the two of them were Russian. She pushed her cart to get closer to their car, but as she passed, the woman stopped speaking.

Irina took her time loading her groceries into the Prius, occasionally glancing their way. The woman got out of the car and headed into the store. The car was a gray Honda, not a bad choice if you were trying to blend in, Irina thought. She returned her cart to the entrance of the store so she could pass by their car again and stared at the man on her way back, but he was looking down now and texting on his phone. The couple gave Irina a bad feeling, so she typed their Arizona license plate number into the Notes app on her phone.

She drove home checking her rearview mirror the whole time. She was surprised Anya wasn't home from dance practice, so she sent her a text. But she couldn't stop thinking about the Whole Foods couple, so she went to the front window and stared out at the street. There was a steady flow of cars, including a couple of gray Hondas. After a few minutes, she went back into the kitchen to put away the groceries. Back at the Agency, she had seen a number of questionable figures coming and going who could have been KGB. They were usually bland-looking, nondescript—like Putin himself, like the couple at Whole Foods.

She went into her contact list and called Sarah, gave her the license number and took her through the sequence of events.

"So. Let me break this down. You were at Whole Foods and you heard some people speaking Russian?"

"They might have been speaking Russian. They stopped when I got close to their car."

"So…"

"They looked Russian."

"Their facial characteristics?"

"Yes. And their behavior seemed suspicious. Just waiting, like they weren't interested in going into the store."

"So they were watching you?"

"Possibly."

"And they didn't go into the store?"

"Eventually the woman did."

"Irina, relocation is stressful. And I know you're concerned about the Special Counsel's indictments. I will run a check on the license number and trace it to the owners. But this doesn't sound like something to worry about. Even if they are Russian, that's not cause for alarm. There are a quarter million Russians in Phoenix. They came here for the same reason you did. Because it's warm."

"You said you would keep us safe."

"Yes, and we will. I promise."

Irina hung up. Her hands were shaking as she stuffed the chicken with lemon and rosemary. Anya hadn't responded to her texts, so she texted her again.

"Special Dinner. When will U be home?"

After 10 minutes, she didn't get a reply, so she decided to check her Find My Phone app. It was the first time she had used it to track her daughter's location. It took her a minute to confirm that Anya was not at dance practice, not at Alexis' house and not at Celeste's either. According to the dot on the app, she was somewhere across town. Irina switched to Google maps, which pinned the location to a strip mall. Irina tried to tamp down her alarm. Anya was perceptive and resourceful. She had grown up navigating the sketchy St. Petersburg subway. But why hadn't she called to tell her where she was going? Of course, there was the possibility of a boy, an older, more experienced boy. That she could easily see. But more likely she was just having an adventure with her friends, a secret escape from the boring boundaries of her teenage life. In America, kids were on such a tight leash these days, almost like they were under house arrest.

When she checked the app again, the dot hadn't moved. She got up and put the chicken in the oven, drizzled olive oil on the carrots and potatoes. Despite her agitation, she felt good to be preparing a home-cooked dinner. If Anya was up to something and there was a confrontation, she would be in a stronger position.

Fifteen minutes later, Irina called Anya, but she didn't pick up. Now she was starting to worry. She went to the window, half expecting to see the Russians' gray Honda with Anya inside, but there was no one in front of the house.

Finally, well after 6, the dot started to move and she got a text. "Sorry. B there in few"

Irina felt a surge of relief. Her daughter was safe. But then she started wondering if Anya would come clean about her afternoon adventure. If she lied, what would Irina do? If she confronted her daughter, she'd have to admit she was tracking her.

Irina sat at the counter waiting, the smell of roasting meat and vegetables filling the room. When she heard the key in the lock, she opened her laptop and tried to appear casual.

"How was practice?"

"We skipped practice."

Irina looked up. She hardly recognized the girl staring back at her. "Wow."

Her daughter had been transformed into someone five years older, maybe more, with dark, smoky eyes and sculpted cheeks, black hair thick and soft on her shoulders like a model's in a shampoo commercial.

"It was Alexis' birthday. Her mom gave us all a spa day."

"A spa day?"

Anya held out her hands to show perfectly sculpted nails with purple pastel polish. "We got makeovers, hair, mani-pedis and a mini massage."

Irina searched for something resembling a compliment.

"Very glamorous."

"I knew you'd hate it."

"I don't hate it. It's very dramatic."

"Mom, it's just a makeover. Get over it. You had a whole face job remember?"

"I'm sorry. If you told me you were going to a spa, I wouldn't be so shocked."

"If I told you, you wouldn't let me go."

"That's not true."

It was true she found the idea of pampering teenagers disgusting. She looked at her daughter, saw how beautiful she was and caught a flash of resemblance to the face in a photo on Vera's living room wall, a portrait of Mila, Vera's mother, with the dark, intelligent eyes and hint of a smirk.

"You look like your great-great-grandmother."

"The one who died in the war?"

"Yes, she was beautiful and a history professor, at St. Petersburg University."

"I know. Why can't I just be myself?"

Be herself, Irina thought, of course. Suddenly she realized how much harder she had made that for her daughter, dragging her around the world, forcing her to take on a new life, a new name—to learn a new language and adapt to a new culture. As frivolous as it seemed to Irina, if a spa day helped her daughter figure out who she was at this moment, there was no harm in that.

"Okay, I'm sorry. I made dinner. Are you hungry?"

Anya stalked out of the kitchen toward her room.

"We had appetizers at the spa. And I have a lot of homework to do."

Irina was sitting at the counter, replaying the evening in her mind, when she smelled the chicken burning.

On Irina's one-year anniversary, Trevor

met with her in a small conference room and presented her performance review, which stated she "exceeded expectations" for efficiency but "needed improvement" for her contribution to team morale. She received a seven percent raise. Twelve minutes later she was back at her desk.

As the months wore on, the world's need for sharing hate and depravity on Facebook accelerated and her days turned into a fevered blur. New moderators were hired and left in droves, so it was impossible for her to keep track of who was on her team. She couldn't remember their names. People started getting high in the stairwells and having sex in the bathroom stalls. Cash and opioids were exchanged openly in the parking lot throughout the day.

To compensate for turnover, Irina was forced to work longer hours, often coming home after 7:00 in the evening. By then, Anya would be in her room immersed, supposedly, in homework, so Irina often found herself sitting at the counter alone, finishing off whatever was left of the quinoa bowl or taco plate Anya had ordered. Sometimes she'd wash it down with a couple of fingers of Stolichnaya from a bottle she kept in the freezer, just enough to soften the jagged edge of the day.

Her check ins with Sarah at WitSec were now only every few months, so she and Anya were pretty much on their own. Irina had started to wonder if this was the new life she'd been given. If so, with the endless stream of frenzied hate speech, conspiracy theories and other madness, it was a lot like the old one.

One day after lunch, one of Irina's moderators asked for a ruling on a series of posts flagged for cyberbullying. Two middle school girls had posted videos of themselves addressing a cantaloupe as Marjorie, then stabbing it with forks and knives. Irina only needed to see a few seconds.

"Take it down."

It was an easy call, but back at her desk, Irina couldn't stop thinking about it, thinking about Anya. Her 16th birthday was coming up. She had requested her own spa day party with friends, to which Irina begrudgingly agreed. She got straight A's on every report card, her English was excellent and she seemed to breeze through her homework. Irina knew there must be secrets her daughter kept from her. That was to be expected. But now she wondered what Anya might be doing with all those free hours every night in her room.

In the afternoon, Irina sent an email claiming she had a doctor's appointment and left the office early to beat Anya home from dance practice. She went upstairs to Anya's room, straight to her computer, which was charging on her desk. Irina entered the password she remembered Anya had once used, @nya2003, but that didn't work, which meant Anya had recently reset it. So Irina would have to wait until Anya logged back in, then try to take a look at her search history before she logged back out. Since Anya spent her evenings in her room, that wouldn't be easy to do.

But before giving up, Irina took one more guess and entered Anya's ID from her old Snapchat account, which Irina had made her cancel when they moved to Phoenix: stpetersgur!

And she was in. She went straight to Anya's browser history. The last item, searched at 1:12 a.m., was a YouTube video recounting the horrible deaths of the stars and crews from famous horror films. It told the story of Sharon Tate's murder by the Manson Family after her husband directed *Rosemary's Baby*, Gregory Peck's near-death experience during the filming of *The Omen* and the unexplained helicopter accident on the set of *Poltergeist*. The video's conclusion was that, clearly, Satan was at work in Hollywood. Did Anya believe such things? Irina found that possibility disturbing. But even more unsettling was what seemed to lead Anya into the dark regions of the supernatural: a sermon titled "Why We Know Satan Is Real" from a Christian pastor at an online megachurch in Ohio. Irina watched it for a few minutes. The pastor cast a wide net to support his case, from opioids to "the scourge of transgenderism" to mass murder. Anya had watched for less than a minute before moving on. Apparently, she knew a phony when she saw one, but Irina still found her daughter's viewing habits unsettling. How had she ended up there?

She scrolled down to the evening's first listing, a Beyoncé music video at 6:37. From there she went to Ariana Grande and Cardi B, then she crossed over to a series of beauty vloggers: Kylie Jenner, Lauren Curtis and Jeffree Star. Some of the videos lasted nearly an hour. Skimming through them, Irina cringed at the breathless attention they lavished on themselves. They seemed like shameless opportunists, shilling their products and rewarding themselves with bottles of Dom Perignon when sales exceeded their goals.

From the beauty vloggers, Anya had moved on to a series of videos from other YouTube influencers: Jake and Logan Paul, Jenna Marbles, Zoella. Irina recognized some of the names. They appeared in each other's videos to boost their audiences and seemed intoxicated with their own popularity. Irina watched, repelled but transfixed, as they pulled silly pranks and shared shallow, passing thoughts, as if they were conveying special knowledge only they possessed. The underlying theme was that traditional media was full of spin and lies. They offered a window to both coolness and truth. Irina skipped from one video to the next, fleeing each of them after a few seconds, but Anya had watched for three hours. That was troubling.

After watching Jake Paul drink beer while jumping on a trampoline, Anya seemed to have fallen into a YouTube battle between Jake and his nemesis, Shane Dawson. That led her to a Shane Dawson conspiracy video about how Cardi B had been hypnotized by the Illuminati. Which led Anya into the dark world of the ultimate conspiracy monger: Alex Jones. At Cogniture there was a joke: "You're never more than three clicks from Alex Jones." Now it wasn't funny. According to her history, Anya had worked her way through his greatest hits: the Pizzagate pedophile ring, the government's gay bomb, gay-making chemicals embedded in juice boxes, symbols of the New World Order in Lady Gaga's Superbowl performance and proof the mass shootings at Sandy Hook and Parkland were staged.

Anya never spoke about such things, so perhaps she didn't believe them, but with hours of viewing every evening, someday she might. The YouTube algorithm was learning what Anya liked, how to keep her eyes glued to the screen. There was no doubt it had the power to shape her. Chances are, YouTube knew Anya better than Irina did.

Irina tried to imagine how the conversation would play out when she confronted her daughter. Anya was a clever debater and would probably try to turn the tables with the usual litany of daughterly complaints. "You're so controlling." "I can't breathe." "I can't believe you violated my privacy like that." "I need more freedom." "You're always so disappointed in me." Irina had to take a careful, measured approach or she'd end up on the defensive.

She checked her watch. She had time to make a quick Walmart run to pick up some things Anya had been asking for: a new memory card for her phone, a colored pencil set for art class, a Hydro Flask stainless-steel water bottle small enough to fit in her backpack. She parked in the lot close to the door, grabbed a cart and quickly navigated the length of the store, adding a few more items for Anya to the cart: a six-pack of her favorite kombucha, some single-serve Greek yogurts, a tub of sour gummy worms.

As she approached the checkout, she saw the Russian couple she had spotted months before at Whole Foods coming toward her. She recognized the man's receding hairline and the woman's small, serious eyes. They looked straight ahead, avoiding her glance as they pushed their cart past, but she was sure it was them. She slipped out of line and followed them from a distance, through small appliances, back toward children's clothing, down the long aisle of paper and plastics and back through the center of the store. They moved along without inspecting any of the merchandise. The only item in their cart was a 12-pack of Aquafina water. For Irina, that was the smoking gun. Nobody went to Walmart to buy one thing.

She followed them into the self-checkout line. Because they only had one item, they finished ahead of her and she lost sight of them as they exited the store. But as she pushed her cart into the parking lot, she saw them sitting in the gray Honda parked only a few spaces from her.

Irina loaded her bags into the car and called Sarah on the way home.

"I saw the Whole Foods couple again."

"Wait. Who?"

"The Russian couple that was following me at Whole Foods."

"We looked into that months ago. Stop worrying about them."

"This isn't a coincidence. They were acting suspiciously."

"How so?"

"Wandering around Walmart with one item in their cart. Who does that?"

There was a long silence on the end of the line.

"Irina, let's move up your next check-in to tomorrow? How about 8 o'clock?"

"Sure."

Maybe she was being crazy. But she knew the ways of Putin's KGB cabal, certain they had many methods unknown to smug bureaucrats like Sarah.

On her way home, she swung by Chipotle and picked up salads to go, chicken for her, tofu for Anya. She also picked up a half-dozen chocolate chip cookies from a local bakery she knew Anya loved. They would eat a healthy dinner, then have a cookie, then she would find a way to broach the question of why her daughter was watching videos about Satan and school shootings.

Anya was quiet over dinner. When Irina asked about school, she mimicked a yawn. When she put the plate of cookies on the table, Anya thanked her but ate only half of one. When she presented her with the memory card and other items, Anya's reaction was a barely perceptible nod.

Irina could remember her own teenage moods. Angry? Yes. Confrontational? Yes. But sullen? Never. The arrogance and passivity so infuriated Irina, she considered reaching across the table and taking back her little gifts, but that would divert her from the important conversation she needed to have.

"Anya, we have to have a talk."

Her daughter calmly looked her in the eye and then stared down at the table.

"I know it was hard to come here and start all over. It's hard to make new friends."

"I have friends. You don't have to worry about that."

"I know. But I know school is boring for you." Irina searched for the right angle to ease into the conversation. "Maybe it isn't easy finding interesting things to do."

"I think I'm doing okay. I'm doing better than you."

Irina had never stopped to consider that her daughter was watching her, passing judgment.

"Maybe so. But the other day you left your computer open and I took a look at your search history. I saw some pretty disturbing stuff."

"You have no right to do that. It's my computer."

"That I bought you. And it's my job to make sure you're not using it to watch the terrible things that are out there."

"So you're spying on me?"

"I'm worried about you. Why are you watching videos about Satan and Alex Jones?"

"Some kids were talking about it. They said the school shootings were fake."

"No, no, no. Many kids were killed. Alex Jones is evil. Please don't watch that stuff."

"Everybody watches it."

"Who's everybody?"

"Celeste. Alexis. Other kids. The moms watch it too."

"Those videos are made by people who make up crazy things to shock people so they can make money. The more shocking and insane it is, the more people watch, the more money they make. And none of it is true."

"What about all the stuff you made up?"

Touché. A long silence hung between them. Irina believed she had purged herself by confessing her crimes, but she wondered if her sins were so grave she would spend the rest of her life trying to untangle herself from them.

"It's true. I posted bad things. But then I tried to make up for it. That's why we came here and we're in this situation."

Anya seemed to sense she had leveled the playing field but wasn't sure where to go from there. "So, what am I supposed to do? Just stop watching conspiracy videos?"

"Yes. They're crazy and dangerous. And you can't watch them at Alexis' or Tara's house either."

Anya nodded. "Okay."

"Okay then."

Anya seemed relieved the conversation was over. She took a cookie from the plate. "You know Celeste's mom is a little obsessed with you."

Irina's guard went up. "What do you mean?"

"She's always talking about what a great athlete you are. She asks a lot about what we were doing in Estonia, but I tell her I was too young to remember."

"Good answer."

"But I might have slipped up once and mentioned St. Petersburg."

Irina felt a surge of panic. "What did you say?"

"Just that the winters are a lot nicer here than in St. Petersburg."

Irina's mind was racing. "Is that all?"

"Yeah. But now she brings it up like she knows we used to live there."

Irina could imagine the thrill a crack in her story would give a person like Tara, a secret that she could somehow use to her advantage or weave into one of her own demented conspiracy theories. This wasn't good. Irina had executed every step in the how-to-start-a-new-life plan, but it didn't seem to be working. The past kept pulling her back.

When she met with Sarah the next morning, Irina didn't know where to start. Sarah brought up the Russian couple first.

"You really have to stop focusing on them. We ran detailed background checks on them, and there are no issues. Russians live here. You're going to run into them."

"But they keep showing up in the same stores I do. Pushing their cart around. Not buying things. That doesn't sound weird to you?"

"No. It sounds like they haven't figured out how to be real American consumers yet."

Irina didn't believe her. Sarah was one of those people who insist there's a simple explanation for everything because they lack imagination.

"I know this is stressful. What else is going on?"

"Tara, that curious mom from school, knows we're from St. Petersburg."

"How do you know?"

"Anya accidently mentioned St. Petersburg. Now she's always asking her about it."

For the first time that morning, she had Sarah's full attention. "That could be a problem for you."

"What do you suggest?"

"Anya is in a vulnerable position. You need to pull her out of that relationship before she reveals anything else. This woman is bad news. She could start spewing wild stories and make things tough for you."

"Anya will be devastated. Tara's daughter is her best friend."

"We have to get this under control. Otherwise we might have to think about another move."

Irina left Sarah's office, climbed into her Prius and sat in the parking lot. It was impossible to still her mind, with all the thoughts swirling around inside it. Tara, the Russians, Anya, the toxic world awaiting her at Cogniture. She decided a workout would clear her head and already had her workout clothes in the car, so she called the office and told them she was running late. Things were so chaotic they probably wouldn't miss her.

She decided she should steer clear of Tara and the Crazies, so she headed to Camelback CrossFit, not far from the office, just north of town. It was a cool space, in an old lumber warehouse, with a totally different crowd. Lots more piercings, and the tattoos were more Maori warrior than Semper Fi. She chatted with a couple of women: Jan, who was straight and serious; Casey, who was funny and coming onto her.

After the workout, Irina drove to the office, savoring her endorphin buzz. Maybe things weren't so bad. Maybe she could figure out a way to pull away from the CrossFit Crazies without her life falling apart. By the time she pulled into the Cogniture lot, Jan and Casey had sent her friend requests, which she happily accepted.

When she got to her desk, she had a message to call Taylor in security. Office drama was the last thing she needed.

"We have an issue with one of your recent hires, Benjamin Moss."

She didn't recognize the name. "Is he one of my moderators?"

"Yes, someone reported he was holding weed in his locker and selling it in the parking lot."

"So has he been let go?"

"No, we didn't find anything. But you might want to look out for any strange behavior."

"Ha!" She thought he must be joking. "You don't have to look hard for that."

But otherwise it seemed to be an average day.

Moderators asked her to make the call on a couple of videos that appeared to be coded threats from a Mexican drug cartel. In the afternoon, they took down what looked like an online catalog posted by animal traffickers, showing captive leopards, orangutans and green turtles.

But as the evening shift began arriving, Irina felt a disturbance moving through the sea of desks and looked up to see Trevor, eyes-wide, coming toward her, shouting "Fish bowl. Fish bowl."

She followed him into the glass-walled conference room, where several people were staring at a Facebook Live video projected on the big screen. The footage was jerky, like it was shot with a head-mounted GoPro camera from inside a car. The driver narrated calmly as he navigated through traffic. "I'm driving to the mosque. Almost there." Then the car stopped, and he jumped outside. There was a repeated popping sound and people started falling down. It took Irina a second to realize what she was witnessing: a real-life, first-person shooter video.

In the room, someone shouted, "Oh, no."

Someone else said, "Stop. Stop it."

"We have to watch this," Trevor said. "It just happened. The shooter streamed the attack on Facebook Live. We have to watch so we can recognize the footage and take it down."

"What?" Irina said. "Why doesn't Facebook take it down?"

"They did. But they didn't get it fast enough. And the shooter made sure it went viral by embedding it with memes and a reference to PewDiePie. There are already thousands of copies out there. People keep uploading them. Get everybody in here. We have to start looking for them and taking them down."

As the video rolled, the gunman went inside the mosque and moved from room to room, shooting as the bodies piled up on the floor. Then he left, changed weapons and started back inside.

Irina turned away from the screen.

They brought all the moderators into the conference room and played the video again. Some looked away or refused to watch. Then they went back to their desks to start searching for the footage. Within an hour after the shooting, it was all over Facebook. They removed dozens of copies from the Facebook pages of white nationalist groups, but it kept popping up everywhere, on Instagram, Twitter and of course 8chan, the world's white-supremacist clubhouse. The Facebook Escalations Team in Menlo Park coded a copy of the video and pro- grammed its AI to recognize it, but determined viewers found ways to edit and reframe the footage so the AI couldn't detect it. The shooter had gotten maximum impact from his efforts. So Irina and the mod- erators stayed at their desks. For every copy they took down, a dozen more popped up.

At 7:30 her phone buzzed. It was Anya.

"Are you still at work?"

"I'm sorry. We have an emergency."

"Is it the New Zealand thing?"

Irina felt a jolt. "How did you know?"

"There's a lot of stuff about it online."

"Don't watch it. It's very disturbing."

"I won't."

"Please. Promise me you won't watch it."

"Okay. I promise."

"Have your friends watched it?"

"I don't know. I haven't talked to them."

Irina wondered if telling her daughter not to watch the video might have the opposite result. She wanted to be with her, protect her from this new horror. But that wasn't possible at the moment.

"I'm going to be here late. Are you okay?"

"I guess so. Celeste was acting weird."

Irina's radar went up, but she couldn't start worrying about the moods of someone else's teenage daughter.

She didn't get home until after midnight. Anya's door was closed and her lights were off, so Irina sat at the kitchen counter and ate cold pad thai. She checked her email to see if there were any additional developments. When she logged on to Facebook, she saw her feed had exploded. It took her a few minutes to unravel what she was seeing. Apparently, Hellfire and Camelback were bitter rivals in the local CrossFit Games. Within minutes of her accepting Jan and Casey's friend requests, Tara had jumped into her feed and a full-on Facebook war broke out between the boxes.

"Irina are you really abandoning us for a bunch of freaks and stoners?"

Jan responded: "Why don't you get into your time machine and go back to the '50s?"

Tara continued: "Just keep tripping instead of lifting. We will own your butch asses this year."

Casey jumped in: "Haven't you girls heard homophobia increases lactic acid buildup?"

Tara shot back: "Don't do it Irina. Don't taste the rainbow."

Finally, Jan tried to shut it down.

"That's enough. Let's save it for the games."

But Tara couldn't resist one last comment.

"Stay with us Irina. Russians are cool. We don't care if you're a spy."

Irina stared at the words in horror. She knew people like Tara from her days at the Agency. She had friended them, stroked them, manipulated them in her previous life, so she knew how far and fast things could spin out of control. She tried to imagine the worst-case scenario. That she'd be cancelled. That Anya would be called out or bullied at school. That somebody would spray-paint "Get Out Spy!" on the front of the house. Such things were possible. She couldn't think clearly enough to know what might come next. She wasn't even sure who she was anymore. The old Irina would have confronted Tara. The new Irina wanted to disappear.

As she sat at the counter, mind spinning, another post went up. It was a photo of the entrance to Camelback CrossFit, blocked with yellow crime-scene tape and littered with broken glass. Someone had thrown a kettlebell through the front door. Apparently, the Facebook fight had spilled out into the real world. Her feed exploded with another flurry of posts.

"Crazy bitches."

"Psychos!"

"You wanna play? Let's play."

A few minutes later another image appeared in her feed. It was a five-second video of Hellfire's front window being shattered by a metal weight bar, hurled like a javelin from somewhere offscreen.

Irina closed her computer and went for the Stolichnaya in the freezer. She poured some in a glass, felt it burn going down, waited for it to still the buzzing in her brain. There was nothing to be gained from thinking. Any conclusions she reached would be fevered and distorted. But she was pretty sure this was the end of their life in Phoenix. If she were honest, she had to admit she hated it. All of it. The nightmare job, endless dirt-colored sprawl and big-box stores. Brutal heat that could only be escaped by retreating into frigid AC. Hovering, wacko moms like Tara and her Crazies. Her sessions with the passive-aggressive, rule-making Sarah. She was done. For the last year and a half, she had been tearing up her life every few months, and the pieces kept getting smaller. What little sanity she had left was too fragile to be torn apart again.

She went back to the fridge, poured herself another inch of vodka. Before she knew what she was doing, her text was on its way to Dez.

"Hi, it's Irina."

She waited. No response. She sat at the counter staring at her phone. It was just after 1 o'clock. She felt lost, hopeless, ridiculous for thinking, after 18 months, he was back in Menlo Park waiting for her.

When her phone buzzed, she jumped, but the call was from a number she didn't recognize and not from 408, probably just more robocall spam. Usually she just declined the call and blocked the number, but this time she decided to pick up.

"Hey, it's Dez."

The sound of his voice cut through her.

"Hi." She realized she hadn't actually thought about what she was going to say. "What's this weird number?"

"Burner phone."

"So you're using burner phones now?"

He paused. "Recent precaution. FUBAR here today."

"What is FUBAR?"

"Fucked Up Beyond All Recognition. Military term. Are you still working at Cogniture?"

"How did you know?

"I have my ways. Are you taking down the video?"

"We took down hundreds of copies. But there are probably thousands still out there," Irina said.

"Yeah, we're trying to code the work-arounds people are using to post the footage. It's like a giant game of Whack-a-Mole."

"Terrible. I can't do this anymore."

"People are walking around shocked and distraught, but a lot of us knew this was going to happen someday. The shooter knew what he was doing. He used Facebook Live exactly the way we designed it."

"I have to get away from this. Go somewhere else. The people here are weird."

"What happens if you drop out of witness protection?"

"I don't know exactly. It's voluntary. They say they can't protect us if we leave."

"Protect you from whom?"

"Whoever. Possibly the KGB. I keep thinking Russians are following me. Maybe I'm just being paranoid."

"Irina."

She remembered the first time he had spoken her name. He understood all the trouble she had brought on herself and couldn't make stop. There was a long pause.

"You can come here," he said. "But there's a lot going on."

"The FUBAR. It's everywhere now."

"So it seems."

"So, I might as well come."

She set her alarm for 6:00 a.m., woke up and loaded the car, filling suitcases and big, black garbage bags with whatever clothes and toiletries she thought they might need for a few weeks. Anya was still half asleep in her pajamas when Irina wrapped a blanket around her shoulders and led her to the car.

"We have to leave."

"Where are we going?"

"Menlo Park."

"Seriously?"

Irina handed Anya her pillow and started the stealthy Prius. "You love it there, right?"

"For how long?"

"Just a little vacation."

"As long as we're back for my birthday."

"Of course."

They drove for 11 hours, almost 800 miles, across two deserts on four hours' sleep, Irina gulping Red Bulls to stay alert at the wheel. Eventually, she felt herself fading, and the road began to look flat and static, like a photograph. For the last few hours of the drive, she bit down hard on the inside of her cheek, using the pain to stay focused until they arrived in Menlo Park.

When they got to Dez's place, Irina

crashed hard. She couldn't control her thoughts and felt as if dark forces were massing inside her, threatening to carry her away. She suspected there was a name for it: panic attack, nervous breakdown. If ever there was a time to see a shrink, this was it. But that wasn't an option now. Better to let it scar over first. So she shut down everything: phone, computer, TV, even her workouts. She took naps, nibbled vegetables and browsed books from Dez's vast collection—*The Modern History of the Olympics, Forests of Northern California*—but didn't attempt to actually read any of them. She ignored all of Sarah's calls and left the house only for short hikes with Anya, during which she tried to avoid any talk of Phoenix.

After a couple of days, the dangerous jaggedness of her thoughts softened, and she became strangely sensitive to sounds. The musical hum of the refrigerator. The scraping of the madrone tree against the side of the house. The chatter of the birds. The bark of the neighbor's Australian shepherd three doors away. The sounds crowded out her tortured thoughts, slowed them down. But when she began to notice an ever-present background hiss, it worried her. Did everyone hear it? Why didn't anyone ever mention it?

One night in bed, she brought it up to Dez.

"Do you ever hear a hiss in the air?"

"A hiss? Like a snake?"

"It's more subtle than that. Listen, can you hear it?"

They listened.

"I don't hear it."

"I do. Always. Am I going crazy?"

"Maybe you're developing animal powers of hearing."

This was what she had missed, his little jokes, the not taking anything too seriously. Irina let her mind drift toward the possibility that she and Anya could stay there, restart their lives again in Menlo Park.

She wondered what his life had been like while they were apart. There were signs someone else had been living in the house—lotions, creams and ointments in the guest bathroom she and Anya were using—all cheap store brands. If there had been a woman in his life, she was of low self-esteem. Perhaps it was none of her business. But still, she was curious.

"Did you have a roommate while we were gone?"

"There were some guys sleeping in the spare bedrooms. We're working on something."

"For Facebook?"

He hesitated and looked away. "No."

"Like a startup?"

"Not exactly. I can't really talk about it."

He was not very good at concealing things.

"Did your friends leave because of us?"

"No, they'll be back. But they won't disturb you. When they come back, they're going to set up in the garage."

Irina started to ask what he meant by that, but let it slide. She had her own problems and couldn't afford to get sucked into thinking about Dez's side hustles or phantom associates. She had to sort out the open wound of her life back in Phoenix. She ignored calls from Trevor and Melanie at Cogniture, first expressing concern, then threatening termination. Let them fire her. She hated the place. No matter what, she wasn't going back. For several days, she ignored calls and texts from Sarah, who she suspected had a list of things Irina didn't want to hear or do. But finally she decided Sarah might be the only person out there willing to help her. It might be wise to call her back.

"First of all, bolting out of town under the cloak of darkness was not your best move."

"I was outed on Facebook. I panicked. What else was I supposed to do?"

"You give me a call and we come up with a plan."

"I have a plan. Anya and I want to stay here."

"In Menlo Park, with your Facebook boyfriend? Absolutely not. You should think of your daughter."

"Anya likes California."

"Think of her safety. Your safety."

"We feel comfortable here."

"That situation has too many unknowns. If you want our protection, you can't live wherever you want. You can't come back to Phoenix, but we will find you another place to live. We need a couple of weeks."

Irina hung up. The idea of moving again filled her with dread. Another strange city. Another unfamiliar house. And now she had to break the news to Anya that they couldn't go back to Phoenix, that her 16th birthday plans had to be aborted and she would never see her friends again. Staying in Menlo Park, in the California glow of Silicon Valley, might have been a plan she could have sold Anya on. Her daughter had been happy there. Maybe she could reconnect with Kirsten or some other friends from her English and filmmaking classes. But telling her she would have to start over again at a new school and make new friends was going to be a terrible conversation. She had to find a way to make it up to her. With teenage girls, everything was a negotiation. To keep her daughter's trust, she would have to give her something in return: freedom, praise, privileges. Obviously, the first step was spending time together. She tried to think of things they might do. There was shopping, of course, but Irina loathed shopping. Maybe she should start by taking her to lunch and feel her way forward from there.

She found Anya lying on the couch watching an old episode of *Game of Thrones*. The red-haired witch was seducing a teenage boy and planting leeches on his chest. Irina sat down at the end of the sofa and watched for a moment. Seeing the competition for her daughter's attention, she began to doubt her plan. But she had to start somewhere.

"I'm feeling restless. Want to grab some lunch?"

Anya kept her eyes on the screen. "Lunch? Since when do we do that?"

"Since today."

Anya stared at her. "Where?"

"You decide."

They watched the witch slowly remove the blood-gorged leeches and place them in a silver chalice. Anya widened her eyes and hit pause.

"How about Juice Girl?"

Under the circumstances, Irina figured an $11 smoothie was a reasonable investment. "Sure."

They arrived at the café before noon, so their orders came up quickly and they found a table in the sun.

"Are we going to have a talk or something?"

"After all the things that have happened, don't you think it would be a good idea to talk?"

Anya shrugged.

"So. I'm sorry we had to leave Phoenix like that."

"You mean jumping in the car and leaving without telling anyone. Yeah, Mom. That was pretty crazy."

"I'm sorry. I know you have friends there."

"Yeah."

"Are you in touch with them?" Irina had told her it was important not to reach out to them.

"I posted once on Instagram after we left. But I didn't tell them where we were."

Irina started to remind her about posting but caught herself. They had to be cautious, but if she was trying to bring Anya closer, she would have to let some things go.

"I know this is boring. Sitting around the house. Nothing to do."

"Yeah." Anya stared at her again as if to underscore who was to blame.

"I promise all the moving will be over soon."

"When are we going back to Phoenix?"

They were having a nice lunch. Irina didn't want to destroy the mood. Besides, it would be better to tell her once she knew the plan. "Maybe another week or so. When things settle down."

"I'm looking forward to that."

Irina looked across the table at her daughter and suddenly saw how much she had changed. She was beautiful and smart, and she knew it. On the surface, they were not alike at all. But suddenly she could see how determined and willful Anya was. That she recognized. Irina knew if she didn't find a way to soften the blow of their next vagabond adventure, she might lose her.

"I just had an idea. Since we might be staying here a little longer, what do you think about learning how to drive?"

"Seriously?"

"Don't you think that would be fun?"

Anya looked at her. "So I could drive places with friends?"

"Not right away but eventually."

"I guess that would be cool."

They finished their lunches and went out to the car. Irina drove to a deserted portion of the parking lot.

"Let's practice."

"Now?"

"Sure. Why not?"

They got out of the car and changed positions. Anya gripped the wheel nervously with both hands.

"Let's start with the feet. On the right is the gas or whatever since it's a Prius. On the left is the brake. You use your right foot for both. Try it."

Anya pumped the accelerator and the engine raced.

"You're pushing too hard."

Anya eased off the pedal. "Nothing's happening."

"It's still running. It's just quiet. Try the brake."

Anya pushed on the brake.

"Okay. Now slide the gear shift down to 'D.'"

Anya moved the shifter and the car started to drift forward.

"Now just give it a little gas."

Anya gently applied her foot to the accelerator, and the car advanced slowly across the lot.

"Try turning."

Anya's knuckles were white on the wheel. She kept turning until she completed a circle. She smiled.

"Now stop."

She hit the brake and they jerked forward in their seats.

"Too hard. Take your foot off the brake, give it more gas and brake more softly this time."

They drove around the parking lot in big loops, turning and braking for nearly an hour. Anya nearly grazed a dumpster pulling into a parking space. To restore her confidence, Irina had her practice the same maneuver again so that the lesson ended on a positive note.

"You look very natural behind the wheel."

Anya shrugged, but Irina could tell she was pleased with herself.

That night Dez called to say he would be home late, so they ordered salads delivered and watched another episode of *Game of Thrones* in which Tyrion the dwarf was having sex with the prostitute girlfriend he secretly loved. It was awkward sitting next to Anya watching people have sex on a big screen, so Irina went into the kitchen and plugged in the electric kettle. She remembered she and Anya had somehow never discussed the subject of sex. When the episode was over, she came back with cups of tangerine tea.

"It's been awhile since we had a talk about boys."

"*Boys.*" Anya put air quotes on the word. "You mean sex."

"Okay, sex."

"We don't have to talk about that, Mom. I know about condoms and I'm already on the pill, so you don't have to worry about me getting pregnant."

"Good." Irina offered a nod.

"Like you did."

That hurt. Irina was willing to admit her recent deficiencies as a mother, but she wasn't going to rewind her apology all the way back to her daughter's birth.

"Very funny. What do you want me to say? That I'm sorry I gave birth to you? That you were a mistake? I would never say that."

"But you might think it."

"No. Never. Where is this coming from?"

"I don't know. Everything just seems so hard."

Her voice broke. Irina could see she was trying not to cry.

"Hard for you or hard for me?"

"Hard for both of us. Sometimes I just want to have a boring life like my friends."

"I know. It's true. All the moving is hard."

"It was hard back home. Before we came here."

It was true. Things had always been hard for them. Never normal or predictable. Irina wasn't sure what that would even look like. Her mother had tried to give her that experience. Unsuccessfully. Protecting your mother by hitting your father in the head with a skillet wasn't normal. Irina never blamed her mother for that, but sometimes she wondered if the violence and anger was something she inherited and maybe explained why she created chaos wherever she went.

"Yeah, Piter was hard too. But Russians are tough."

"Right. Don't you get tired of being tough?"

Irina thought for a second.

"Yes. But I know I have to do it anyway."

Irina wasn't sure if that was the best answer. She reached across the sofa and squeezed her daughter's skinny calf.

"But that doesn't mean you have to be like me."

Early the next morning, two men pulled up in front of the house in a white van, unloaded a stack of flat brown shipping boxes and placed them on a dolly. Irina watched them roll the dolly around the side of the house and heard them enter the garage through a side door. Then they went back to the van, and each of them returned dragging a roller bag. From inside the house, she could hear their voices and the sound of power tools. She went through the kitchen and opened the inside door to the garage. The two men were assembling a metal rack against the far wall of the garage. They looked at her and froze. One was short with a beard, muscles bulging from his T-shirt. The other wore a sweatshirt and had hair pulled back in a ponytail. They looked like all the hipster men she'd ever seen at Facebook.

"Hi, guys."

She waited for them to introduce themselves. Instead of offering their names, they said, "We're friends of Dez."

"He's not here."

"Right," the short one said. "We're just setting something up. The noise won't last much longer."

"Don't worry about that."

The two men said nothing. Clearly, they did not want to converse. Irina scanned the garage. There were stacks of shipping boxes like the ones that had just arrived against one wall and two memory foam mattresses lying on the floor. She closed the door and called Dez.

"Was it a bad idea for us to come here?"

"No, why do you ask?"

"Because it looks like two guys are sleeping in the garage."

"There's a lot going on. I can't talk now. We'll talk tonight." Then he hung up.

Who were the men? What were they doing? Was it going to somehow interfere with her possible plan to stay in Menlo Park? To push these thoughts out of her mind, she threw on her sweats and went for a run. Then she and Anya went for a drive, this time through the neighborhood, which was illegal, of course, since Anya didn't have a permit, and risky, given their quasi-fugitive status. But their rogue excursions seemed to build Anya's confidence and intensify their bond.

When Dez got home a little after 11, Irina was waiting for him.

"So what's the story with the two guys?"

"We used to work together at Facebook."

"I thought everybody at Facebook was rich. How come they're living in your garage?"

"You don't want to know."

"Maybe I do."

"We're going to bring it all down."

"What?"

"Facebook."

After everything she had done and witnessed at the Agency, after the insanity at Cogniture, nothing really surprised her.

"So this is the FUBAR you were talking about? You and your friends are going to hack Facebook?"

"Somebody has to."

She looked at him. He seemed calm, committed.

"Remember the day Zuck went to Congress and had to explain how Facebook works. 'Senator, we run ads.' That's when we realized a bunch of old white men weren't going to stop him. We decided it was up to us."

"When is this happening?"

"Soon."

"So Anya and I can't stay here?"

"You can stay for now. Then leave with us when we execute."

"And go where?"

"Mexico. Canada. Ecuador."

"What about Anya?"

"She can come."

"So you do the hack and we all drive down to Mexico?"

"Just the three of us. Anton and Erik have their own plans."

Irina tried to imagine the three of them driving dusty roads, living the fugitive life in some ramshackle Mexican town. Corrupt cops in dark sunglasses showing up and throwing them into a hideous Mexican prison. "And what if we get caught?"

"We won't. I know how to do this."

Irina believed him. He was so smart, so methodical. No doubt he already had sources for fake IDs and passports, and once they got to their destination, he would know who to pay off, how to disappear. But she couldn't do that to Anya. She had put her through enough already. A fugitive road trip to Mexico would be the end of their relationship for sure.

"We can't. It's too crazy."

"No crazier than anything else."

"I can't do this to Anya."

"It will be an adventure for her."

"We've had enough adventures."

The next morning she called Sarah for the latest status on their relocation.

"We're finalizing the details. I need a few more days."

"I don't want to do anything with technology anymore. No Facebook, Instagram, Twitter. I want to go back to being a personal trainer."

"Okay. Let me work on that."

"And how about someplace not so hot this time?"

When she hung up, she knew she had to tell Anya. The longer she waited, the worse it would be. She changed into her sweats and went out to the kitchen. Anya's door was still closed, so Irina decided to go for a run to clear her head.

She headed out the door and started toward the hills above town. The houses became larger and statelier as she climbed. A Porsche, a Ferrari and a couple of Teslas zipped past, the drivers no doubt on their way to exalted positions in the world's technology capitol. Irina wondered who they were, but of course, she knew. They were the same people she'd met at Facebook, the ones who ran the world everybody else lived in now.

As she approached the top of the hill, an enormous Mercedes rolled past, driven by a tiny girl, obviously on her way to school. She couldn't have been older than Anya. Her mother sat in the passenger seat, and they were laughing. Irina felt a stab of envy. She didn't want their car or their house, but she wanted the ease that came with these possessions. She wanted to be in a car with her daughter, laughing as they drove.

When she reached the top of the hill, she turned around and ran back to Dez's house. If they only had a week left in Menlo Park, she wasn't going to ruin it by telling Anya the news now. Besides, it was better to wait until Sarah told her the plan. Maybe they could enjoy a couple of carefree days together before blowing up their lives again.

When she got back to the house, Anya was sitting at the kitchen counter drinking juice, her long legs dangling beneath her T-shirt.

"Do you want to do some more driving today?"

"Sure. I guess so."

They practiced backing the Prius down the narrow driveway. After several tentative attempts, dodging plants along the edge of the drive and gouging the tires on big rocks, Anya finally made it to the street.

They headed off through Menlo Park. The streets were wide, so Anya had plenty of room when she passed oncoming cars. Occasionally Irina had to remind her not to veer too close to cars parked along the curb. They drove all through the neighborhood, practicing smooth stops at traffic signals and when to give other cars the right of way.

While they were waiting at a light, a police car pulled up beside them and one of the cops glanced in their direction.

"Just keep your eyes to yourself," Irina said.

She met the cop's gaze and nodded. He nodded back.

They practiced signaling, smoothly executing turns, how to use the emergency brake and make sure the car was in park. By the time they got back to the house, Anya had stopped white-knuckling the steering wheel.

Inside, Irina went online to check the rules for getting a driver's license. In Russia a bribe would suffice, but this was America, where there were rules to be followed, requirements to be met, including 30 hours of driver education. This seemed ridiculous, excessive. But she found a company that let you take the course and receive an Official Certificate of Completion online for $49 and, with her 16th birthday looming, Anya was old enough to apply. She knew Sarah could call at any moment and give her the news that would scuttle her plan. But it seemed important to keep their momentum going and make as much progress as they could.

They sat at the counter together as Anya filled out the online registration, entering her name, email, age and address. Irina winced as she entered "Buckeroo Road." Hopefully, that wouldn't matter. But on the payment page there was a drop-down menu for selecting the state where you were applying for a license. Irina watched silently as her daughter selected ARIZONA. She realized there must be different tests for different states. If so, this was a pointless exercise, because they weren't going back to Arizona. Anya would have to do the course all over again. But Irina couldn't mention that now. That would make it look like she had been lying to Anya all along. When Anya finished, Irina entered her credit card information and clicked PURCHASE.

Anya sat at the counter and started working through the training modules.

"If I finish this, I can get my permit right after my birthday?"

Irina nodded. She felt like a lying, terrible mother, a worthless person. However badly Anya would have taken the news about Phoenix, now it was going to be worse. Now she would have to cover this lie with another one. She'd have to pretend to be surprised they weren't going back to Phoenix. She would have to blame the rules and the people in witness protection, blame Sarah.

The call from Sarah came early the next morning.

"Great news. You're going to Colorado Springs."

"Okay." The city's name meant nothing to Irina.

"You don't seem very excited. Colorado Springs is great. There's a huge fitness culture. This is a perfect fit for you."

Perfect? Now she would have to stop lying to Anya. She would have to leave Dez. "When do we go?"

"You need to be there in 72 hours."

"We have to go back to Phoenix and pack."

"You can't. You have to go straight to Colorado Springs. We'll gather all your things and take care of the rest."

"Anya needs to say goodbye to her friends."

"You know it doesn't work that way."

"What if we need more time?"

"Irina, you are out of time. This move is so far out of protocol. You're lucky we're keeping you in the program."

Lucky. It hardly seemed so. But she had no other options.

"We'll send you an encrypted email with the address and other particulars. I'll see you in 72 hours."

Irina sat on the edge of the bed. Dez had already left for the office or wherever he was going these days. She would have to tell him. But first, Anya. She went into the kitchen and found her back at the counter watching a video on how to calculate safe driving distance.

"It's like I'm cramming for finals."

Irina was furious with herself for being so stupid. By delaying and trying to soften her lie, she had dug herself in deeper. But she didn't want the closeness they were having to be over. If she could come up with one grand gesture, at least they could hold onto that.

"Why don't you take a break and we'll go get some lunch?"

This time they drove straight through the neighborhood with Anya behind the wheel. As they approached Sand Hill Road, Irina entered the name of a sushi place in the San Francisco Richmond District Dez had mentioned

"Want to try a little freeway driving?"

Anya's eyes widened. "Is that a good idea?"

"The rush hour is over. Traffic won't be bad. Let's go get some sushi."

As the friendly voice of Google Maps directed them toward I-280, Irina could see her daughter gripping the wheel hard. Her eyes darted nervously between the mirrors and the road as she prepared to merge.

"You're doing great. We're in no hurry."

Mile after mile they proceeded. Anya stayed in the right lane all the way, driving just below the 60-mph speed limit, until they reached the outskirts of the city. To exit she had to cross three lanes of traffic, so Irina had her start the maneuver in advance, easing to the left one lane at a time.

Anya let out a big sigh as she turned onto Junipero Serra Parkway. "Well done."

They drove through heavy traffic up 19th Avenue to the north edge of Golden Gate Park, then headed west on Fulton Street. To avoid the drama of parallel parking, they pulled into a spot with plenty of space around it a couple of blocks from the restaurant.

Irina requested a table instead of the sushi bar. The waiter brought them a bowl of edamame and mugs of tea that tasted like grain. Irina resolved to tell Anya the news, to stop putting it off. But first she wanted to revel in the moment.

"See, you are a good driver."

Anya beamed. "That was a little scary. But it was cool."

The sushi arrived on smooth wooden planks.

"We should do this more often," Irina said.

"You mean when we get back to Phoenix?"

Irina stared at her sushi. Fat, moist slices of fish hung over the mounds of rice. She knew she wouldn't be able to enjoy it.

"We have to talk about that."

"Yeah. My birthday is coming up. We have to make plans. Shouldn't we leave like, tomorrow?"

Irina let the question hang there.

"Yes. But we can't go back to Phoenix."

"What?"

Irina lowered her voice. "The people in witness protection said it's not safe for us anymore. We can't go back."

"Why not?"

"Celeste's mom caused big problems for us in Phoenix."

"Are you serious?"

"I know how much you were looking forward to your birthday. We'll do something really nice in the new place."

"What new place?"

"We're moving to Colorado Springs."

Anya put down her chopsticks and dipped her head. Tears fell on the sushi.

Irina started to say something about how much better Colorado Springs was than Phoenix. That they wouldn't have to put up with the furious heat and the air wouldn't dry their skin. She thought about mentioning that Russians had been tailing her there. But she knew nothing she said now could possibly matter. All the trust and closeness they'd built over the last few days was gone.

On the way back from the city, Irina drove. Anya stared out the window and sent a few texts. When they reached Dez's place, she went straight to her room. Since they only had the things they'd brought from Phoenix, there was little to pack or prepare. Irina plotted their route and decided they could spend a night in Las Vegas as a perk for Anya, even though it would mean a 12-hour drive the following day. Irina was dreading it, the driving and the tension of being trapped in the car with Anya. When she stuck her head into Anya's room to tell her of the 7 a.m. departure time, her daughter was texting and nodded without looking up.

Irina knew she would have a hard time sleeping, so she rummaged in the medicine cabinets and found one of Erik's old Ambien prescriptions with one capsule inside. She fell asleep hard just after 10 o'clock and didn't wake up until her alarm went off at 6 a.m.. She put on comfortable clothes for the drive and made coffee. At 6:45, she tapped on Anya's door and opened it to an empty bed. She checked the bathroom at the end of the hall, and Anya wasn't there either.

She found Dez in the garage conferring with Erik and Anton.

"Have you seen Anya?"

When she saw the baffled looks they gave her, she felt a surge of panic and circled through the house, checking every room and calling out her name. No Anya. She went back and searched her daughter's room. Her roller bag was gone, along with her purse and her computer. Irina tried calling and sent several texts as she went back through the house again, even checking closets, looking for something, anything, a goodbye note or a clue. It wasn't until she looked out the large living-room window that she saw the Prius was gone. She ran out to the street and noticed the tire tracks across two azalea bushes along the edge of the driveway.

Now she was furious. She called and texted again, leaving the same message, "ANYA WHAT THE FUCK!!!! CALL ME NOW!!!!!"

But there was no reply.

She paced the house, frantic. Dez came in from the garage.

"What's going on?"

"She took the car."

"I didn't know she had a license."

"She doesn't. But we've been practicing. I can't believe she did this."

Dez waited with her for another hour, then left for Facebook, where he was still showing up to avoid suspicion. For the next couple of hours, Irina paced the house on edge, waiting for some word. What could she do? If she called the police and they stopped Anya for driving without a license, that might ruin her driving record, adding to the list of ways Irina had made her life miserable. But she could threaten to call them.

"Anya this is terrible. I'm worried about you. If you don't call me in the next five minutes I have no choice but to call the police."

She waited five minutes, then 10, then 15, then 30 and still couldn't bring herself to make the call because, if anything, she was more to blame for this than Anya.

Anton burst in from the garage.

"You should take a look at this. I think she just posted something on TikTok."

He held out his phone and there was Anya. Behind her, a wide gate opened and she walked up a driveway toward an enormous Mission-style mansion. She started speaking to the camera.

"So here I am. Just arrived at the Powerpuff Girls house. Looking forward to doing new dances and making new friends. Let the adventure begin."

The video lasted only 20 seconds. It had been posted only a few minutes before. Irina watched it three times in disbelief. She had heard of TikTok, but she didn't really have a sense of how popular it was. She certainly didn't suspect that when she'd told Anya not to post on Instagram, she was now posting on TikTok instead.

It was all so shocking and strange. At least her daughter was safe—that was a relief. But she was also a liar who had stolen the car and betrayed Irina's trust. Irina should have been furious about the lying and the sheer selfishness of it, but she knew it wasn't just some case of a teenager telling lies and taking off with the family car. It was more complicated than that. Really, who had betrayed who?

But Anya was not yet 16. Living without her mother in a house full of other young girls was unacceptable. Of course, Anya wouldn't see it that way. She could possibly make the case that Irina was a dangerous, unstable mother, dragging her around the world, fleeing from her own mistakes. Irina imagined the two of them each pleading their case before one of those TV judges, Anya describing the dumps they'd lived in back in Piter, the flight to America, being pulled out of bed in the middle of the night in Phoenix. It wasn't entirely clear whose side the audience would be on, but Irina guessed the judge would side with her. A 16-year-old girl belonged with her mother, case closed. But playing the legal card, Irina knew, was a last resort. Much better to persuade Anya to come of her own accord. Since Anya wasn't picking up any of her calls, she sent another text.

"I saw your TikTok. I'm glad you are safe. We have to talk."

A few minutes later her phone buzzed, a call from Anya.

"I'm sorry for taking the car."

"Anya, that was crazy. So dangerous driving down there."

"It wasn't that bad. It just took forever. I stayed in the right lane all the way. Just like you showed me."

Irina wanted to scream.

"I know you're tired of all the moving. But stealing the car and driving to LA doesn't change our situation. We have to stick with the plan."

"I have my own plan, Mom."

Irina could feel her anger and frustration rising. She couldn't let it get the best of her. "I see. And what's your plan?"

"One of the other girls invited me to stay here. We're going to make videos together."

To Irina that didn't sound like a real plan. More like a girlish wish that would collapse if she kept her cool and applied her maternal wisdom, such as it was.

"I don't know about that, Anya. I will come down and we can talk about it."

"When?"

"I can be there in a few hours."

"I'm too exhausted from all the driving."

"Okay then, tomorrow morning."

There was a long pause. Finally Anya said, "Not too early."

Irina felt hopeful when she hung up. Disaster had been averted. She would fly to LA in the morning, make her case for starting their new life and not succumb to Anya's slippery logic. Then they would drive to Colorado Springs, a day late perhaps, but basically as planned.

She still had to say goodbye to Dez. She had done it once before, but this time was harder. He had asked her to join him. She wanted to be with him. But she couldn't be part of his fugitive-hacker scheme. She had enough problems of her own.

When he came home late that night, she told him she was leaving. But she couldn't bring herself to tell him how she felt or even find the words to say a real goodbye. Instead she left it loose and said she'd call him from LA.

She'd never known sex could be sad. But they ended the evening with too much wine and a heavy, heartbreaking fuck. If she couldn't name what she was feeling, her body knew.

The Uber pulled up in front of a massive gate she recognized from Anya's TikTok video. This was the right house, unbelievable as it seemed. Irina lifted her bag from the trunk and pushed the buzzer on the keypad embedded in the stone post outside the gate. She waited a couple of minutes. Nothing happened. She could see the Prius inside, wedged between a black Range Rover and a silver Mercedes convertible.

She texted Anya: "I'm outside."

She heard a buzzing sound and the gate parted from the center. Her roller bag clacked across the flagstone driveway as she started toward the house, even bigger than it appeared from the street. It seemed impossible a bunch of teenagers could be living there, but Dez had explained that houses like this were popping up all over Beverly Hills and Bel Air, managed by Hollywood agencies looking to cash in on kids who were celebrities in their own world, a world Anya seemed to be part of and Irina didn't know existed until now.

As Irina climbed the wide stone steps, Anya appeared in the doorway, looking half asleep in her low-cut tank top and short pajamas. Irina stepped into the marble entryway and put her arms around her, but Anya's arms felt limp on her back.

"Mom, why did you bring luggage? You can't stay here."

"We're going straight from here to Colorado Springs."

Anya looked around. "We should go outside if you want to talk."

They walked down the main hall, through the center of the house. They passed what looked like an office with two smartly dressed women behind glass desks, what looked like a small dance studio with full-length mirrors along one wall and several sparsely decorated bedrooms, each with clothes scattered around and a mattress on the floor. She followed Anya to the end of the hall, through the sprawling kitchen and out a row of sliding glass doors. They sat down in a couple of wrought-iron chairs next to a matching table beside the pool. There was a purple inflatable raft floating on the placid surface.

Irina's mind was spinning, trying to understand how her daughter could be part of this. "A pool?"

"All the houses have pools. One of the girls said she'd loan me a swimsuit."

Irina felt like she'd entered a different world with its own rules. She couldn't allow herself to get distracted by its strangeness. She had to stay focused.

"I'm glad you're safe."

"You saw the gate. This place is totally safe."

Starting with a show of concern didn't seem to be working. She was going to have to try a more direct approach.

"You should never have taken the car without permission. You could have had an accident or been arrested. I was worried something had happened to you."

Anya glanced at her, then looked away. "I'm sorry if you were worried."

"I know this might look appealing to you. But you can't stay here. We have to go to Colorado Springs."

Anya looked out toward the pool and shook her head. "I'm not going with you."

"You're too young. You can't stay here on your own."

"One of the other girls just turned 16. We have chaperones."

Irina leaned toward her so that their faces were close and Anya would be sure to get her message. "Don't be ridiculous. How are you going to pay for this?"

"We get sponsors and earn money. One of the other girls invited me to make videos with her. We're going to work together."

"So you just hang out at the pool and make videos all day? What about school?"

"We take classes online."

Irina wanted to avoid falling back on the heavy hand of parental authority. When she was growing up, that had never worked on her. But she felt like she was running out of cards to play.

"Anya, I will go crazy worrying about you."

"You can call me whenever you want."

"It's not safe for you to be here. We need to stay together. We need protection."

"From who?"

"From the people I used to work for in Russia."

"That's your problem, Mom. I can't keep moving all my life to get away from that."

The sliding doors opened and two girls in bikinis bounded out with towels over their shoulders. They glanced at Anya and Irina and ran back into the house.

Irina reached for Anya's hand.

"Do you really expect me to go to Colorado Springs without you?"

"If that's what you have to do. I don't want to be part of it anymore."

"We don't have a choice."

"I do."

"You can't just do whatever you want, Anya. You're still a minor. You can't stay here without my permission."

Anya turned and seemed, for the first time all morning, to really look at her. "Mom, I keep waiting for all the craziness to stop but it never does. I'm done."

"I'm not leaving without you."

"What are you going to do? Call the police?"

"I could."

"And then what? Keep me prisoner in Colorado Springs? Do you think that's going to work?"

Irina stared at her. This was madness. She wanted to reach across the table and wipe the smug expression off her lovely girl's face. But she could imagine the cost of creating such a scene. Her eyes drifted toward the pool. Once again, she found herself in an impossible situation. What could she do? Throw her arms around Anya and drag her to the car? Walk away? In the long silence that followed, Irina realized how much she had underestimated her daughter. Anya had played out the arguments and built the stronger hand. There was something ingenious, almost Gandhi-like about it. Irina could only win by destroying their relationship.

They stood up, went inside and walked back through the kitchen and down the hall to the marble entryway. Irina felt light-headed, wondered if all this was really happening. Was she actually leaving her daughter behind?

As they stepped out onto the stone porch, they saw the Prius was still blocked by the black Range Rover.

"That's Mia's car. I'll go get her."

Anya went back into the house and returned with another girl, not much older, holding a key. She scurried barefooted down the steps and backed the Range Rover out of the way.

As her daughter handed her the key to the Prius, Irina threw her arms around her in a fierce hug. She was strong enough to carry her away but that would never work.

"Come with me."

Anya shook her head. Tears came up but she wiped them away.

Irina carried her roller bag down the steps and put it inside the car. As she backed the car out onto the street, the gate closed smoothly behind her. She looked up at the porch, but Anya had already disappeared inside.

Irina drove in a fog, following the voice of Google Maps for the route she'd entered in advance. She drove down through the last of the super mansions and descended into the sprawl of LA. Before she hit I-405, she pulled over to the shoulder of the freeway and called Dez.

"So Anya isn't coming with me."

"Seriously? What are you going to do?"

"I don't know."

"You can come back here."

"And do what?"

"Up to you. Be part of the plan."

Maybe it wasn't the worst idea. Facebook had become a monster. Taking it down was a noble cause.

"My hacking skills aren't the best."

"We've got that covered."

Irina closed her eyes and listened to the traffic racing past. The car was already pointed north. If she kept driving in the same direction, she'd end up in Menlo Park.

"I can't do it. Too much FUBAR."

"I'm sorry to hear that."

She waited for the joke, but this time he didn't have one.

She merged back onto the freeway and headed north, then east on I-210, past signs for Disney, Warner Bros. and Universal Studios, places she and Anya had planned to visit when they first came to America but had never reached. Perhaps now Anya would explore them with her new friends instead. In all the back-and-forth, she had forgotten to mention Anya's 16th birthday. She suspected the Powerpuff Girls could stage quite a bash. She imagined a life of dancing, parties, makeovers, bikini lounging at the pool and sex with clueless teenage boys. Who knew what kind of Anya would emerge on the other side? Perhaps one she wouldn't recognize. The thought made her incredibly sad. But as she drove along the northern edge of the great American glamour factory, she thought about what a mess she'd made of her own life. *Who am I to judge?*

When she hit I-15, she drove north into the Mojave Desert, a gray emptiness for miles in all directions. She passed an abandoned, graffiti-covered rest stop with a giant "EAT" sign sticking up from the curled shingles on the roof. She realized she hadn't had breakfast and was thirsty from the desert heat pressing through the windshield. A little further she passed an exit for Zzyxz Road, which looked like gibberish, a meaningless word from some made-up language, which she found disturbing. She passed road signs for Alien Fresh Jerky and recalled the comments from Facebook groups obsessed with UFOs landing in the desert. She finally stopped on the other side of the Nevada state line in a town called Jean, picked up two bottles of water and a couple of Clif Bars and filled the tank. As she started back toward the interstate, in the distance she noticed strange columns of rocks stacked in a vivid, psychedelic rainbow of red, blue, pink, orange, green and purple rising from the sand. Irina thought it might be some sort of mirage. Or perhaps she was losing her mind. If so, she needed to know. She veered off onto a frontage road and followed it into the parking lot for Seven Magic Mountains, apparently some kind of art installation. In the distance she could see people posing and taking selfies against the brightly colored rocks. Irina sipped her water as she watched from the car. Now they were painting rocks to make them Instagram worthy.

Without Anya, there was no reason to stop in Las Vegas, so she pressed on, gladly skirting all but a slender wedge of Arizona, driving north instead into Utah canyon country. North of St. George, she pulled into a scenic overlook, got out of the car and stretched. She was exhausted from the drama and the driving and sat down on a bench, sipped her water and nibbled on a Clif Bar. Towers of red rock filled the horizon to the west, carved into majestic, mystical shapes, so massive and intricate and surrounded by so much space, it was hard to believe they hadn't been shaped by some sentient being. They almost begged to be worshipped. The scene reminded her of American cowboy movies she'd seen growing up, like *The Magnificent Seven* and *Butch Cassidy and the Sundance Kid.* That was a country everybody, even the Russians back home, wanted to live in. If it ever existed, it was long gone now.

She stopped for the night a little further on at a Comfort Inn in Cedar City, where she had a dry, tasteless burger and fell asleep in her clothes. Knowing she had a long day of driving ahead of her, she got up early and was on the road with her morning coffee just after 6. She wanted to think about something besides the unknown she was heading into and the wreckage she was leaving behind. But she was already tired of her playlists, so she tuned in AM radio whenever she got near a town. Across Utah it was mostly Mormon stuff, local services, prayer groups and readings broken up by long stretches of nothing but static. When she crossed the state line into Colorado, Rush Limbaugh took over, followed by local stations with people calling in to share their thoughts on the Global Warming Hoax.

Outside Grand Junction she managed to get a signal from the local public radio station with news about the Special Counsel investigation. She fiddled with the dial to filter out the static. The attorney general was speaking. He rambled on, thanking people, saying things she couldn't follow until he finally said, "No collusion."

It took her a moment to process what exactly that meant, but he kept repeating the same words—"no collusion, no collusion"—and there was no mention of anyone new being charged with a crime. She could guess what would happen next. The criminals they had already arrested for talking to the Russians would be pardoned and everybody would get off. In the end, her testimony had amounted to nothing.

What did she feel? For the first few seconds, rage. Then anguish, hopelessness, fear and despair swirled through her all at once. The tears started flowing and she just let them come. She thought of everything she had given up, everything she had risked. She thought about why she had come to America, how things might have turned out differently, but she couldn't really see it clearly or make sense of it. From the moment she arrived, it felt as though she was being swept along by deeper currents over which she had no control. Maybe Putin, Trump, Facebook, YouTube, Twitter, Cambridge Analytica and the rest weren't exactly working together, but somehow they were on the same side, all trying to keep their money-making machines running and the power in place.

She hadn't felt this low since her fall into the pit that night in Budapest. Nothing was the same after that. Now the idea of starting a new life again seemed like an American fantasy. Russians didn't believe in such things. She could move to a new city, find a new job, a new house—but a new life was another story. She would never escape the old one.

Colorado Springs

Even midway through her second winter, she couldn't get used to driving in the snow. She always imagined a dark, lethal sheet of ice lurking beneath the whiteness, ready to wrest control of the Prius and send it spinning sideways into the path of one of the massive pickup trucks or SUVs everyone else in Colorado drove, always accelerating and tailgating to demonstrate their snow-driving prowess. Car accidents were one of the things she feared most because there were so many ways to end up broken, inching through life in a wheelchair or on forearm crutches. She'd rather be dead.

The snow had stopped before she left home, but now the sky was low, so there was likely more on the way. The foothills to the west looked white and scrubbed, and peaks further in the distance were crowned with a fresh dusting of white. Scenic as they were, the mountains blocked the afternoon sun, so the winter darkness came early, just like in Piter. With the way the days and months now blurred into each other, sometimes for a moment, she imagined she was back there.

Her life in Colorado Springs had started promisingly enough. She got a job at a local fitness club, landed a few private clients. By her first Christmas, she could imagine how her new life might work out. But then the virus jumped from bats to humans, people started dying and she got pulled into that nightmare with the rest of the world. Hospitals turned into war zones, with patients on gurneys filling the hallways and morgues so overflowing they stored the bodies in refrigerated trucks. Within a few months, the virus traveled around the world and left 10 million people infected, half a million dead. People became dangerous to each other. Gatherings were banned, so of course she lost her job, and her social circle shrank to zero. The world became unrecognizable, and she wondered if it was ending, if the virus was how nature was finally taking its revenge.

She found it impossible to escape the news. Wildfires erupted across California and turned the skies deep orange. Riots broke out in the streets to protest police killings of unarmed Black men—her former colleagues at the Agency were no doubt cackling with glee. With nowhere to go and nothing to do, people were glued to their screens, consuming fake news and increasingly preposterous conspiracy theories 12 hours a day. Strange factions formed and multiplied into millions. QAnon members decoded secret messages. Right-wing groups planned attacks on the government. White supremacists, right-wing militia, anti-Semites, Zionists, Hindus who hated Muslims, Muslims who hated infidels, old Khmer Rouge generals staging a comeback, radical vegans, angry animal protectionists—all cultivated their holy wars. At the center of it all, of course, was Facebook. With everybody's eyes locked on screens, doom scrolling through daily reports of the mounting chaos, Facebook earnings reached an all-time high. The pandemic that was killing people by the thousands was good for guys like Zuck and their shareholders. They were practically printing cash. Irina heard some of them were cashing in their chips and retreating to walled compounds in New Zealand, leaving it for others to clean up the damage from their brilliant inventions.

Dez's attempt to bring it all down had failed. The last Irina heard from him was more than a year before, when he sent a cryptic, one-word text: "Tomorrow." The next day reports of his hack appeared in the news, noting its clever three-pronged approach. The hackers exploited a vulnerability in Facebook's 20,000 Apache HTTP servers, disabled the servers' management software to conceal their efforts, and burrowed into the Siemens HVAC systems, turning Facebook's eco-friendly, water-cooled data centers into molten metal. Although they succeeded in crippling the operation in Prineville, Oregon, Facebook's load-balancing architecture simply rerouted the traffic to their other five massive data centers around the world. Aside from a brief delay in page loads, the company emerged from the assault unscathed. She imagined Dez dejected and drifting somewhere off the grid in the Canadian wilderness, but she heard nothing.

Now after 10 months, the virus was still raging, and just after the New Year, she was desperate for spring. If things didn't get better by then, she was in serious trouble. Her last check from Witness Security had come the previous summer, and she had burned through what little savings she had. Aside from her government stimulus checks, the only money coming in was from a few remaining private clients and that wasn't nearly enough. Her situation was *unsustainable*, a word she heard increasingly often. Almost every day something new—the shrinking water table, ozone layer, city budget, global fish stocks—was added to the list of unsustainables, signaling a threat to the town, state, region or species. But in her case, it definitely applied. Her latest plan was to get by on bulk carrots, spinach, rice and steel-cut oats. By her calculations, a few hundred dollars would buy a six-month food supply.

Irina imagined what it would have been like if she had persuaded Anya to come live with her. She had to admit, as much as it hurt to think of her living in the daily depravity of the Powerpuff Girls house, Anya was better off there. This was no way to live. Thanks to her daily

TikTok posts, it was easy to keep up with what was happening in her daughter's life.

Seeing the clever, confident face Anya presented to the world, Irina considered the possibility that perhaps she wasn't such a horrible mother.

Meanwhile, Irina spent most of her days alone, so she was grateful for her occasional training sessions, even if it meant driving across town in the snow. That morning her session was with Adam, a 50ish fitness junkie who at their first workout was too friendly and refused to wear a mask. She had tried to schedule an outdoor cardio session for that day's workouts, but the snow had prevented that. Adam decided he wanted to do weights and machines, so she had to rent another trainer's gym for $10 an hour, which meant she was clearing $30 for driving across town and watching Adam lift dumbbells.

He showed up wearing a T-shirt with a fist holding a bicycle pump and the words "Bike Lives Matter" on the front. He worked through three sets of curls and shoulder presses with Irina counting off the reps, correcting his form and offering her standard encouragements: "Keep your back straight"; "No cheating"; "Finish every rep."

While he rested between sets, Irina let her eyes drift up to the big TV mounted on the wall just above his head. Some event was underway in Washington. She thought Trump was gone already, but there he was, addressing the usual motley crowd--a sea of red MAGA hats, American flags and yellow banners with a snake curled around the words, "Don't Tread On Me."

"Triceps next?" Adam asked.

"Right, sorry." Irina nodded. Her eyes went back to the screen.

"Is it twelve reps or fifteen?"

Irina looked down at the workout card in her hand. "Twelve."

Adam started his reps and Irina counted them off, "One… two…three…four. Square your wrists." Her eyes drifted back to the screen. A crowd was gathering around the Capitol Building. With the sound muted, she couldn't tell what was happening. She glanced up at the screen but kept counting until he finished his 12th tricep kickback.

"Okay, good. Thirty-second rest."

Adam lowered the weights to the floor. Irina turned up the volume as Trump ended his speech.

"Fight like hell or you won't have a country anymore," he told the crowd.

After the election, Irina had tried to block out stories about the lawsuits and Democrats stealing the election. She didn't understand the fine points of how American politics worked, and back home Russians were always talking about fraud, so it was all noise to her. But as she watched the crowd growing and thickening around the Capitol, she realized the Pussy Grabber in Chief had no intention of going away quietly. Instead he was saving his worst for last. The camera cut to the crowd pushing through a flimsy barricade, past a row of unarmed police.

Adam lifted the dumbbells and stared at her. "I thought we were doing a workout."

Irina hit the mute button. "Sorry. It looks like there's a riot happening."

"More fake news. Can we just focus here?"

"Okay, sorry."

Adam sat down on the bench and started his arm extensions, but Irina's eyes kept returning to the screen. Protestors were marching toward the Capitol. She recognized the symbols on their jackets from her days back at the Agency. The dripping skull of the Punisher, vests with the crossed hatchets of Vanguard America stitched above the breast. These had been her people. Now they were marching up Pennsylvania Avenue in an angry mass.

She stopped counting, and Adam let the weights clang to the floor. "You can watch TV on your own time. I'm not paying for this."

Irina shook her head and kept watching. "I understand. I apologize."

"I'm going to be posting about this. Just so you know."

She thought she heard him shout "Bitch!" on his way out, but it hardly registered. Onscreen the crowd kept advancing. A man in a gas mask waved a banner with the face of the alt-right mascot, Pepe the Frog. She had once gotten likes from Pepe's followers. By now the crowd had grown to an angry mob. Outnumbered police swung their clubs, trying to fend off the crowd converging on them with flagpoles, sticks, crutches, whatever was at hand. She felt a flash of panic, wondering if chaos might be sweeping the country. She looked outside and saw it was snowing again. As the crowd surged up the Capitol steps, she decided she needed to get home.

Although her mind was racing, she drove slowly, tires making fresh tracks on the snow. She called Anya and left a message. "There are lots of weird things going on right now. Crazy people out there. You should stay inside." She wanted to call Dez, but she had no idea how to reach him. She had no one else to call.

Back in her apartment, she dragged a chair from the kitchen into the living room and positioned it in front of the TV. Still wearing her puffy down jacket, she watched the crowd thicken around the building. People climbed up scaffolding that had been erected around the Capitol and broke windows on the upper floors. A young woman in a pink hat passed a "STOP THE STEAL" sign to an older man above her and climbed up behind him, then he handed the sign back to her.

They made an odd couple. In a simpler world, the two of them would have been back home living their separate lives, annoying friends and relatives with their extremist ideas—but probably thanks to Facebook, they had found each other. When Irina saw how the conspiracies accelerated in the months leading up to the election, she knew her old friends at the Agency had to be involved. They were master amplifiers, constantly trolling the dark corners of the web, looking for new toxins to germinate and spread.

By now the rioters had the building surrounded and were probing for the weakest lines of defense. They started posting their own videos to social media, and the cable networks began to mix them with their own feed, so the chaos of the coverage matched the chaos of the crowd. Gunshots were fired, and there was a huge thrust from the crowd as they streamed into the building, hysterical and elated. Irina leaned toward the screen and watched in horror. She recognized the orange beanies of the Proud Boys in full body armor, prepared for battle. Others were dressed like cowboys, carried pitchforks or wore three-cornered hats. Some cloaked themselves in animal skins. One wore the sculpted head of a bald eagle over an American flag suit and tie.

As camera crews were jostled and assaulted, coverage became choppy. The crowd fed off its own frenzied energy. People shouted, "Hang 'em! Hang Mike Pence!" Shocking images filled the screen. A man casually chatted on his cell phone with his boots on a congress-woman's desk. A bearded man in camo paraded through the halls waving a Confederate flag. A policeman was dragged down a flight of steps and set upon by the crowd as a woman was trampled underfoot. The camera jerked back and forth, then suddenly focused on a face Irina recognized. At first, she told herself it couldn't be him, but as the camera lingered, she was sure. It was Lonnie Jensen, or Lone Lonnie, as he called himself, wearing a helmet with a chin strap and a sweatshirt with the words "Trust The Plan" inside a giant "Q." He had a cluster of zip ties hooked to his belt. They had exchanged likes and links many times on the Stop All Invaders Facebook Page. His comments ranged from mildly eccentric to mad-dog crazy, and as best Irina could remember, she had offered encouraging replies. Now he was shouting instructions to the crowd about taking hostages.

Irina felt a pain in her chest. In an instant, the last four years of her life collapsed, and she felt the madness pull her in, pure and raw, as if she were inside the crowd. From her travels among the followers, she knew the millions of views and engagements were only part of the story. The real truth was in the collective madness that grew and festered as people exhorted one another online. Alone in a frozen, starving city, they wouldn't last a week. But in their tribes, they found each other, found the courage of the mob. Back at the Agency, they knew it was only a matter of time before the rage they stirred up spilled out into the world. The forces they had set in motion before the election were just a spark. This was the fire, one that couldn't be stopped. A wave of guilt and shame rose up and swept over her as she stared at the screen.

She went to the kitchen and pulled the quart of cheap Finlandia she kept for emergencies from the freezer. She sipped from the bottle and stared at the screen, watching scenes of the mob in an endless loop. She watched for hours, unable to look away. After midnight, she stood up unsteadily and put the vodka back in the freezer. She took three Advils, dimmed the lights and dragged the chair to the front window. The snow had stopped. She closed her eyes and waited for the Advil to take effect. After a few minutes, she decided a walk in the cold air might help. She put on gloves, checked her pocket for keys and headed outside.

The street was deserted in both directions and covered with several inches of fresh snow. She walked a couple of blocks, cold air cutting her lungs like a knife. Her left temple began to throb. With each step, the pain shot across her skull. She wondered if she could give herself an aneurysm, trigger a sudden, irreversible explosion in the brain that would kill her on the spot. She started to jog and decided if she felt something burst, she would lie quietly on the ground without calling for help, so there would be no hope of reviving her.

She ran along the center line for almost a mile until the throbbing became unbearable. Then she lowered her head, put her hands on her knees and after a couple of heaves, threw up a patch of vodka-tasting vomit onto the snow. She took a few deep breaths, made her way to the sidewalk and leaned against a car. She rubbed snow on her face, put a handful in her mouth to clear the vile taste and slowly started back toward her apartment.

Her thoughts circled back to the scenes of mob. She dreaded going back inside alone, so she walked slowly, feeling the cold and silence deepening around her. She wondered how she could ever forgive herself, knowing the chaos she had helped unleash upon the world. Although she had tried to atone for her actions, she doubted she would ever feel absolved for what she'd done. She'd given everything she had to Facebook and to Mueller and his team, even given up her daughter. And they'd done nothing. Maybe that was the problem: She'd chosen the wrong confessors. They were all too compromised, too vested in their own interests to care about the cost of what she'd given them. That was her mistake.

Since there were no cars, she veered into the street and walked where the snow wasn't as deep. The darkness was broken by huge circles of light from the street lamps. She thought for a moment. Maybe it wasn't too late. So many crazy things had happened in just the past few months—the impeachment, the pandemic, Black Lives Matter—the trolls had been forgotten. But now there was a straight line running from the 2016 election to the riot. Maybe it was time to really come clean, not to some bureaucrat, but to the world. Remind them: Russians started this. The Agency's goal was to spread conflict in American society. Mission accomplished. She could present her story as a kind of apology to the rioters and crazies who stormed the Capitol. Apologize for manipulating them, for planting and nourishing the beliefs they thought they were rioting for. Apologize for planting seeds about a Deep State conspiracy run out of a pizza parlor. Apologize for working for the real masters that pulled their puppet strings—the Putin-Trump-Bannon-Mercer-Murdoch-Zuckerberg cabal. That might get someone's attention. With so many voices out there, would anyone actually believe her? She had been there, could explain precisely how and what they had done, so perhaps they would. She was the Russian troll who had helped get Trump elected, spilled her guts to the Special Counsel and been forced into hiding. That was a good story. And, for what it was worth, the facts were on her side. If she only changed a few minds, that was better than nothing.

Back inside she made a pot of coffee and sat down at the counter. She had to think of the best way to create a buzz for her story, make certain it was news. After some searching, she ended up on the personal page of a *New York Times* reporter, Alexandra Donovan, who had tracked the story of the trolls and the Facebook saga from the beginning. Irina was sure she would be interested. She sat down at the keyboard and started typing.

Dear Ms. Donovan,

My name is...

She stopped. The safest approach was to remain anonymous. But that would cast her as a shadowy figure whose account would be easy to dismiss. She asked herself again why she was doing this. Did she actually think she could save America or make a difference in history? Of course not. She was doing this for herself. The only way to come clean was to empty herself and tell her story, not some mysterious troll's.

She started typing again.

My name is Irina Zakharova, a former employee at the Internet Research Agency in St. Petersburg. I came to the United States after the 2016 election. I consulted with Facebook, provided testimony to the Special Counsel and entered the U.S. Witness Security Program. But my story has never fully been told. Details were omitted that now seem important after today.

I would like to share my story with you now.

Sincerely,

Irina Zakharova

She stared at the words onscreen, then hit "send." Within a few minutes, the reporter replied. It was impossible to know what would happen, once her story ran. A long list of crazies could come for her, possibly Russians, and she would be easy to find. But she had so little to lose. The only way to free herself was to step out of the shadows.

So let them come.

Bel Air

At first, it was thrilling to live in an actual mansion with girls her age. It felt unreal, so much like a dream she was sure one morning she would open her eyes and it would all be gone. The idea that so many people out there were waiting for her next post was pure fantasy, the kind of thing that only happened in movies.

Everybody said the key to being TikTok famous was to find your niche, but for her it was almost too easy. From Day One she was the hot/funny/nerdy Russian girl. Her dance and lip-synch videos had a self-deprecating quality that made her sexy to the boys and nonthreatening to the girls. It was unbelievable to watch her number of followers climb to 1, 2, 3 million and see the endorsements roll in from Lululemon, Free People, Jo Malone and Super Salads Plus. Her check from the talent agency got bigger every month, and she hardly had to spend any of it, because companies kept sending her products to try and designers kept giving her free clothes. She had lost track of how much money she had saved, but she knew it was a lot.

Initially the girls in the house felt like a circle of sisterhood, hanging out in their bikinis beside the pool. They all appeared in each other's videos, which was a quick way to boost everyone's followers. Although no boys lived in the house, they were always around. She'd had sex with a few of them, but it hadn't lived up to her expectations. Even the boys who knew what they were doing seemed mostly in it for themselves. She wondered if it might have been more enjoyable if she liked them more, but it was hard to know what to like, when they all said the same things, wore the same clothes, had the same hair.

Of course, TikTok fame didn't come as easily as it looked. It was hard to constantly come up with new material, and everyone had to post at least two videos a day. Although the chaperones from the talent agency took care of the food and made sure the house wasn't too filthy, with no adults around, the girls often resorted to their worst behavior.

After a few months the drama started. Everyone said drama drives engagement, so the more she tried to stay out of it, the harder they worked to pull her in. When she kept her distance, that became the story, with other girls calling her out as the cold Russian bitch. It was crazy how it exploded, with their followers taking sides—attacking her, attacking the other girls, attacking each other. She finally stopped reading the comments. It was like they had all lost their minds. Listening to the other girls, she cringed at the thought of never being any smarter than she was now. She started buckling down with her online classes, thought about maybe leaving the house in a year and applying to colleges.

Even when things were closing in on her, she never regretted running away from the frantic life with her mother. She'd had enough of their wild adventures, and the friction of spending so much time together had worn them both so thin that finally Anya couldn't stand being around her, the way she lived on high alert, obsessed with her morning workouts, never caring how she looked with her air-dried hair and not a speck of makeup. But when the other girls complained about *their* mothers—how vain they were, what liars and terrible cooks they were, how they spent fortunes on boob jobs and Jimmy Choo shoes—her list of grievances seemed shallow. It was more like a list of things she missed.

When her mother's name popped up in her news feed, she was shocked. But there she was, using her real name, Irina Zakharova, describing her life as a Russian troll, her travels to Facebook and Washington, telling secrets to the government and going into witness protection. Anya was even more amazed a few nights later, when she watched her mother share her story with Rachel Maddow and tangle with some nasty blonde on Fox who tried, unsuccessfully, to make her look bad. That was fun to watch.

Maybe when the time is right, they'll be together again, but at the moment, she has tuition to save for and a job to do. She's moving in a new direction with her content, leaning into her Russian heritage. She dissects clips of movies with Russian stereotypes, usually super-villains and spies. Occasionally, she offers her followers helpful book reports on classic Russian novels.

"Today's assignment, *Crime and Punishment* by Fyodor Dostoevsky. Here's the message: Get over yourself. If you think you're special, it's going to catch up with you. Being an arrogant jerk is a serious crime!"

Sometimes she takes over the mansion's gourmet kitchen and cooks Russian recipes like *Vatrushka* buns, *syrniki* or Russian crepes. One day she decides to bake something special, something she knows her mother would like. "Today I'm going to make a secret family recipe."

Anya charms her followers with running commentary as she combines the ingredients. "A cup and a half of butter. You might want to think about a bigger bikini. Try not to confuse the sugar and salt, okay?"

She pours the batter into a loaf pan and places it in the oven. Then, demonstrating the familiar cooking-show magic, she reaches under the counter and lifts up a perfect, golden cake.

"Here it is. The family secret: Stolichny cake."

She sprinkles it with powdered sugar, cuts a slice and presents it to the camera. She can't remember the last time she and her mother made the cake together, but she knows, somewhere, Irina will be watching. So she repeats the words her great-grandmother, who she barely remembers, would say.

"It's very filling. One slice is enough."